A Riverside Christmas

Copyright ©Caroline Green 2024

All rights reserved.

Author's note: The village of Redfield is a fictional creation. All other locations are real.

For Matt, who makes everything possible.

One

'It's beginning to look a lot like Christmas...'

Zoe watched the changing view from the train window, eager to catch her first glimpse of the river. There was a feeling of nervous anticipation fluttering in her stomach. She had seen the skyscrapers of London slide out of sight to be replaced by tangled hedgerows and glimpses of the fields beyond, many looking somewhat bleak and empty in the weak December sunlight filtering through the grey clouds above. A sudden burst of laughter from a family a few seats away caught her attention for a moment and she automatically turned her head towards them to see the dad making a game of tickling his young son. She smiled at the reindeer antlers adorning his head – after all, Christmas was only just around the corner – and turned back to the window.

Shifting the focus of her eyes, she could see her own face reflected in the glass. She saw a young woman with very straight dark hair, a rather upturned nose and a wistful look in her hazel eyes. Zoe had been told that she looked young for her thirty-two years, but recently she had finally crossed the border into feeling like an adult. An early marriage, buying a flat and even turning thirty hadn't done it, but restarting life as a single, divorced woman had brought on a new feeling: that she was a proper grown-up now. It was both terrifying and exhilarating.

As they rounded a bend in the track she caught sight of the river Deben for the first time and a shaft of sunlight pierced the grey clouds like a good omen, casting glittering golden light across the water's surface. The tannoy announced their imminent arrival at Woodbridge and Zoe gathered her things together as the train slowed on its approach to the station.

Zoe stepped down from the train and found herself on a small, well-kept station platform. She could hear the calls of seabirds, and the clanking of masts in the boatyard as a chill wind blew through them. Exiting the platform and stepping outside the station building, she looked around. To her right was a handsome building housing a theatre and restaurant, with an ice-cream kiosk outside, now shuttered for the winter. To her left she could see a shop selling local beers and kitchenware, beyond the car park full of people in town for their Christmas shopping. The arrangement had been made that someone would pick her up from the station but no one seemed to be waiting for her and her heart started to sink. Thankfully it was only a moment later that a smiling woman in her mid-forties hurried towards her. She wore a turquoise padded jacket and had curly red hair sticking out from under a bright turquoise bobble hat.

"Zoe?" the woman asked breathlessly, then on receiving an affirmative answer unleashed a torrent of words that left Zoe blinking in surprise.

"I am SO sorry I wasn't here sooner, the parking is just mad today, I had to go round the back and then run through, totally out of breath, now I feel like I'm having a hot flush even though it is *freezing*! But thank goodness your train was a little later, I saw it coming along the tracks. I know Simone felt dreadful about not being here to meet you and show you around the house but they had to catch the plane and they were just so relieved that you were able to step in at the last minute and save the day!" Here she paused and beamed.

"My name's Isobel and I live in the village too, just a few doors down from where you'll be staying. Can I help you with one of those bags? Let's get back, get the kettle on and then I can show you the lie of the land, so to speak."

Zoe smiled back at her, feeling the warmth of Isobel's personality. "Thanks, that'd be great," she replied, handing a small case to Isobel. "This one's mostly warm jumpers so it's not super heavy. I thought it might get pretty cold out here in the sticks."

They walked together towards Isobel's car. "Well, it can certainly be colder than London – all that concrete tends to hold the heat – but so far this winter it's not been too bad. I'm afraid you're not likely to have a white Christmas, if we get snow it's usually in January or February. It looks so beautiful falling on the river."

Zoe smiled again. "I bet. I've been in London for quite a few years but I'm a country girl at heart."

"And so lucky you were available to take over the house-sitting job when your friend couldn't," Isobel commented as she unlocked the car doors of her slightly battered Land Rover and they climbed in.

"Yes, Katie is one of my neighbours and she's become a good friend. She does a lot of these house-sitting arrangements, in the UK and abroad, and she's always made it sound fun. Then she got knocked off her bike and broke her leg, and wouldn't have been able to walk the dogs."

Isobel tutted while reversing carefully out of the parking space. "I think I'd be scared to ride a bike in London. There are some crazy drivers out there."

"Absolutely," Zoe agreed, rolling her eyes. "Although I don't think crazy drivers are limited to London! The guy was on his mobile phone, not watching the road. Anyway, luckily she is largely ok but she'll be on crutches for a few weeks so she and her fiancé are going to hunker down and enjoy Christmas at home in the flat for a change. And I had no plans because my mum's been invited to stay with an old friend in Scotland over Christmas."

"So here you are," Isobel said, as they left Woodbridge and headed towards Redfield.

"So here I am," Zoe confirmed, "And I can't wait to get started."

The drive to the village was only a few miles in distance. Zoe admired the houses of Woodbridge as they headed away from the station. Those closest to town were clearly old, some featuring slanted walls leaning out across the street. They drove up a hill past larger properties set further back from the road. Zoe spotted wreaths on doors and lights twinkling brightly behind bay windows. They passed under a railway bridge and followed quiet lanes taking them deeper into the countryside.

The road into the village of Redfield took them past a row of houses that gave way to a small convenience shop and then the village green. On the other side of the road was the old red brick school, snowflake decorations adorning the windows, and Isobel drove past this slowly then turned off into a smaller road heading east. She was soon turning into the driveway of a beautiful Georgian house with a sign on the gatepost identifying it as "The Old Rectory". The front borders contained the bare sticks of rose bushes that Zoe knew must be covered in fragrant blooms in the summer months. The Land Rover's wheels crunched on the gravel drive and Zoe heard a faint sound of barking coming from within the house.

"The dogs know me well and they're very friendly," Isobel told her. "I've got the back door key so we'll go round that way; I've never known Simone and Neil to use the front door anyway, although you might find that delivery drivers come that way."

They unloaded Zoe's bags and headed through the garden gate to the back door, where the sound of barking intensified as Isobel extracted the key from her coat pocket and fitted it into the lock. In her emails with Simone, Zoe had already heard all about the dogs and their friendliness so she felt excitement rather than apprehension as the door opened and three furry bodies leapt towards them, tails wagging furiously.

"Hello, hello, steady on there, I'm pleased to meet you too!" Zoe laughed as she held out her hands to be eagerly licked by the three small pink tongues.

"They're rather indulged," Isobel said, a little disapprovingly. "I won't let my Jasper jump up like this."

"Oh, they are gorgeous though. What kind of dog is Jasper?"

"He's a golden retriever but he is quite a big one and I wouldn't want him to knock anyone over! He's a big softy though."

Zoe knelt just inside the back door, still surrounded by dogs. "I love dogs – well, all animals really – and I couldn't have one in my flat so this is such a treat."

"Well these three should give you all the walkies you've been missing! The black lab is Bella, she's the eldest and most sensible, the cockapoo is Henry and the little terrier is Barney."

Barney was attempting to jump up and lick Zoe's face so she gently shooed him away and stood up straight.

"Come into the kitchen," Isobel suggested. "We'll make a pot of tea and I'll show you around."

The kitchen was more modern than Zoe had expected, while remaining sympathetic to the style and period of the house's architecture. A large island dominated the middle of the room, creating a breakfast bar area with high stools, and Zoe immediately decided that this was where she would sit to eat her meals during her stay. Having taken off her shoes, she could feel the delicious warmth of underfloor heating radiating through her socks.

"The heart of the home! What a lovely room."

"Isn't it just? I have major kitchen envy every time I see it." Isobel was switching on the kettle as she spoke. "This cupboard is where the mugs are kept, look, and the fridge is over here. There's some milk but not much food in… will you need a lift to the supermarket?"

Zoe shook her head. "That's really kind but I'll be ok, I've ordered an online shop to be delivered here later today. I'll be getting around on foot or maybe by bus if I need to go further afield but I think I'll mostly be here anyway. There are the animals to look after and then I'll be plugging into my laptop and working as well."

"What do you do for a job?" Isobel asked as she poured out the tea.

"Website design. I can work from anywhere really as long as I have a laptop and internet connection, so I'm hoping to get plenty done while I'm here as well as walking the dogs and so on."

"Sounds interesting. I'm a primary school teacher. I work part time but even so, it's pretty demanding. Thank goodness there's only a few days to go until the holidays! We're all dropping with tiredness at this time of year, kids and teachers alike."

"I can imagine. One of my uni friends is a teacher and I know she works really hard. I enjoy my job and it's great to be able to manage my own time, but then it can be hard to keep the boundaries between work hours and time off."

Tea now finished, they began the tour of the house. As well as the large kitchen and adjoining boot room, the ground floor contained a formal dining room and two reception rooms. The smaller of these was a very pleasant cosy room with views through French doors onto the garden. Despite the wintry outlook, Zoe knew that she would enjoy curling up here and watching the trees and birds. It was such a refreshing contrast from her city flat.

The smallest dog, Barney, followed them from room to room until they started to head upstairs, at which point he lay down in the hall with a sigh. Isobel smiled approvingly.

"I know that the dogs aren't allowed upstairs but I did wonder if Barney would try to pull the wool over your eyes by scampering up innocently as though it was normal practice!"

They looked into each of the four bedrooms and the bathroom, all of which were generously proportioned and tastefully decorated. The main guest bedroom had been made up ready for Zoe. Located at the back of the house, she was drawn immediately to the window to have another look at the garden and then gave an exclamation of delight.

"I can see the river!"

"Lovely, isn't it? Even on a grey day like this."

Zoe nodded, still staring out at the view. "There's something about living near water, isn't there? So calming."

The two women made their way back to the ground floor where Barney greeted them with more licks and a happily wagging tail.

"Ok," Isobel said, "I'll just show you the chickens and then I'd better be getting off home. I promised Steve that I'd make mince pies today."

"It's really kind of you to show me around..." Zoe began but Isobel cut her off with a dismissive wave of her hand.

"Not at all, happy to help. I know you'll want some time to settle in and unpack but do come round for a coffee and a mince pie tomorrow morning? Since we're winding down to the holidays I don't need to do any planning or marking and I'll just be pottering about. Say ten o'clock? You can meet Jasper."

Zoe wondered whether to protest that she had work to do, but the firm look in Isobel's eye told her that her new friend wouldn't take no for an answer. And of course, tomorrow was Saturday – it would be good for her to set more boundaries with work and leave the laptop closed for the weekend.

"That sounds great," she replied.

They had a quick look at the chicken coop, then Isobel headed off to her baking and Zoe closed the back door behind her with a grateful sigh.

"Right, dogs," she addressed the three furry faces looking up at her, "give me a few minutes to unpack and pop to the loo and then we'll go for a you-know-what." Even with her careful avoidance of the word "walk", tails wagged and Barney let out an excited whine. Zoe leaned down to scratch his head.

"Just a few minutes," she reassured him. "I want to get out and explore this place just as much as you do!"

Two

'Snow is falling, all around me...'

Up in her new bedroom, Zoe unzipped her bags and unloaded the contents into the empty drawers and wardrobe. As she placed her book on the bedside table she glanced out of the window and noticed that the sky was darker than before, threatening rain. It was around three o'clock but she knew that at this time of year she didn't have long before the daylight would be gone, and she drew the curtains before hurrying back downstairs to the waiting dogs. Zoe shrugged on her coat and pushed her feet into sturdy walking boots as Barney skipped around excitedly.

She spotted the leads hanging on a hook by the back door and clipped one onto Barney's collar and another onto Henry, the cockapoo. He had a sweet, rather simple expression on his little furry face but his owners had warned her that he was just as likely as Barney to race off after a squirrel or rabbit and ignore her calls. Bella, on the other hand, was very well behaved and wearing a lead would be entirely beneath her dignity. Zoe was slightly concerned about this but as they closed the garden gate behind them and set off up the lane, she began to feel reassured by Bella's steadiness. She would trot ahead or fall behind a little to sniff all the interesting scents, but quickly returned to Zoe's side every time.

"You're a good old girl, aren't you? Are you going to help me keep these boys in line?" Zoe asked her.

Bella sneezed in response.

"Let's hope that means yes," Zoe said, smiling.

The walk up the lane took them past a few houses before they approached the church. It was a pretty medieval building like so many village churches of its kind, although Zoe was interested to see the unusual octagonal tower. A large tree to the side of the tower had been decorated with brightly coloured lights. Bella led the way along a footpath which took them along the edge of the graveyard, heading down towards the river. It seemed likely that this was a walk they took often.

The footpath wound its way through a tangle of brambles and hawthorn, creating a tunnel above Zoe's head. It was rather dark and narrow and Zoe nearly tripped over a rogue bramble before the path suddenly curved and she emerged into the light once more.

She was standing on a small beach where sand and pebbles gave way to several feet of mud and then the river Deben, the water shimmering in the last rays of the winter sunlight breaking through the dark clouds. Several small boats bobbed on the water, pulling against their buoys as the tide lifted them. She knew that upriver to her left was the town of Woodbridge, where her train had arrived earlier that day; to the right, if you kept going far enough, you would eventually come to the North Sea. Zoe shivered a little in the cold breeze and allowed the dogs to guide her on along the beach. There was a small group of beach huts set up the bank next to the yacht club, and further along they came to the Mulberry Tree, the local pub she had heard was popular for its good food and beautiful riverside setting.

Bella trotted ahead and they passed several very smartly renovated houses. Zoe caught the scent of woodsmoke on the air and turned her head to see smoke curling from the chimney of a smaller redbrick cottage, set further back from the river. It was part of a terrace of three similar dwellings. Although it was somewhat overshadowed by its gentrified neighbours, there was something charming about this particular cottage and she found herself wondering about all the occupants of this pretty little village. Still following Bella, Zoe and the other two dogs headed away from the beach up another footpath and out onto a quiet lane. It was now becoming quite dark and although Zoe's sense of direction wasn't always the most reliable, she was pretty sure that they were heading back towards the Old Rectory. However she thought she'd better just check, so she called to Bella to wait while she took out her phone and consulted a map.

"Looks about right, dogs," she said, beginning to walk again while watching the blue dot on the screen to make sure she was going the right way.

They rounded a corner and the phone was nearly knocked from her hand as she collided with a large, glowing, fast-moving shape in the darkness. Zoe couldn't help letting out a small scream before realising that this was not some mythical East Anglian beast roaming the fields, but just a man in running gear, hands on hips and frowning down at her while he caught his breath. His t-shirt was made of reflective fabric, bouncing back any light that touched it.

"Sorry," she said automatically, then instantly regretted it. Why did she have to be so British and apologetic? This man wasn't apologising despite the fact that he was the one who had run into her!

"Probably best to look where you're going rather than at your phone," he suggested drily.

Zoe opened her mouth to make some retort but he was already moving past her. "And maybe some light clothing or a torch?" he called as he started to run off down the road again. "Not many streetlights round here."

Zoe was so cross she couldn't think of a single thing to say before it was too late and he was already too far away. "Honestly, how rude!" she complained to the dogs. "It was at least as much his fault as mine and I was only checking where I was going, it's not like I was live-streaming my lovely evening walk to millions of followers." Bella looked at her with huge chocolate eyes. "Not that I'm not enjoying it," Zoe reassured her. "Oh, forget him. Come on, let's get back to the house."

Back inside the Old Rectory, Zoe hung up the dogs' leads and was grateful for the warmth of the underfloor heating as she padded in her socks through the kitchen. She made another cup of tea and went round closing the curtains as it brewed. The doorbell rang about five o'clock and she was pleased to find a supermarket delivery driver standing on the step with her food delivery. She quickly unpacked the crates onto the breakfast bar. There seemed to be rather a lot of food, but she had tried to think of most things she would need for the next three weeks so that she didn't have to struggle out to a supermarket without a car, and with only an intermittent bus service. There was no way she would get another delivery slot this close to Christmas.

Once the crates were returned to the driver and Zoe had closed the door, she went back to the kitchen to put everything away. As well as the usual practical items that she would need for her meals, she had chosen some seasonal treats: a box of mince pies, shortbread biscuits, a selection of cheeses, chocolate truffles... She decided to make a simple pasta carbonara for dinner that evening. First she had to pop outside to feed the chickens, which she did as quickly as possible because a cold drizzle had started to fall. On her way back inside she grabbed a few logs from the wood store and took them through to the sitting room. She had noticed the wood burner earlier, and seen that there was a basket of kindling ready next to it. She made up the fire and was delighted when it only took one match to get it going – clearly those years of camping with the Guides were not wasted! Once she was happy that it was burning well, she went to make dinner.

Three pairs of eyes drilled into her as she fried bacon to add to her pasta. Zoe looked at the dogs sternly.

"I'm sure you are not supposed to beg for human food. I've had instructions, you know."

Barney fidgeted and let out a small whine.

"I'll put a tiny bit of bacon fat in your bowls when I've finished eating. Now leave me alone!" The rest of the bacon went into the freezer to save for another occasion.

The staring continued for as long as she was cooking, but although the dogs followed her to the warmth of the sitting room, they lay down near the fire and were too well mannered to expect feeding from her plate. Zoe switched on the TV for a bit of company and ate while watching the last half hour of *Elf*.

Her mother phoned just as she was fulfilling her promise to the dogs. They munched joyfully as she answered her mobile. She was pleased to hear from her mum; they had always got on well, and had become even closer since her father's death a few years earlier.

"Hello darling, everything ok?" Astrid's gentle voice reached her ears.

"Hi Mum; yes, everything's fine. I'm here, I've got food and a fire, and the dogs are gorgeous."

"Oh good, I am glad. What's the place like?"

Zoe climbed the stairs as she spoke, remembering a task that she needed to do. "It's beautiful. The house is Georgian, lovely well-proportioned rooms and I can see the river from my bedroom."

"That sounds nice. Is it warm enough?"

"Yes, it's fine. I've lit a fire to be properly cosy in the sitting room but the rest of the house is ok. There's underfloor heating in the kitchen!"

"Ooh, what a treat. I'm definitely packing my woollies for this trip to Scotland. There's snow on the weather forecast."

"You might have a white Christmas! That would be amazing." As she spoke, Zoe carefully extracted a snow globe wrapped in a scarf from a side pocket of her bag. She had forgotten to take it out earlier. It was an ornament she had had for years, and although she couldn't be with her mum or her friends this Christmas, it was a little piece of tradition that she could bring with her.

They chatted on for a while longer until Astrid said that she'd better finish her packing, and they said their goodbyes. Zoe put down her phone and looked around the room where she would be sleeping. She was sitting on a double bed with an oak bedframe, on a sumptuously thick duvet with a cream coloured cover. Two plump pillows lay waiting for her to rest her head. A soft, sage green woollen blanket laid across the bottom of the bed echoed the colour of the room's walls. A freestanding oak wardrobe stood in one corner of the room, and there were matching bedside tables on either side of the bed. It was a wonderfully calm, comfortable, and sophisticated space.

Zoe picked up her snow globe, and turned it gently upside down. The sparkly flakes inside floated delicately down over the tiny snowy scene. It was a fantasy to think of waking up to snow on Christmas Day but Zoe had an optimistic nature. There was nothing wrong with hoping that a little Christmas magic might find its way into her stay here. She would miss her mum but she knew that Astrid would be having a good time in Scotland. Looking at the snow globe sat on the bedside table, she thought that she was glad to be experiencing the adventure of exploring a new place for a few weeks, even if it was likely to be a very quiet Christmas compared to usual.

Three

'I saw three ships coming sailing in...'

The following morning Zoe sat at the chunky oak table in Isobel's kitchen, watching her bustle around making coffee and putting mince pies on plates. Isobel's husband Steve was sat opposite her with an already-empty mug and plate and a newspaper in front of him. The kitchen was wonderfully warm and cosy, with a cheerful scarlet poinsettia on the windowsill and the gentle hum of the dishwasher running in the background. It wasn't as smart as the kitchen in the Old Rectory but it was certainly a room in which you felt instantly comfortable. Zoe had already been introduced to Jasper the dog who had greeted her with the dignity of an elder statesman, and was now curled contentedly in his bed in the corner.

"We're one person short for the pub quiz on Tuesday; can I persuade you to come along?" Isobel asked as she set a large mug of coffee down in front of Zoe. She was wearing a saffron-yellow sweater that complemented her fiery hair.

"Umm, maybe," Zoe hesitated. "I don't know if I'd be all that useful."

Isobel waved a hand dismissively. "Of course you will, you're bound to know a few answers. Anyway it doesn't really matter, it's just for fun. And for glory if we actually win! But I'm positive we have more chance with a full team."

"What time does it start?"

"Eight thirty, but we want a good table so I'll knock for you about quarter to eight and we can walk down together. Steve will be there too and a couple of other locals."

"Ok, sounds great."

Steve had the close cropped hair of many middle aged balding men, perceptive blue-grey eyes, and a deadpan manner. He glanced at the pair of them now over the top of his paper.

"Watch out; now she's adopted you, she'll be trying to convert you to her religion next."

Zoe raised her eyebrows as Isobel turned to her with shining eyes.

"Oh, I'm not really into anything religious," she began cautiously.

"No, he's teasing, he means my swimming. I may be somewhat evangelical about it…"

"Just a bit," Steve replied dryly without lifting his eyes from the newspaper.

Isobel stuck out her tongue at him.

Zoe grinned. "I do like swimming. I even brought my costume just in case there was chance to use it. Do you go to the pool in Woodbridge?"

Steve snorted with laughter but Isobel ignored him. "No, in the river!"

Zoe's eyes widened as she turned briefly to look out at the bare branches of the trees being buffeted by the wind. A few leaves clung on stubbornly here and there, but nearly all had now been stripped away. "But not at this time of year, surely?"

"All year round. It's so amazingly good for you. You have to try it, it's such a buzz. I can lend you a wetsuit!"

"Umm, maybe…" Zoe replied, thinking that the real answer was 'Absolutely not'.

Steve folded his paper and got to his feet. "No point fighting her. Personality like a juggernaut. Once she gets going, there's no stopping her." He dodged the squeaky dog toy that Isobel lobbed at his head and left the room.

Isobel shook her head. "He's always got to have the last word, that one. He's not wrong though, I'll definitely get you in the river before the year is out."

Zoe took a sip of her coffee and thought she'd better change the subject quickly.

"So, when do the schools break up?"

"Tuesday is the last day, so going out to the quiz will be a nice way to kick off the holidays for me. It's been so full on with all the Christmas crafts, the concert, the school fair, the Nativity… Monday will be a normal-ish school day but Tuesday is really just playing games and doing a party in the afternoon. I will need to do a bit of lesson planning later in the holidays but I'm definitely switching off entirely for a while."

"I've got a couple of deadlines still to hit before Christmas Day itself, but once those are taken care of I can relax a bit more. Although having said that, I often end up doing a few hours even when I've scheduled a day off, if I haven't got anything special happening: I think that's the problem with being self-employed."

Isobel nodded as she took a bite of her mince pie. "And what do you actually have to do at The Old Rectory?"

"Walk the dogs twice a day, feed them and the chickens, and just look after the house. Simone explained that the dogs hate staying in kennels, and with them taking such a long holiday this time they wanted to keep things easy and familiar for them; especially Bella as she's getting on a bit now."

"Makes sense. Their cruise does sound special but it's not the sort of holiday I've ever much fancied myself. I do sometimes think it would be nice to go and visit the Christmas markets in Europe."

"Oh yes! I did manage to go for a weekend in Germany last December and the markets were wonderful." She hesitated, then decided to tell the story. "It was sort of a celebratory trip really; my divorce had just been finalised and I wanted to do something positive."

Isobel looked sympathetic. "What happened?" she asked. "Oh, don't tell me if you don't want to! Sorry, I'm being nosey."

Zoe toyed with the handle of her mug. "You know it's funny, I didn't really want to talk about it for a long time but I feel like I'm finally over that now. I guess I just felt kind of ashamed, you know? Like I'd failed. But it was definitely the right decision. We just got married too young really, and then we grew apart instead of growing together."

"Steve and I were quite young when we met but luckily it worked out ok for us. I think if it's the right person, it doesn't matter when you meet. If it's meant to be, you just... know."

Zoe nodded. "Anyway, I've tried some internet dating but it's mostly been pretty disastrous! At least being single meant I was free to drop everything at home and come here. I'm trying to say yes to new things."

There was a glint in Isobel's eye now. "Like wild swimming?"

Zoe laughed. "We'll see!"

The kitchen door opened and a young man slouched into the room. He strongly resembled Isobel but from the unbrushed look of his mop of red hair, and from the pyjamas and bare feet, Zoe guessed that he had only just got out of bed. He had that gangly teenage look of a boy who has grown so quickly that he hasn't yet got used to his long limbs. Zoe guessed that he was about seventeen.

"Morning, sweetheart," Isobel greeted him brightly. "This is Zoe, our new temporary neighbour."

The lad gave her a nod of acknowledgement as Zoe said hi, then he swooped down on the tray of fresh baking.

"Ooh lush, mince pies." He grabbed two before Isobel could jump in to stop him.

"Charlie, not for breakfast!" his mother admonished, but Charlie had already taken a huge bite of his prize and was backing out of the room again. He grinned.

"Thanks, Mum!" he called before disappearing again.

Isobel sighed. "That was Charlie, my youngest. He's at sixth form. Bit of a rebel. I can't say I had so much trouble with his sister although I've worried about her in different ways, I suppose." She picked up a photo frame and showed Zoe the picture it contained: a smiling young woman in a prom dress, with long strawberry blonde waves of hair cascading onto her shoulders.

"Lauren is backpacking in Australia at the moment. This will be the first Christmas that she's not been here." Isobel looked downhearted and Zoe instinctively reached out and rested her hand on Isobel's own in sympathy.

"It must be very strange."

"Very! My baby, on the other side of the world." Isobel shook her head as if to clear it, and smiled at Zoe. "Well, she's a sensible girl and she's with friends. She'll be ok. So I'm determined not to sit around moping. I've got lots more plans for things to bake – that's going to keep me busy. Especially at the rate that Charlie gets through food." She rolled her eyes.

Zoe grinned. "I'm happy to help if you need a more discerning taste tester."

"You're on! Tomorrow I'm going to try a batch of mince pies with a spoonful of cream cheese at the top of each one."

"Ooh, that sounds interesting! Well, today's mince pie was absolutely delicious but I'd better get back to the dogs now. They're just getting used to me so I don't like to leave them for long."

Isobel accompanied her to the door. "Ok, well remember to keep Tuesday night free for the quiz. And let me know if you need anything."

"Will do," Zoe smiled, waving goodbye as she walked away.

The three dogs wagged their tails happily at her return and she let them into the garden for a run around. It wasn't exactly warm, but the weather was mild for December, and she wandered around the large garden while the dogs sniffed around and marked their territory in strategic spots. The garden had a fairly traditional layout with a patio area near the house leading onto a lawn with generous borders. Even in winter the owners had managed to create some interest with tall grasses and plants with colourful stems. They had also left some seedheads for the birds, rather than cut back all the flowers as they finished for the season, which gave more texture to the relative emptiness of the borders. Zoe could imagine that in the spring and summer they would be full of flowers, with bees and butterflies everywhere.

Towards the bottom of the garden there was an arch which led to a small vegetable plot and the enclosure for the chickens. Zoe stepped inside and the three chickens pecked busily around her feet as she checked their food and water. She opened the lid of their nesting box and found just one speckled brown egg nestling in the straw. Picking it up with care, she replaced the lid and took her treasure with her. Fresh eggs were such a treat, she thought, so much better than the ones you could buy in the supermarkets.

At the very bottom of the garden she stretched onto her tiptoes to see the glint of the river. There was an old tree stump which had been left in the ground, perhaps for use as an occasional seat, and she climbed onto the top of this to get a better look. There it was, a ribbon of silver grey flowing through the quiet countryside towards the open vastness of the North Sea. Her phone in her pocket buzzed and Zoe swiped it open to find a message from Katie.

Hope everything is ok with the house and dogs? Wish I was there but glad you could take over x

Zoe replied: *House and dogs beautiful! Check out the view:*

She attached a photo of the river then turned around the other way and took one of the dogs with the house in the background.

Oh, gorgeous! Katie quickly pinged back. *Heading out for lunch now but talk soon xxx*

Zoe put the phone back in her pocket and stood in silent contemplation of the view until Barney bounced up to her, bringing a ball, and Zoe jumped down to play with him.

The freshly laid egg would make a good addition to her lunch but a single egg wasn't going to be enough for a meal on its own. Zoe knew that hens laid less frequently in the winter and Simone had mentioned that one of the hens was quite old and didn't lay at all any more, so this one alone was definitely a bonus. Rummaging in the fridge to see what she could put with it, she found an avocado from her online shop. This was beginning to look a bit more substantial. She cut a thick slice of crusty bread and popped it into the toaster while she quickly scrambled the egg and cut open the avocado. Once all of this was assembled on a plate, she sat up at the breakfast bar to eat.

She may have had a mince pie earlier, but Zoe felt she needed something sweet to finish off her meal. She was rather a fan of the concept of "lunch pudding", especially when the main part had been fairly healthy. A shortbread biscuit with a cup of tea would be just the job.

Despite the fact that it was Saturday, Zoe took out her laptop after lunch. Tucked into the case was an advent calendar that her mum had posted to her a few weeks before. It was just a little one, like a greetings card, with a picture behind each door. She had forgotten about it earlier but she now found door number seventeen and opened it. The image behind was a snowman with a carrot nose and a red hat.

She propped up the advent calendar on the worktop then settled down to work for an hour or so. She had a few emails to answer and some designs to work on. Normally, at home, she would sit at a proper desk or sometimes go out to work in a café for a few hours. There was a cute little independent coffee shop just around the corner from her flat, and she bought coffee there often enough that they were happy for her to sit at the window seat and use the wifi. As she largely worked from home, for Zoe it was nice to have that connection with people. The staff knew her usual order and they would exchange a few pleasantries before she absorbed herself in her work. Here in Redfield, she chose to settle herself comfortably in the snug with her legs up on the sofa and the laptop resting on her knees. She had a suspicion that this might not be particularly good from an ergonomic point of view, but she was enjoying the break from normal routine.

By about half past two she had had enough and thought it would be good to do some more exploring with the dogs in tow. As it was dry she could wear her favourite teddy coat; it was lovely and warm but not really suitable for wearing in the rain, so she had also packed a sensible waterproof option in her suitcase. She whistled for the dogs and soon they were all trotting out into the breezy afternoon.

Zoe decided to set off in the opposite direction from that which she had taken yesterday, heading through the village and along a quiet lane in a more-or-less northerly direction.

Everything looked different when approached from the other side, but she was fairly sure that this corner was where she had bumped into the brusque runner – or rather, he had bumped into her! The houses here were older cottages with small, neat front gardens, and she could see glimpses of Christmas trees through the windows as she passed.

She was admiring the various decorations when an old lady with bright white hair, wearing a long camel coloured coat, came out of her house and closed the front door. Zoe gave her a friendly smile and was a little surprised when the woman merely narrowed her eyes and glared at her in response. She supposed that in a place as small as this, some people might view outsiders with suspicion. She shrugged it off and continued on her way.

The lane wound back towards the river and suddenly she found herself facing the water again. There was a group of small yachts – was that the right word? – racing against the wind. They were crewed by children and Zoe marvelled that they knew how to manage the little boats, expertly steering their crafts with rudder and sails. From this distance she guessed the age of the sailors to be around ten to twelve years. She realised that there was an adult supervising from another boat and saw that the children all wore life jackets, so it seemed to be an organised group. It didn't look like any of them were likely to fall into the water anyway, but she was glad that they weren't on their own. Excited shouts carried to her ears across the grey water.

Zoe took the riverside path and continued north around a bend in the river. A moment later she could see the town of Woodbridge in the distance. The historic white Tide Mill gleamed in the late afternoon sun, beyond a collection of boats moored on the river. It was further than she wanted to walk this afternoon, but Zoe reckoned the distance to the town along this path was probably no more than two miles. She could walk in without the dogs on another occasion to have a look around and visit a few shops. She pressed on just a little further to a small promontory where a bench had been placed, to sit and drink in the view for a moment before turning back. , Henry sat down by her feet while Barney sniffed around the bottom of the bench and cocked his leg to add his own scent to the myriad others that he could no doubt smell.

Various birds flew over the water or bobbed upon it and Zoe thought that she must download an app that her mum had mentioned, that identified birds by their songs. There were several birds here that she would have described as seagulls, but that was a generic term; from their different sizes and different coloured beaks she knew that they weren't all the same species. Long-legged wading birds stalked through the mud at the edge of the water. She was interested to watch them but it was too cool to sit still for long, and she soon got to her feet again and called to Bella, who was sniffing around a short distance away. Together they walked back along the quiet lane, which was so small and narrow that there was a strip of grass growing down the middle of the tarmac. Although the hedgerows along the verges were less full of leaf than they would be in the summer, they still provided good cover for all sorts of small birds which darted around seeking out berries.

Zoe felt a little lonely returning to the empty house. Although she lived alone in her flat in London, she had neighbours all around in the same building and she was used to more background noise. It was so quiet here. The sky was growing dark and she went round the house shutting curtains and turning on lights in the sitting room and kitchen. That made the place feel more cosy. The dogs were a comforting presence too.

In the absence of any Saturday night plans whatsoever, she decided to run a bath. She only had a shower in her London flat so a bath was a novelty that she intended to enjoy. She switched on the mixer tap and dug out the travel-size bath soak that she had brought with her. Simone had said that she was welcome to use anything in the house, but she felt more comfortable just using what she had brought with her as much as possible. She added a dollop of the lavender-scented liquid to the running water and swirled it around with her hand. She undressed and lowered herself slowly into the hot water.

 Zoe reflected that this was one of her favourite parts of being single: she could do what she wanted, when she wanted, without having to consider a partner's needs and wishes. Her ex had been quite demanding when it came to her time. He hadn't necessarily wanted to them to go out and do anything, but he wanted her nearby. At his beck and call, she supposed, looking back. It was a subtle manipulation but somehow they always seemed to end up eating the meals that he wanted to eat, and watching the films that he wanted to watch. If Zoe made plans to go out and do something that didn't involve him, he would sulk and be so difficult that she would end up cancelling. Eventually she realised that she couldn't keep going like this and they had separated.

 In many ways she enjoyed her new-found freedom and she felt that she was living more fully than she had in years. But she had to admit that there were things she missed, or rather things she longed to find with someone else. Companionship and closeness – someone to share both the adventures and the small quiet moments. She wanted a partner who shared her outlook on life and would stand alongside her. She wanted to have a family someday. And a physical connection... she felt that things had been adequate in that department in the past but she rather suspected that 'adequate' didn't begin to cover the connection that some couples had. She wanted that too.

 As Zoe stepped out of the bath and wrapped herself in a large, white, fluffy towel, she decided to try harder with dating once she got back home. There had to be *someone* out there who was right for her.

Four

'Whence comes this rush of wings afar, following straight the Noel star..."

Zoe opened her eyes and found that it was still quite dark although the digital display on her bedside clock read 7:40. Of course, it was nearly the solstice, and sunrise came slowly on these dark winter mornings. Curiously, she had heard a bird singing – she thought it was a robin – just after six, but when she had glanced at the clock it was definitely too early to get up, and she had dozed off again. She was surprised to hear birdsong so long before dawn.

She lay in bed enjoying the warmth for a few moments, and stretched her limbs to shake off the sleep. She supposed that she could doze off again for a while – after all, it was Sunday – but the dogs would be waiting to go out in the garden and relieve themselves. There was also something exciting about waking up somewhere new and she wanted to make the most of the day.

She let the dogs out the back door and made coffee with a cafetière while they sniffed around the garden. Today's advent calendar door revealed a picture of a Christmas tree, complete with star at the top. By the time she had drunk the coffee and got dressed, the sky was lighter and she decided to seize the moment and take the dogs for their walk before she made her breakfast.

It was cold but less windy than the previous day. There weren't many people around this early on a Sunday and Zoe was humming 'Winter Wonderland' to herself as she and the dogs started their walk. They took the brambly footpath next to the church then emerged onto the beach. A splashing sound caught her attention and she turned to see what had made the noise. There were a couple of swimmers in the water, brightly coloured swimming caps clearly visible as they bobbed along. Just beyond them, a little further down the beach, a tall male figure began to emerge from the water. He was clearly used to the cold of the river water as he wasn't wearing a wetsuit, just a pair of fairly long, tight, black swimming shorts. He strode through the shallows to the sand, water pouring off his broad shoulders and muscular chest as he ran a hand through his dark hair. He had the sort of physique that she associated with surfers; lean and strong from natural movement rather than the pumped up muscles some men worked for in the gym.

Henry gave a short bark and the man looked up and saw Zoe. She gasped and quickly turned away. She didn't want him to think she was staring at him! Even though, to be perfectly honest, that was exactly what she'd been doing. Too long without a date, she told herself sternly, her cheeks turning pink. A glimpse of a good-looking man and you lose your head completely!

She bent down to fix a shoelace that had come untied, hoping he would have disappeared by the time she had finished. Straightening up, she risked a quick glance in his direction. Of course, he was still there, now briskly rubbing a towel over his dark hair. Zoe hastily grabbed a stick, threw it in the opposite direction for the dogs to chase, and made her escape as swiftly as possible.

Back at the house, she hung up her coat and the dogs' leads and made toast and another pot of coffee. She sat at the breakfast bar to eat, trying not to drop crumbs although she knew that the dogs would eagerly hoover up anything that fell to the ground. When she had finished she took her laptop through to the snug sitting room and set herself up comfortably near the window. She decided to get a couple of hours' work done, then to relax a bit later in the afternoon. Through the window she could see a bird feeder station with a number of different containers holding different types of seeds and peanuts. She made a mental note to locate the stores of seed – in the shed, perhaps? – and keep the feeders topped up.

As she watched, a gang of little birds descended from the trees en masse and fluttered around, taking turns to peck at the food. She recognised blue tits, great tits and the sweet teddy bear-like faces of long-tailed tits. They swooped and hopped around the feeders. The peanuts seemed particularly popular. The birds darted around for a few minutes before soaring off in a flock again, as if in response to some signal that was invisible or inaudible to Zoe. She turned back to the laptop again but allowed herself to be distracted whenever she caught movement out of the corner of her eye.

By lunchtime she felt that she had been productive enough for a Sunday, and closed her laptop and put it safely away. She had done some rough meal planning to make sure that she ordered the right sort of things from the online supermarket shop; there was nothing more frustrating than doing a big shop and then feeling like you still didn't have the right combination of ingredients to make anything decent to eat! She had a recipe for a simple stew with prawns, red peppers and new potatoes, and decided to try it out. Zoe tipped all the new potatoes into a saucepan of water. She would cook these separately, then those that she didn't use today could keep in the fridge ready to be used for another quick dish later.

Zoe found a Christmassy playlist on her phone and hummed along while frying onion and adding garlic, peppers and paprika. Stock and tomato purée went in next, and the prawns just needed a few minutes at the end. It wasn't long before everything was ready and she sat down at the breakfast bar to enjoy the fruits of her labour.

Lunch finished, Zoe took a cup of tea through to the snug and curled up on the sofa. There were a few Christmas magazines on a side table and she picked these up and leafed through them. The first had lots of lovely gift ideas. Zoe had already bought all the presents she needed for her mum and a few friends, but she still enjoyed flicking through the pages looking at all the shiny treats. As always, she saw several things that she would rather like for herself!

She put it aside after a few minutes and picked up another. This was focused on food and Zoe saw several recipes that she was interested in trying. Some of the dishes looked far too elaborate and she wasn't about to start making canapés or complicated desserts when she was spending Christmas on her own, but there were soups and some different ideas for vegetables.   She was intrigued by the suggested combination of parsnip and pear fritters. She took photos with her phone of the ones she fancied the most, in case she wanted to refer back to them once she was back at home in her flat.

A third magazine was more of a general lifestyle publication, with fashion and beauty as well as sections on the home, food, and wellbeing. Zoe admired the stylish outfits that the models were wearing. They made glamour look very easy. Zoe's style tended towards comfort; she had a fair amount of smart-casual clothes that were suitable for workwear or going out, but she was happiest cocooned in snuggly knitwear. Today she was wearing a chunky crimson jumper, jeans, and thick cosy socks. Now that she had been invited to the pub quiz, she was glad that she had brought a few smarter tops just in case she needed them. Zoe didn't really like to be the centre of attention so avoided sequins or showing a lot of skin, but she did want to look nice if she was going out.

Once the dogs had had their afternoon walk and she had gone round and shut the curtains, Zoe switched on the TV in the snug. She was interested to see what was on the local news and to catch the weather forecast. There were a few serious stories at the start of the programme but these soon gave way to more cheerful and seasonal items. The channel covered the whole of East Anglia and as Zoe watched a segment about the cathedral and lights in Norwich, she thought that it looked an attractive city to visit. There was a large outdoor market throughout the year and the centre looked busy with shoppers and other visitors.

The next report was about a Christmas fair and art exhibition in the seaside town of Aldeburgh. Behind the reporter, Zoe could see a row of brightly coloured buildings facing the sea across a pebbly beach. She liked the sea but it had been a long time since she had last been to the coast.

There was a few minutes about sport, which didn't much interest her, before the weather presenter came onto the screen with a map of the region. It looked set to stay fine and dry for several days, possibly with a change on the way as they headed into next weekend.

"It's looking relatively mild for the next few days," the presenter declared, "but we do expect some unsettled conditions bringing more wintry temperatures for the Christmas weekend and beyond."

The newsreader flashed a dazzling smile at the weather presenter. "As always at this time of year, Andy, the big question is whether we can expect a white Christmas?"

"That is the big question, Charlotte! I have to say it's looking unlikely, but the weather does have a habit of surprising us and we've still got a week to go, so keep your fingers crossed if you're hoping for some snow this year!"

The credits rolled and Zoe was about to switch off when the voiceover announced that the news would be followed by *The Snowman*. Zoe loved the classic animation and decided to stay in the sitting room and watch it before making dinner, especially as it was only half an hour long. As soon as the music began and the first flakes of snow swirled on the screen, she was transported back to her own childhood, snuggled on the sofa between her parents watching the adventure with wide eyes and dreaming that something magical would happen to her one day, too. She had a tear in her eye at the end when the snowman had melted away and the boy was left kneeling, bereft, in the snowy garden. Bella pressed her head against Zoe's knee sympathetically, and she laughed.

"I'm ok, Bella! Just a big softy when it comes to things like this. Come on, let's go and rustle up some dinner."

****

The next day was Monday. Zoe decided to take a short walk to the little convenience shop by the village green, to see what sort of items they stocked. She left the dogs behind, unsure whether they would be welcome in the shop. She had enough food for the time being but if it was the sort of place where you could buy a pint of milk and a loaf of bread, that would be useful.

The shop window held a small, carefully curated Christmas display which she admired for a moment before going inside. Cotton wool and tinfoil had been used to create a miniature snowy landscape with an icy pond, and small toy animals stood around it in groups; a little herd of cows, a flock of sheep, a duck on the pond and two reindeer at the rear of the scene. Above this hung a twiggy branch of twisted willow, decorated with shiny baubles and a few very beautiful carved wooden decorations that looked handmade.

Zoe pushed open the door and a bell tinkled as she stepped inside, closing the door behind her. The shop contained a curious mixture of practical and whimsical items; to one side, store cupboard essentials, a few loaves of bread and a chiller cabinet with milk and cheese; to the other, a selection of pocket money-friendly children's toys, scented soaps, dream catchers, and a few other things that looked like they were made by local craftspeople.

Behind the counter a woman in her fifties with short purple hair looked up and gave her a friendly smile. "Good morning. Let me know if there's anything I can help you with."

Zoe thanked her and took a few minutes to wander round, exploring the shop. There was a selection of greetings cards and she chose one with a picture of a Highland cow to send to her mum. Taking it up to the counter, she handed it to the shopkeeper.

"That's a nice one," the woman commented.

"Yes, it caught my eye because my mum's in Scotland at the moment. I thought she'd like it."

In her peripheral vision Zoe caught sight of a movement and glanced to the side to see what it was. An enormous black cat with large, pointed ears was making its way towards her. It was the biggest cat that Zoe had ever seen, and had thick fur and the most spectacular tail. Inscrutable green eyes stared at Zoe as the cat drew closer, then wound itself around her legs. She reached down and gently stroked the creature's thick coat.

"What an extraordinary cat."

The woman stood on tiptoes to see over the counter. "Interesting. Nova's very particular when it comes to which humans she'll tolerate. Looks like she's decided you're one of the good ones."

"What breed is she?"

"Maine Coon. She's a great companion. And very good at catching mice. You might see her patrolling around the village sometimes, she likes her freedom."

Looking at the shopkeeper, Zoe thought to herself that the woman's personal style seemed to match the eclectic nature of her shop, a mixture of practical and eccentric. She was wearing dungarees and chunky boots, and her purple hair coordinated with a scarf loosely draped around her neck. Long dangly silver earrings completed the look.

"Are you the young woman who's staying at the Old Rectory?" the woman enquired.

"Um, yes," Zoe said, taken aback.

The woman smiled understandingly. "It's a small village! I'm afraid everyone knows everyone else's business around here. Pleased to meet you. I'm Poppy."

"Zoe," she replied. "Pleased to meet you too."

"Has anyone mentioned the Yule celebration to you yet?" Poppy asked as she rang up the purchase on the till.

"No, I don't think so. What's that about?"

"It follows an ancient tradition of celebrating the winter solstice and the return of the sun. We have a bonfire at the village green and share a drink and something to eat. Everyone's welcome."

"It sounds interesting," Zoe replied, intrigued. "Kind of... pagan?"

The cat completed its circling of Zoe's legs and stalked off again towards the back of the shop.

Poppy smiled. "Well, it's a festival that pre-dates Christianity." She lowered her voice slightly as though someone might overhear, although they were the only ones in the shop. "There are one or two of the older, shall we say... um, 'traditionally-minded' members of the village who disapprove. There's one particular lady... you might see her walking, she always wears the same long beige coat..."

Zoe remembered the grumpy-faced woman who had glared at her outside her cottage the other day. "I think I know who you mean."

Poppy grimaced. "Yes, she's definitely not a fan of the event. Or of me, for that matter! But for the most part everyone enjoys it. We've been doing it for, oh, at least six or seven years now."

"And when is it?"

"Thursday, the twenty second. We start at six so it's not late for the little ones to join in."

"Do I need a ticket?"

Poppy laughed. "No, it's very informal. But there will be a van selling slices of pizza so you might want to bring some money for that."

Zoe thanked her and put the card in a large pocket of her coat. "I guess I'll see you there, then."

"See you," Poppy echoed, and Zoe pushed open the door, making the bell tinkle again as she did so.

Five

'Deck the halls with boughs of holly, fa la la la la, la la la la...'

In the late afternoon Zoe wrapped up in her coat, scarf and hat, and took the dogs along the river path, passing the pub on her left and heading up past the smart modern-looking houses. The sky was fading through pastel shades of pink, blue and grey. The moored boats bobbed gently on the turning tide and a flock of starlings was making its way to a group of trees on the other side of the water, ready to settle and roost for the night.

There was still enough daylight to see by when you were outside, but people were starting to switch on the lights in their houses, and Zoe was able to enjoy a sneaky peek into the interiors of the houses she passed. The first of these had a huge expanse of glass at the back, facing the river, revealing a large open plan space with a dining table at one side and a seating area at the other. The kitchen was just visible beyond. Although the lights were on there was no one in sight so Zoe could admire the interior without feeling that she was spying on anyone.

The owners had decorated in shades of warm white and added texture to make the look more cosy. The large corner sofa had a knitted throw laid across one arm as well as knitted scatter cushions, and there was a soft-looking rug on the floor. The dining table was made of a pale wood and sat on top of another rug, zoning the space. A tall Christmas tree was decorated with white and silver baubles and other ornaments, with a silver star glittering at the very top. The effect was very beautiful and classy but Zoe could only imagine that this was a household without dogs or children, to keep all those pale colours so pristine.

She moved on to the next property. This was on a slightly smaller scale but again featured large picture windows affording a good view to an inquisitive passer-by. This one looked more like a family home. Again, the underlying palette was neutral, but the tree was decorated in Scandi-style bright red and white, and Zoe could see a few homemade decorations amongst the shop-bought baubles and wooden reindeer decorations. She smiled, remembering all the glittery toilet-roll angels and cotton wool snowballs that she had created as a child to grace the family Christmas tree. The window here had homemade paper snowflakes stuck to it, echoing the three large and intricate snowflakes (presumably shop-bought) which hung from the ceiling above.

She had only a glimpse of the jewel-bright baubles on the tree belonging to the next house as she could see people inside and didn't want to disturb their privacy. After that there was just the row of cottages. The first looked unoccupied; its windows were dark. She wondered if perhaps it was just used as a summer holiday let. In any case there was clearly no one home tonight. The middle cottage was rendered and painted white. This one, and the third, had more signs of life. She couldn't see anything of the interiors; the terrace was set further back from the river and featured smaller windows than the large houses, and the curtains at these were already closed.

The third cottage was the one that attracted her attention the most. Its walls were the original red brick and there was a wreath hanging on the red front door. She wondered what it looked like inside. She imagined a cosy, modern country style lounge, perhaps with a Shaker style kitchen. It looked like the kind of house where tinsel would be allowed, not banished for being too retro and un-stylish. It looked like the kind of house where she would like to live.

Zoe and the dogs continued with their walk as she daydreamed about how she would decorate her ideal space. She liked natural materials – wood, rattan, greenery – and definitely lots of fairy lights. It was a shame she couldn't decorate this year but it just hadn't been practical to bring anything except her snow globe. It did seem strange to have Christmas without a Christmas tree. At home in her flat, she had a small artificial tree that she brought out each year. If she lived in a characterful cottage like that one, she would have fairy lights in every room. She wondered if it had a garden where she could watch the birds. In the spring she would take her morning coffee outside to sit in the warming rays of the sun.

She allowed her imagination to embroider the scene still further; perhaps she would plant sunflower seeds with a toddler and they would watch the flowers grow taller than all of them, even the handsome husband who came into the garden to kiss her cheek and swing the toddler, laughing, into the air. Perhaps a small scruffy brown dog would scamper across the lawn after a ball. Perhaps, perhaps.

She was so lost in thought that she didn't see the tabby cat trot across the lane in front of her. Barney did, however, and jumped forwards to chase it with such enthusiasm that she lost her grip on his lead. He dashed after the cat, barking furiously, with Henry trying to follow. Even sensible Bella pricked up her ears in interest.

"Barney!" Zoe ran after him and grabbed the end of the lead. "That was very naughty," she scolded him, as Barney ignored her and continued to bark at the cat. It had leaped lightly up a fence and onto a brick wall, and now sat looking down at them imperiously with unblinking eyes, apparently entirely unafraid.

"You're a very lucky dog that there were no cars around," Zoe went on, relieved that nothing more serious had happened on her watch. "I can see that I'm going to have to be on my toes when it comes to you."

Barney kept barking for a while as she dragged him away from the cat. "And you can stop taunting him!" she called back to it as it continued to sit smugly above them on its pedestal like an Egyptian deity, watching them with its green eyes.

Zoe was still feeling a little put out with Barney for running off as they made their way back through the garden gate at the Old Rectory. She unclipped the leads and he bounded off into the almost-darkness towards the chickens' enclosure. There was some scuffling and a sound as though pots near the shed were being knocked over.

"Barney! What are you up to now?!" Zoe walked towards the shed and was met by Barney trotting proudly towards her with something in his mouth. "What have you got?" She switched on her phone torch and then nearly dropped it in horror. Barney had caught an extremely large rat. From the way it was hanging down, Zoe could see that it was dead.

"Oh god. It's enormous. Well, good work, boy, I suppose. We don't want rats sniffing around the chickens so I guess we can say that you've redeemed yourself from your earlier naughtiness. Ok, drop the rat now. Drop it."

She moved towards him and Barney took a step back and gave a small growl. "You can't bring it in the house! Drop it. Drop the nasty rat." Barney kept a firm grip on his prize and Zoe wondered despairingly what she was supposed to do. A thought struck her like a lightbulb switching on above her head. Treats! That was what she needed. Zoe fished out a plastic poo bag and wrapped it around one hand, then took a treat out of her pocket.

"Good boy, then. Come and have a biscuit." Barney promptly dropped the rat to receive his reward, and Zoe quickly scooped up the dead rat in the plastic bag, shuddering in disgust. She tied the bag shut and put it into the wheelie bin. "Oh, that was gross. Come on then, you three. Let's get inside. I can't handle any more excitement tonight!"

****

Tuesday passed quietly. Apart from taking the dogs out and feeding the chickens, Zoe spent most of the day working on her laptop. She was looking forward to some socialising in the evening at the pub quiz. After taking the dogs for their afternoon walk, Zoe went round the house shutting the curtains and decided that she had done enough work for that day. Isobel had said that she would call for her at about seven forty-five so there was still plenty of time to cook and get ready. She prepared a tray of vegetables to roast, drizzling them with olive oil and sprinkling over some rosemary that she had collected from the garden. She saved the leftover odds and ends of vegetables and took them out to the chickens.

Once the tray was in the oven, she took a cup of tea through to the snug and switched on the TV to look for something Christmassy to watch. A cheesy telemovie was just beginning, featuring a very beautiful woman with unnaturally white teeth who was drafted in to help save a struggling country hotel. From the look of the handsome hotel owner in the lumberjack shirt, who was of course not keen on the beautiful woman's interference, Zoe knew exactly how the story was going to play out.

"And I don't care," she told Henry, who was sat at her feet looking up at her. "Maybe trashy TV movies are a guilty pleasure, but it's a pleasure nonetheless."

She got up during an advert break to start cooking some rice, then came back in to pause the TV when she realised that while she didn't want to miss the film, she might let something burn if she neglected the cooking for too long. She took out the finished vegetables when the oven timer beeped, and was soon back in the snug enjoying her dinner, and watching the developing relationship between the couple on screen. By the time the credits rolled she was feeling well fed and so comfortable that it was almost tempting to stay in, but she was also in need of some company.

Looking through her wardrobe, Zoe chose a burgundy coloured top to replace the hoody she'd been wearing all day. She selected a cardigan to go over the top so she could easily take off a layer, as she suspected that it might be quite warm in the pub. She made sure to feed the dogs and chickens and was ready to go when she heard Isobel's knock at the door.

There were shadows under Isobel's eyes but she had accessorised with snowflake earrings and she was looking relaxed. "All finished!" she announced happily. "The holiday starts here."

"All right, don't rub it in," Steve grumbled. "Some of us don't finish until Friday."

"Sorry, love." Isobel patted his arm sympathetically.

Zoe smiled. "I'm with you, Steve. Still lots to do. Although I have to admit, I am winding down now."

"Think you've got time to join in with a solstice swim on Thursday?" Isobel asked hopefully.

"I'm not sure it's lack of time that's putting me off swimming in a freezing river! I did meet Poppy though, in the shop, and she told me about the Yule celebration in the evening."

"Oh yes! I should have mentioned it before. We always go, it's lots of fun."

They had reached the pub. Lights shone cheerfully in the mullioned windows and a faint sound of chatter and laughter came from inside. The old wooden door was hung with a rustic wreath, studded with pinecones. Steve went first, pushing open the door, and Isobel and Zoe followed.

Inside it was lovely and warm, and a buzz of sound rouse from the conversations of all the patrons sat at scrubbed wooden tables or leaning on the bar. The building was clearly very old; fairy lights hung from the original beams and the stone floor beneath their feet was slightly uneven through long years of use. The bar was decorated with a long swag of greenery and tartan ribbons, and decorations adorned every alcove and window. The effect was enchanting.

Steve led the way to a small table where a sandy-haired man in a navy cable-knit sweater was sitting with a pint in front of him.

"Alright Rob?" he greeted him. "This is Zoe, she's house-sitting at Simone and Neil's so Isobel's press-ganged her into joining the team tonight."

Isobel swatted at her husband in mock annoyance as Rob stood, smiling, to shake Zoe's hand.

"Good to meet you, Zoe," he said. He had an open, friendly face and was stockily built. The large hand that shook hers was warm and calloused and she recalled that Isobel had mentioned that Rob farmed some land nearby.

"What can I get you two to drink?" Steve asked. "They've got mulled wine tonight if that takes your fancy."

"Ooh, yes please," Isobel replied, and Zoe nodded.

"That sounds great, thanks."

Steve headed to the bar and the two women sat down with Rob.

"So, what are you bringing to the team, Zoe? Any specialist subjects?" Rob grinned.

"Oh wow, I'm not sure! I usually do ok on music questions. And maybe anagrams, if they have those? I'm not much use on sport though."

"Me neither!" Isobel put in. "But Steve is good at those questions. Between us all we'll smash it. Not that I'm competitive," she finished.

Rob laughed as Steve returned with the drinks. He set steaming glasses of mulled wine in front of Zoe and Isobel.

"Oh no, you're not competitive at all, my love," he teased her.

Zoe watched in amusement as Isobel put her face in her hands.

"Oh, fine! I admit it! I am horribly competitive. But honestly, who doesn't like to win? Last time we were beaten into second place by just a couple of points and the winning team looked so smug, so I really want to show them how it's done this time." She nudged Zoe's shoulder.

"I have a feeling that you are going to be our secret weapon."

"Harsh," an unfamiliar voice commented. "I thought you said I was your secret weapon."

Zoe turned to see that a tall man had approached the table from behind her. He looked lean and fit and was wearing jeans and an unbuttoned checked shirt over a t-shirt. Zoe guessed that he was in his early thirties. He ran a hand through his dark curly hair and with a jolt of recognition she realised that this was the man she had – hmm, admired? – coming out of the river yesterday. She blushed, hoping that the heat of the room would excuse the colour rising in her cheeks.

"Tom!" Isobel got to her feet and kissed his cheek. "You know you're an integral cog in the team machine." He rolled his eyes slightly at this. "Anyway, this is Zoe."

Turning to Zoe, he nodded in greeting and his blue eyes held hers for a moment.

"Nice to meet you," he said briefly.

"Better get a drink quick mate, I think we're nearly ready to start," Rob advised as the quizmaster approached their table with question sheets and pens. Tom headed to the bar and ordered a pint from the slender young barmaid with a halo of Afro hair framing her pretty oval face. Zoe took a sip of her mulled wine and felt the warmth of the spices and alcohol spread through her body.

The first of the question sheets was an anagram round which they could get started on immediately. There was a Christmas theme so before Tom had even returned to the table, the team had quickly sorted out LAWN SLOB into SNOWBALLS and SNOG TICK into STOCKING.

They were hesitating over HYENA PIP when Tom returned and sat down with his own glass of mulled wine.

"Write the letters in a circle," Zoe suggested, but Isobel had barely put pen to paper when Tom spoke.

"Epiphany."

"Oh, well done!" Isobel said cheerfully. "That's a bit of an obscure one."

After that they just had time to spot that CAN ASSAULT should become SANTA CLAUS before the quizmaster switched on the microphone and began to speak.

"Good evening everybody, and welcome to this festive edition of our monthly quiz here at the Mulberry Tree. Just a friendly reminder before we start that phones should be out of sight throughout the quiz; we don't want any cheating!"

Zoe picked up her phone to check that it was on silent before slipping it into her bag. Tom leaned a little closer to her.

"Think you can manage without your phone for a few minutes?"

She frowned at him uncomprehendingly. "Um, yes, I think I'll survive."

His voice was cool. "I thought perhaps it was glued to your hand."

She still didn't understand – she wasn't even holding her phone when she'd seen him coming out of the river – then she suddenly gasped as she realised what he was talking about. "It was you I bumped into on Friday night!"

He raised an eyebrow. "Glad I was so memorable."

"Well, it was really too dark to see your face. But I'd hardly forget nearly being knocked over by a glowing beast in the darkness!" She glared at him.

Steve was listening with amusement. "A glowing beast?"

Tom answered before Zoe had a chance. "I was out for a run and Zoe and I bumped into each other – literally. She was looking at her phone, rather than where she was going."

Zoe bristled. "I think you'll find you were the one who bumped into me, I was just minding my own business. I'd only picked up my phone for a moment to check directions."

Rob shushed them both. "We're going to miss the first question!"

"So let the fun begin! Now some of our rounds have a Christmas theme but we've got some regular questions too. Round one: flags and capital cities of Europe."

The first round began and Zoe tried to ignore Tom and focus on the questions. She wasn't about to let him spoil her evening.

"Question one: what is the capital city of Estonia?"

"Tallinn," whispered Steve, and Isobel wrote it down.

"Question two: which country's flag is this?"

The quizmaster held up a flag with a blue cross on a white background.

"Is it Norway?" Zoe whispered. "I think it's one of the Scandinavian countries."

"Finland," Tom answered confidently, and Zoe felt a pang of annoyance at his certainty. Maybe I'm more competitive than I realised, she thought to herself. But I'm not supposed to be competing with my own team!

Several more rounds followed with questions on sport, music and TV. They stopped for an interval so that people could refresh their drinks and the points so far could be totalled up. Their anagram answers were collected along with the other four sheets.

"So, at the halfway point, our leaderboard stands as follows," the quizmaster announced. "The Snow Hopers; twenty-six points." A cheer rose from a table near the bar. "The Naughty Elves; twenty-nine points." Another cheer from across the room. Isobel was looking tense.

"Flying the flag for the youngsters, the Gen Z Snowflakes have thirty-one points. All Present and Correct; well not quite, you lot, you've got thirty-two points. So, currently in a close second place with a very respectable thirty-six points, we have the Christmas Crackers."

"That's us!" Zoe exclaimed, pleased.

Isobel winced while Steve patted her shoulder reassuringly. "It's all good, love. We've still got time to take them."

"Ooh, look at their smug faces," Isobel hissed to him. "I *so* want to beat them."

The table near the fire was now the only one not called, so they knew they were in first place and were exchanging grins as they waited to hear their team's name. "Which means," the quizmaster continued, "that in first place, just one point ahead with thirty-seven points, is Ice Ice Baby!"

The first-placed team whooped and clapped. Looking at the self-satisfied faces, Zoe suddenly felt that she wanted the Christmas Crackers to win just as much as Isobel did.

Six
'It's the most wonderful time of the year...'

"Right, on with the show. Round six: film. And this is one of our Christmas-themed rounds, so question one is: on which number street does a miracle take place when a courtroom finds in favour of Kris Kringle?"

Isobel wrote down '34th Street'.

"Question two: in the film *Mean Girls*, the Plastics perform a dance to which Christmas song?"

"Maybe 'Santa Baby'?" Tom whispered.

"It's 'Jingle Bell Rock'," Zoe answered.

"Definitely?" Isobel asked, pen poised ready to write.

"Definitely," Zoe confirmed. She blushed furiously as she admitted; "When I was at high school my friends and I learned the dance."

Rob was grinning. "Can you still remember it?"

Isobel swatted him with the answer paper.

"Question three: which Christmas film have UK audiences voted as their favourite for the last three years in a row?"

"*Elf*," Steve suggested.

"What about *It's a Wonderful Life*?" Isobel chipped in.

"It's good but I don't know if it's still so popular these days. *Muppet Christmas Carol*? That's my favourite," Zoe offered.

Tom shook his head. "It's got to be *Die Hard*."

"*Die Hard*?!" Zoe was incredulous. "Is that even a Christmas film?"

"Of course it is," Rob agreed. "Have you never seen it?"

Zoe was forced to admit that she hadn't. Rob was dismayed. "Oh, you have to watch it! I think I've got the DVD somewhere, I'll have to dig it out."

In the end they decided on *It's a Wonderful Life*, which turned out to be correct when the answers were read out at the end of the round.

Three more rounds followed in quick succession before the final round was announced. This was one purely focused on

Christmas-themed questions. The teams conferred in whispers and scribbled their answers intently. Soon there were only two questions left.

"Question nine: what do Swedish children leave out for Santa?"

"Could be a trick question," Rob whispered. "Maybe they leave a mince pie too?"

Zoe shook her head, smiling. "I know this one! I have a Swedish friend and she told me that they leave out a cup of coffee, to help him stay awake."

Isobel duly wrote down the answer.

"And finally, question ten: in the first Harry Potter book, what gift does Harry receive from the Dursleys?"

"Socks," Tom answered immediately.

"No," Zoe countered, "I'm sure it's a fifty pence coin."

"How sure?" Tom challenged her. "Because I really think it's socks."

"Really sure," Zoe insisted. Isobel looked dismayed.

"Come on team, what am I going to write?"

The quizmaster was coming round to collect the final answer sheets. Tom grabbed the pen and wrote '50p' and handed in the sheet.

Oh god, thought Zoe, I hope that was the right answer! She didn't want to let the team down, but she was almost certain that she was correct.

Again a short interval ensued while the scores were totted up. Isobel, Steve and Rob chatted cheerfully, but Zoe felt tense. She was aware of Tom's silent presence by her side. Soon the quizmaster was ready to announce the scores. He started with the last placed team which turned out to be the Snow Hopers. They seemed unfazed and loud cheers and laughter came from their table. Zoe suspected that their generous intake of mulled wine might not have helped their score!

The quizmaster continued to read out the rankings until only two teams remained. As at the halfway point, it came down to the Christmas Crackers versus Ice Ice Baby. Isobel gripped Steve's hand tightly.

"It was a very close race at the top of the leaderboard, with just one point between the top two teams. I'm happy to announce that the winners, with a fantastic score of seventy-six points, are... The Christmas Crackers!"

Their table erupted in cheers as the Ice Ice Baby team looked crestfallen. Isobel's smile spread from ear to ear and Zoe was buzzing. They were presented with their prize – a bottle of champagne – which Isobel pushed towards Zoe.

"You should take this, you really were our secret weapon. I'm sure we wouldn't have aced that last round without you."

Zoe demurred politely. "That's really kind but I don't think I can drink a bottle of champagne on my own."

"Not with an attitude like that," Rob quipped.

"You and Steve take it," Zoe suggested. "There are two of you, after all."

"Well, ok, but only if you promise to come round and help us drink it," Isobel conceded.

Some of the other punters were heading to the bar for another round but others were starting to put on their coats and prepare to leave. Rob stretched and stood up reluctantly.

"I'd better head off, early start tomorrow."

"Me too," Zoe said. "I've got to get back to the dogs."

They all headed outside together into the cold night air. Zoe glanced back towards the river. A bright moon, nearly full, floated not far above the horizon. The river reflected its light and scattered it in ripples. Tom and Rob said their goodnights; they were taking a path off to the right. Tom held out his hand to Zoe.

"Well played," he told her, his expression inscrutable. Zoe reached out to shake the proffered hand and felt a jolt, almost like an electric shock, as they touched for the first time. The next moment Rob was kissing her cheek and saying goodbye and it was all over so quickly that she barely had time to register what had happened. Too much wine? she asked herself as she began to walk up the lane with Isobel and Steve.

"I assume you don't have any plans for Christmas Day itself?" Isobel asked as they walked past houses decorated with fairy lights. Zoe liked the houses with strings of warm white lights hanging down. The blue and white ones looked more like icicles but they weren't as welcoming, in her opinion.

"Well, no," Zoe admitted. "I've got a small chicken in the freezer so I'm planning to make myself a simple version of Christmas dinner. I might just stay in my PJs for most of the day although, come to think of it, I do still have to walk the dogs. I suppose I'll get dressed for that."

"You can't be on your own on Christmas Day! Come to ours for lunch."

Zoe was torn. She really didn't want to be alone for the whole of Christmas Day – she'd rather been dreading it – but she didn't want to butt in where she wasn't really wanted.

"I'll be ok. I'm not going to impose on your family Christmas."

Isobel shook her head. "You wouldn't be imposing at all, and I love a big crowd around the table at Christmas. You'd fit right in."

Zoe was about to protest some more but Steve stepped in. "She's quite right, we do usually have a few waifs and strays. You'd be very welcome."

That swung it. Isobel had that firm look in her eye again but Zoe would have stood her ground if Steve hadn't been happy to join in with the invitation.

"Ok, in that case I'd love to. Thanks very much."

"Fab! It'll be great fun," Isobel beamed.

They continued past more lavishly decorated houses. Zoe rather wondered why Santa had forsaken his usual sleigh and seemed to be travelling in a hot air balloon on one, and by train on another, but she was certainly amused by them all.

They said goodnight outside the Old Rectory and Zoe went in to see the dogs. They were all pleased to see her return after an absence of a few hours and she let them out into the garden briefly before locking the back door for the night. Yawning, she headed upstairs to brush her teeth and get ready for bed. It had been a fun evening. She was delighted to have helped the team to victory, especially because it seemed so important to Isobel. Rob seemed like a really nice character. She wasn't sure about Tom. At first he had seemed to take her for a frivolous city girl, glued to her phone. But he had given way and written down her answer in that final round, and shaken her hand afterwards.

Snuggling down under the thick duvet, she sighed as she shut her eyes. Unbidden, an image of his fit body rising out of the river floated across her mind's eye. She pushed it away. That's enough, she told herself firmly. No more nonsense tonight. Whether it was the fresh air from all the dog walking that did the trick, or perhaps the mulled wine, within moments she was sound asleep.

****

Wednesday dawned clear and bright, and Zoe woke refreshed from a deep and restful sleep. She went downstairs and opened door number twenty-one on the advent calendar to discover a picture of an angel, dressed in white with a shining halo above its head.

As she pottered around the kitchen making porridge with honey and berries for breakfast, she reflected that today would be a good day to walk into Woodbridge. She had been planning to go at some point for a wander around to explore the little town. Now that she was invited to Isobel and Steve's for Christmas lunch, she thought that it would be a nice gesture to get them something. She ought to be able to find something suitable in Woodbridge.

The dogs still needed their morning walk first, so once she'd finished breakfast Zoe clipped Barney and Henry's leads to their collars and together they headed out of the back door,

Bella trotting slightly ahead. Zoe had been looking at a map of the area and thought that they might try a different footpath this morning, following the edge of a field in a southerly direction and skirting an area of woodland. She found the path easily enough, beginning at a break in the hedgerow with a finger post pointing the way up a slight hill.

The field edge turned out to be rather muddy and Zoe was beginning to regret her decision – she would certainly have to clean some muddy paws before letting the dogs back in the house – when the path bent to the left, there was a break in the trees next to her, and a new vista opened up. She was now some way above the river and there it was below, shimmering in the winter sunshine, the moored boats bobbing gently as the water flowed past them.

"Beautiful!"

The bare branches of the trees swayed slightly in the light wind, framing the view over the water. It was so quiet that Zoe almost felt she might have been the only person for miles around. The opposite bank of the river looked untouched by humans at the first glance, although when Zoe looked harder she spotted a couple of isolated houses nestled into patches of woodland. The view from their windows must have been stunning.

She was still lost in the moment when Henry let out a quick bark and she turned to see a runner coming towards them, down the hill. The sun was behind him, silhouetting him, so that he was almost upon her before she realised that it was Tom. She felt unreasonably annoyed that he was interrupting her peace, and prepared to give him just a brief hello as he ran past. However as he drew closer, he slowed to a walk and paused his running watch. Barney moved forwards immediately to say hello and to attempt to lick Tom's legs. He seemed unperturbed and gave the little furry head a scratch.

"Morning, Zoe," he greeted her.

"Morning," she replied coolly, wanting to be polite but reluctant to start a conversation. Barney was still trying to lick Tom. "Barney, stop that!"

"Oh, he's all right, I don't mind. I probably taste salty because I'm running. Listen, I was hoping to bump into you. I was out of order last night and I wanted to say that I'm sorry."

"Oh," she said, wrong-footed. This wasn't how she was expecting this to go!

"Did Isobel tell you I'm a teacher? High school, not primary like her. Anyway, some of the kids are always on their phones and it's become a pet peeve of mine. And when I ran into you the other night I was particularly tired and grumpy and I'm thinking now that I was being unfair."

Zoe didn't know what to say. Tom looked sheepish.

"Do you think we could start again? Your knowledge of Harry Potter and random Swedish customs is very impressive, even if you haven't seen *Die Hard*." His eyes twinkled.

Zoe relented. How often did you hear a sincere apology?

"Ok, maybe we can start over," she conceded with a small smile.

Tom's own smile was wide and genuine. "Great." He looked out at the view she had just been admiring. "Isn't it beautiful? I'm so lucky to live here."

Zoe had to agree. "It's stunning. So peaceful. I'm really enjoying it here."

His eyes were warm as he looked down at her. "I'm glad. Now, I suppose I'd better get on with this run. See you around?"

"Yes, see you," Zoe replied, as he started his watch again and headed off down towards the river.

"Curiouser and curiouser," she commented to Bella, who was sat patiently at her side. "First he practically knocks me over and is rude to me, then he as good as calls me an airhead, then he's all charming and apologetic." She shook her head in bewilderment. "Well, come on then, let's get on." They carried on up the hill, following the path that Tom had approached from, and found a crossroads of footpath signs at the top. Not wanting to go too far with plenty more walking ahead of her later, she took the right hand fork that looked likely to take her back to the village by the quickest route. She soon spotted the church and found her bearings, and Bella led the way back to the house.

Zoe took the dogs back inside and had a cup of tea and a satsuma before getting ready to set out again on her own. Following the river path, she headed upriver towards the white beacon of the Tide Mill. She became quite warm as she walked and undid the buttons on her coat. As she drew closer to the town, there were plenty of people strolling along the river wall and enjoying the mild day and the winter sunshine. She was looking forward to exploring all that the town had to offer.

Seven

'Oh the weather outside is frightful, but the fire is so delightful...'

Zoe kept walking along the river path until she saw a footbridge over the platforms and track of the railway station. A train was approaching from the north and she hurriedly climbed the steps with a sense of childish excitement to watch it pass underneath the bridge. Zoe loved trains and while her enthusiasm for them had been slightly dampened of late by the squashed conditions of the London Tube, out here in the open air she could enjoy them once more. The sight of a steam train would have been even better, but this was a working line, not a heritage line. Her dad had been particularly keen on steam trains and many of her childhood holidays had featured a train ride. In her imagination she could still smell the smoke puffing from the chimney and hear the shriek of the whistle.

She walked down the far side of steps and headed straight up a road opposite, taking her to the end of the main thoroughfare. Shoppers were milling around carrying bags of their purchases, and lights were strung across the street, glimmering in the shadows where the low sun didn't reach over the buildings. Real Christmas trees – small ones! – were affixed to the shops above head height, leaning out diagonally across the street. A bearded busker was singing and playing guitar outside one of the shops and Zoe paused to listen for a moment. He was singing 'Fairytale of New York', one of Zoe's favourite Christmas songs. She dug a pound coin out of her pocket and tossed it into his case, and he gave her a nod and a smile as he continued singing.

Zoe wandered along slowly, stopping to look in shop windows to admire their displays and seek some inspiration for the gifts she planned to buy. There were quite a few of the usual chain stores but also plenty of independent, local businesses. She couldn't resist a look inside one particularly interesting-looking shop that had shelves piled high with scarves, soaps, candles and jewellery. There were certainly lots of things here that she would like to buy for herself... Examining each display with interest, she spotted a mug featuring a print of swimmers that would be perfect for Isobel.

A few doors down was an authentic chocolaterie with a tempting display of Belgian chocolates. She wondered about buying something for Charlie but had a feeling that perhaps he might prefer quantity over quality. These exquisite little morsels would be gone in a flash, from what she'd seen of his appetite. She wandered in and out of a couple of bookshops, pausing for quite a long time in the charity bookshop. Tinsel was draped over the top of the bookshelves and music was playing; Zoe hummed along with 'Santa Claus is coming to town' as she browsed the shelves. She had a quick scan through various sections but fiction was always her favourite genre. Tilting her head to one side to better read the names on the spines, she saw quite a number of books that she had already read. She picked up a Christmassy story set in Scotland, thinking of her mum, and flicked through a couple of pages. This looked just the thing for curling up with on the sofa in the evening. She took it up to the till and was served by a friendly older man wearing a Christmas jumper emblazoned with a snowy scene.

Moving on, she came across a small supermarket that sold a range of local produce as well as the usual big brands, and she found some nice-looking lemon drizzle biscuits and a big slab of chocolate for Charlie. That just left Steve. She remembered seeing the shop near the station that was run by a local brewery, and thought that she could call in there before heading back to Redfield.

Winding her way down towards the river to get her bearings, Zoe found herself near the Tide Mill. A tall white wooden building, the shape of its red tiled roof reminded her of an upturned boat's hull. There were five windows up the side almost to the apex of the roof, hinting at the different levels within. She walked past it to take a look at the still surface of the mill pond behind. The mill itself was closed to the public for the winter but she had a look at the information board outside. It explained that the mill still produced flour, and there were pictures of the huge machinery inside. She wondered if she could come back some time in the summer to see the town in a different season. Turning to her right, she saw a café and a few more shops and decided to grab a sandwich for lunch. It was just turned midday and her stomach was rumbling.

The café was bright and modern and busy with customers, many with bags full of their own Christmas shopping, but Zoe managed to find a free table. Soon she was tucking into a cheese toastie with red onion marmalade, accompanied by a pot of tea. Suitably fortified for the walk home, she exited the café and spent a few happy minutes looking at the Christmas activities that were taking place in the square outside. Children were running around following a 'find the Christmas elf' treasure hunt and there were gazebos set up with local crafts and goodies for sale. Zoe couldn't resist treating herself to a bag of mince pie flavoured fudge to enjoy later.

Zoe carried on walking downstream along the river's edge, past houseboats moored along the quay. She admired the boats, wondering what it would be like to live on one. Some had little porthole windows; some had chairs set up on their outside deck areas. A small white terrier padding busily around on the deck of one boat made her smile. Perhaps they would be more appealing in summer than winter, she reflected, though smoke rose from several chimneys suggesting a cosy cabin within.

She passed a sign advertising a free children's craft workshop. It was only the first day of the school holidays but she could see several parents following the signs and taking their young children into the building to keep them occupied for a while with glueing and colouring. She suspected that there might be rather a lot of glitter and cotton wool snow involved, if it was anything like the crafts she remembered from her own childhood.

She soon spotted the railway bridge and crossed over to the brewery shop. This was a real treasure trove of beers, wine, gin and kitchen equipment. They were having a special Christmas shopping event with free samples being handed out to customers. Zoe accepted a shot glass of Prosecco and sipped it slowly, enjoying the bubbles. Steve had been drinking beer at the pub quiz so Zoe chose a gift pack with bottles of local ale. She was glad that she had her rucksack to load these into; it would certainly be easier to carry home. Having paid and been wished "Merry Christmas" by the smiling assistant, she shouldered her bag and set off on the return walk.

Back at the Old Rectory Zoe made a cup of tea before laying out her present haul on the breakfast bar along with some star-print wrapping paper. She found scissors and tape in a drawer. With Christmas tunes playing on the radio, she set to work wrapping the gifts. Luckily they were all easy shapes to wrap and she was soon finished. She decided to keep them upstairs in her bedroom. She didn't think the dogs were likely to smell the biscuits and decide to eat them while she wasn't around, but better not to take any chances. It wasn't like she had a Christmas tree to put them under anyway.

It felt like the perfect evening for getting cosy and Christmassy. Once she'd eaten dinner, complete with a couple of pieces of fudge for pudding, Zoe changed into her pyjamas and got ready to settle in for the evening. She lit the fire and coaxed the flames into life until it was burning well. She switched off the bright overhead light and turned on a couple of lamps for a softer glow, and lit a candle. With the curtains pulled and the dogs curled up on the hearthrug, she settled on the sofa under a blanket with a glass of red wine and switched on the TV. A programme showing Christmas crafts was just beginning and Zoe watched the presenter and guests making their own stockings, table centrepieces, and Yule logs. She enjoyed these sorts of programmes even though she wasn't very skilled at crafts herself.

"I'm not too sure about these table centrepieces," she told the dogs. "They're certainly very pretty, but they do seem like a lot of work for something that you have to move out of the way the minute you sit down, to make space for all the dishes on the table!"

Bella laid her head on her paws and sighed.

"I think you agree with me, don't you?" She sighed herself. "I don't know what makes me seem more crazy, talking to myself or having a one-sided conversation with you three. Good job there's no one else around to hear!"

She was feeling upbeat after her successful shopping trip, and a definitely a little more Christmassy than she had the day before. She rather wished that she had bought herself some of the beautiful Belgian chocolates from the shop earlier, but then she remembered that her online food shop had included some chocolate truffles and she went to root through the kitchen cupboards to find them. Snuggled back under the blanket, a couple of chocolates were the perfect addition to her cosy evening. She switched off the TV after the craft programme finished, and picked up her new book. She was soon completely absorbed in the story and the next thing she knew, an hour had passed and she was ready to make her way up to bed.

Eight

'In the bleak midwinter...'

Zoe had no intention of joining the swimmers in the water for their solstice sunrise swim, but she was awake just after seven and decided she would take the dogs down to the river to watch the sun rise. She could have breakfast when she got back. She dressed and made coffee, pouring it into a thermal travel mug to take with her, and set the washing machine running before she left the house.

The sky was beginning to lighten as she made her way along the footpath to the beach, coffee in one hand and dogs' leads in the other. It looked set to be another fine day and although Zoe was glad of her warm coat and woolly hat, there was only the lightest touch of frost in more sheltered spots.

She emerged from the tunnel of branches onto the beach and into the light. The sun wasn't yet above the horizon but the deepest indigo of the night sky was giving way to lighter blues, with stripes of orange and peach where the first rays touched the clouds. On the other side of the river the trees were silhouetted black against the glowing sky and she stood transfixed.

"This was worth getting out of bed for," she told the dogs.

She heard shouts and laughter and headed along the beach a short way to where the swimmers were gathered. They had already entered the water and were swimming up and down, bright hats bobbing above the water as they cruised along. Zoe counted ten – no, eleven – people in the river and there were several more standing on the beach watching. She went over to join them, spotting Steve amongst the group.

"Morning, Steve."

"Good morning! Come for a recce, before you try it yourself?"

Zoe laughed. "Maybe. I'm yet to be convinced that this is a good idea. But they all seem to be having a good time."

"They do. You still wouldn't catch me doing it, though. I only make an exception when we have a heatwave."

Zoe sipped her coffee and watched the swimmers while the dogs sniffed around the pebbles and driftwood washed up on the river's shoreline.

"Are you working today?" she asked Steve.

"Yes, and tomorrow. Then I'm off until after New Year, so it's not too bad." He checked his watch. "I'll have to head off to work soon actually but I expect Isobel will be out in a minute". Sure enough, within seconds Zoe spotted Isobel wading out of the water and up the beach. Steve handed her a large changing robe and she made quick work of getting out of her wetsuit and into her warm clothes. Her bobble hat stayed firmly on her head throughout the whole process. Zoe was impressed.

"Isobel, you're positively glowing! It looks like that did you some good."

Isobel was beaming and rosy-cheeked. "It always does! I'll feel great all morning now. Revitalised!"

Most of the other swimmers were also coming out and drying off. As Zoe looked around she recognised Tom. He looked just as fit as he had the other day but this time she was closer and had a better view. She looked away quickly so that he wouldn't think she was ogling him.

"Still up for joining the Yule celebration tonight?" Isobel asked.

"Yes, definitely."

"We'll see you there. I'm not sure exactly what time Steve will get in from work and if we're running late I wouldn't want you to miss the start of the ceremony."

"It all sounds very interesting."

Tom came over to join them, pulling a t-shirt and then a fleece jumper over his athletic torso.

"You'll be at the bonfire tonight, won't you, Tom?" Steve asked him.

"Yeah, I reckon. Are you all going?" He looked particularly at Zoe as he spoke and she nodded. "I'll see you there, then."

"Come on then love, I need to get off to work." Steve picked up Isobel's bag and Zoe and the dogs followed them back through the village.

Back at home, Zoe's washing had finished and she hung out the clothes on the line in the garden. It looked like a sunny enough day to make it worthwhile. Even if the clothes didn't get completely dry, they would have a pleasant freshness from drying outdoors. She had very cold fingers by the time she had finished and she rubbed them together briskly as she went back inside.

She made a cup of tea and decided to do a little research into cold water swimming. She read that just a couple of minutes in cold water seemed to have a beneficial effect, helping with stress and mental strength, and possibly a natural boost to the immune system. Apparently you shouldn't stay in long – certainly no more than twenty minutes and probably much less – to avoid hypothermia. It was best to start swimming outdoors before the temperature dropped, and then to keep going at least once a week to gradually acclimatise your body to the cold. That obviously wasn't going to be an option here!

Zoe sat back from her laptop and looked down at Bella who was lying near her feet.

"It's a completely mad idea, obviously, but I have to admit I do want to try it! I think it would be a real buzz."

Bella gave a long sigh and Zoe laughed and leaned down to rub the black dog's belly.

"Maybe next time Isobel asks me, I'll say yes."

As darkness fell Zoe's thoughts turned to the solstice celebration. It sounded quirky. She wasn't big on organised religion but at the same time she felt that ritual and tradition were interesting concepts and she was keen to see how this local version played out. Close to six o'clock she put on her teddy coat and pulled on a hat over her dark hair. Barney wagged his tail and looked hopeful.

"Not tonight, Barney. I'm not sure this event is dog-friendly. You stay in the warm now."

Zoe could see her breath hanging in clouds in the cold, still night air as she shut the door and set off into the darkness. With few street lights it really would have been very dark, but the moon was full and cast a silvery light over the village. The haunting call and response of a pair of tawny owls echoed through the bare branches of the trees and she shivered slightly despite her warm coat. It felt like a night for magic and mysticism.

Zoe was getting quite caught up in fantastical thoughts of supernatural forces surging through the darkness when she turned a corner, emerging at the village green, and her strange imaginings melted away in an instant. A crowd of people was already gathered, children shrieking and running around the edges of the group in excited anticipation. Poppy from the village shop was there, swathed in a long green cloak-like coat and wearing a garland of greenery on her purple hair. She was handing out glow sticks and the children holding them were like fireflies darting through the blackness.

Light shone cheerfully from the pizza van, drawing her in with its glow and with the tempting smells emanating from within. As she made her way over to it, she spotted a familiar face. Rob was standing near the van, wearing a green weatherproof jacket and a navy beanie hat over his blonde hair. He was already halfway through his slice of pizza.

"Hey, Zoe!"

"Evening. That looks good."

"Mm, it's great. Are you going to get a slice?"

"Definitely! I'll be back in a sec."

She joined the small queue and was soon rejoining Rob with her own piece of pizza. She took a large bite, savouring the rich cheesy taste.

"Oh, you were right, that's delicious."

Rob grinned. "Worth coming out in the cold for, isn't it? I always think that food tastes better when you eat outside."

"Your job must suit you well, as you're so keen on the outdoors."

Rob nodded. "Yeah, most of the time I think I've got it pretty good, although the hours are long. The idea of going to an office every day brings me out in a cold sweat – I'd hate it." He pointed to a smaller vehicle next to the pizza van. "Do you fancy a coffee or something?"

Hot drinks were being served from a small modified van. Its side opened up like a wing to reveal barista-style machinery, containers of milk and other ingredients, and disposable cups.

"It's so cute!" Zoe exclaimed.

Rob ordered coffee – "It won't keep me awake, I'm always out like a light the minute my head hits the pillow" – and Zoe opted for hot chocolate. This was served with a swirl of cream and a sprinkling of marshmallows over the top. She wrapped her cold fingers around the cup and took a sip. It was creamy and silky smooth.

"I love sweet things," she confessed to Rob, "and normally I try to eat quite healthily... but it is Christmas."

Isobel and Steve joined them, holding slices of pizza. Together they made their way over to the edge of the unlit bonfire. Branches and unwanted rough wooden pallets had been piled high.

"Just made it in time! I think they must be nearly ready to start," Isobel commented. The crowd certainly seemed to be drifting over in their direction.

Steve looked around. "Tom's going to miss it if he's not here soon," he remarked.

Looking around, Zoe saw the sour-faced old woman in the beige coat walking past the village green, looking very put out. Isobel glanced over too.

"Uh oh," she said quietly. "I think Barbara has come out for a walk at this time deliberately, just so that she can look at us disapprovingly."

"Poppy did mention that she's not a fan of this celebration," Zoe whispered back.

"No kidding! She tried to get it banned after the first year, but there was too much support for the event so it carried on."

The assembled villagers were now spread in a circle around the pyramid of wood. Poppy approached and stepped up onto an old tree stump, waving glow sticks to get their attention. There was a smattering of applause, then a hush fell.

"Welcome, friends!" she called in a clear voice. "We gather each December on this long dark night to celebrate the turning of the year and the return of the sun!" There was some clapping and cheering.

"John and Marie are now circulating with drinks for the toast so please help yourselves to either a cider or an apple juice." An older man came their way holding a tray with plastic shot glasses filled with amber liquid and Zoe took one and thanked him.

"May you find rest and peace in the darkness; balance, harmony and connection in winter's embrace, and may your path be illuminated as the light returns!" More clapping followed. Zoe was fascinated. It seemed like a lovely ritual, celebrating and embracing the cycles of the natural world.

"We will now light the bonfire, then raise our glasses in a toast."

Poppy hopped down and lit a torch which flamed brightly, illuminating her face. A few of the smaller children gasped and she smiled at them as she approached.

"Let's have a countdown, please. FIVE" – Everyone joined in – "FOUR, THREE, TWO, ONE!"

She thrust the flaming torch into the pyramid. The wood caught quickly and soon the whole pile was burning brightly, flames licking up from the top into the black night. The smallest children jumped up and down with glee and everyone cheered.

Zoe was just as entranced as the little ones at the great glowing beacon of the bonfire pushing back the darkness.

"Now, please join me in raising your glasses," Poppy called. "To new beginnings!"

As she raised her glass Zoe suddenly spotted Tom for the first time that evening. He stood almost opposite her, his face glowing in the firelight. He looked directly at her and their eyes met as they echoed the toast, "To new beginnings."

"Happy Yule everybody!" Poppy finished and there was more cheering and applause.

Tom came over to join Zoe and the others.

"Hey, there you are!" Rob greeted him. "I thought you weren't going to make it."

"I was busy in the workshop and lost track of time," Tom explained. "Just made it in time to see the bonfire lit."

"It's quite the full social calendar here in Redfield, isn't it?" Zoe commented. "What's next on the agenda?"

"We'll be going for Christmas Eve drinks in the pub," Isobel said. "To which you are, obviously, invited. And there's a Boxing Day swim. After that I think it's just a quiet few days until the New Year's Eve party."

"That takes place in the village hall," Steve chipped in. "Dancing, drinks and buffet food. It's usually a good laugh."

"You should come," Tom put in suddenly. She looked at him and was startled by the blueness of his eyes shining in the firelight.

"Yeah, definitely," Rob said. "Can't be here for New Year and miss out on the fun. I'll show you some moves." He wiggled his hips.

Zoe laughed. "Is that right?! Ok, sounds good."

They stayed for a while to watch the bonfire, then Tom and Rob went their separate ways home and the other three started to walk back towards their houses. Isobel was talking about what she wanted to do when they got back.

"There's a new show I want to watch – have you seen the trailers? – ghost stories for Christmas."

"Ghost stories? Aren't they more for Halloween?" Zoe asked.

"No, they often feature at Christmas too. Like Jacob Marley and the ghosts of Christmas past, present and future in 'A

Christmas Carol'? And what's that song, I can't remember all the words; 'There'll be something and something and something and something, and carolling out in the snow...'"

Zoe joined in. "'There'll be scary ghost stories and tales of the glories of Christmases long long ago...' Yes, you're right."

"Of course, they're only fun if you enjoy being scared."

"Well, in the comfort and safety of a locked house, I suppose I do quite enjoy a scary story. I'll look for it when I get in. What time does it start?"

"Nine, I think."

They were almost back to the Old Rectory now.

"Great to see you tonight, Zoe," Isobel said as she gave her a goodnight hug. "See you for Christmas Eve drinks if not before!"

Back in the house, Zoe decided that she felt a little peckish. The pizza had been delicious but it wasn't really a full meal. She made a plate of cheese and biscuits and cut an apple into slices. Sitting down on the sofa, Zoe switched on the TV and found that the ghost story programme was about to begin. She started to watch. By the time half an hour had passed, she was completely gripped. The chilling story built up the suspense little by little. It was too good to stop watching – she had to know what was going to happen – but she was starting to feel rather nervous. Suddenly the house seemed to be full of strange creaks and she could feel the weight of the black night outside pressing against the windows. Stop it, she told herself. You're being silly! But that didn't change the rapid beating of her heart, and even having Henry laid across her feet didn't quite banish the creeping sense of unease.

By the time the programme finished and she was ready to go up to bed, she was avoiding looking in mirrors in case she spotted a ghostly presence looming behind her, and when she climbed into bed she lay for a moment with her eyes open in the dark room. The silence of the countryside pressed in on her. A jacket hanging on the back of the bedroom door looked like a stranger standing there. A sudden scream from outside made her jump, and even knowing that it was probably a fox was little comfort. She pulled the covers right up over her head like a scared child and felt very alone.

Nine

'Three French hens, two turtle doves, and a partridge in a pear tree...'

Zoe opened her eyes and was surprised to find that it was morning already. She had expected nightmares after scaring herself silly with ghost stories last night, but once she managed to drop off she had slept deeply. In the dim morning light the whole thing seemed completely ridiculous and she chided herself for her behaviour. Door number twenty-three of the advent calendar held a picture of a present wrapped in green paper and topped with a gold bow.

It was rather a grey, misty morning. Walking the dogs towards the church, rooks cawed harshly from the treetops and she glared at them. "Stupid birds," she muttered. "Stop being so menacing." Henry looked up at her with his head tilted to one side. "You'll protect me, won't you, Henry?"

Henry's quizzical look made her smile and she leaned down to scratch his head. "Sweet boy. Somehow I don't think you'll make much of a guard dog but you are a cutie." Barney barked loudly and the rooks rose, still cawing, from the tree and flew away. "Oh, good job, Barney! Come on, let's walk up the hill today." They found the field edge footpath and climbed up the hill, above the river. At the crossroads of footpaths at the top, Zoe considered her options. She knew that the path to the right would bend back round to the village fairly quickly. The path to the left seemed to lead into an area of woodland which looked a little spooky in the mist. With ghost stories still in her mind, she decided to leave that for another day but to go on further with exploring the footpath straight ahead.

"Come on Bella, this way." Zoe set off along the new path and Bella followed, stopping to sniff every so often. The path climbed a little higher still above the river, running through the middle of a field. It seemed rather barren at this time of year but she guessed that crops would grow here in the summer. The soil was sandy and the path had become somewhat muddy so she had to walk slowly to avoid slipping and sliding with every step. She was relieved when she came to another junction where she was able to follow a grassy path to her right, which looked like it would lead back towards Redfield.

She passed a field where two horses stood, one black and one bay. They were wearing rugs and munching on a pile of hay, and raised their heads as she approached in order to keep an eye on her and the dogs. She could see clouds of their warm breath in the air. Zoe was fond of horses and had ridden as a child but it had been years now since she'd been on a horse. It was a pleasure to see these two.

She found herself coming back into Redfield near the village green and wondered if it would be possible to pop into the shop with the dogs in tow. Luckily her dilemma was solved when she spotted Isobel's son Charlie walking Jasper across the green towards her. He waved to her.

"Hi Charlie! Could you do me a big favour and just keep an eye on these three while I pop in to the shop for some milk? I'll only be a minute."

"Yeah, no worries." He took the leads from her hands.

"Thank you!" She pushed open the door and stepped into the shop. Poppy was nowhere to be seen but by the time Zoe had picked up some milk and a loaf of bread, she had come out of the back room and was ready behind the counter. She was wearing her purple scarf again, this time with a chunky-knit cardigan and a long skirt.

"Good morning," she smiled. "I hope you enjoyed our celebration last night."

"Very much," Zoe replied. "It seems a really lovely tradition. Although maybe I shouldn't have followed it up with ghost stories when I got home!"

Poppy laughed. "But it is the perfect night for them! When the veil between the worlds is thin. Anyway, I'm glad the celebration was positive for you. New beginnings." There was a wise look in her eyes.

Zoe thanked her and paid for her groceries, while feeling that she didn't quite understand everything that Poppy was saying. As soon as she stepped back outside to Charlie and the dogs, the feeling was forgotten.

"Thank you so much, Charlie."

"No problem. See you around." He handed back the leads and headed off with Jasper trotting alongside. Zoe made her way back to the Old Rectory and let the dogs inside where they all went straight to their bowls to have a drink.

"Good idea, gang. Must be coffee time."

After her cup of coffee, Zoe thought she would pop out to check on the chickens. She cut an apple into chunks to share with them, popping a piece into her own mouth as she did so, and put on her coat again. It was chilly to be without one for even a few minutes outside the house.

Zoe opened the door to the chicken coop and stepped inside. The enclosure was tall enough for her to stand comfortably and was enclosed above and on all sides by a wire mesh. The chickens had a nest box filled with straw where they laid their eggs. There were food and water containers and a couple of small shrubs as well as a little holly tree standing about five feet tall. The black and white chickens pecked around her feet as she put out their food and checked their water, but she couldn't see the brown one anywhere. Puzzled, she looked around. Where had it gone? She lifted the lid of the nest box and found two eggs but no chicken. She looked down at the other two in confusion.

"Where's your friend gone?"

Her first thought was the fox she had heard last night, but there were no signs of a struggle. She went out of the coop, closing the door carefully, and started walking around the outside looking for a gap in the wire where a determined chicken might make an escape. She was about halfway round, engrossed in the task, when a voice made her jump.

"Everything ok?"

She gasped and stood up suddenly, stumbling back a little and nearly losing her balance. A strong hand gripped her arm, steadying her, and she found herself staring up at Tom.
"I'm sorry, I didn't mean to startle you."
Zoe felt cross. "Don't sneak up on me then!"
He raised an eyebrow. "I'll remember that next time I'm trying to do a good deed." He released her arm and offered a tin that he held in his other hand. "I was just passing Isobel's house and she asked me to bring you some stollen." He looked down at the tin. "I think she's going a bit overboard with baking this year."
Zoe's anger melted away as quickly as it had come. "I'm sorry I snapped at you. I think I'm still jumpy from watching ghost stories on TV last night. I'm just..." She looked at the coop again and frowned.
Tom tilted his head slightly to one side and regarded her quizzically. "What were you doing?"
She looked at him quickly and decided to tell the truth, strange as it was.
"I've lost a chicken."
His surprise was genuine. "Lost a chicken? Did it get out somehow?"
"That's what I'm trying to work out. The black and white ones are there but the brown one has disappeared completely. It's not in the nest box. I was just looking at the wire trying to work out if there's a hole."
Tom nodded. "Well, you go back round that way and I'll go this way, and let's see what we can find."
Relieved to have an extra pair of eyes on the case, Zoe agreed and they carefully examined every inch of the coop. Coming back together at the other side, Tom was now equally confused.
"Nothing. And if there was, the other two would probably have made use of it too."
"A fox? I thought there'd be a scene of carnage, feathers flying and all that."

Tom shook his head. "It would have taken the others as well, and we've still got the problem of how it would have got in and out. Let's take a look inside."

Together they searched the coop, checking the nest box again and bending down low to check beneath the shrubs. Zoe was on the point of giving up entirely when Tom gave an exclamation as he peered into the holly tree.

"I've found it... but I'm afraid this chicken has laid its last egg."

Zoe gasped and looked into the tree as he held aside a few of the spiky leaves for her. The chicken was there, lying on its side. She reached in gently and extracted the soft feathery body.

"Oh dear. Simone did mention in her emails that one of the chickens was very old. It must have perched in there and just passed away. What am I supposed to do with it now?"

"Roast it?"

Zoe looked sharply at Tom but his eyes were dancing and his mouth twitched as he struggled not to smile. She sighed. "I suppose I'll have to bury it – her, I should say really – I think that Simone sees them as pets. Definitely not as dinner," she finished firmly.

"Let me help," Tom offered. "At least the ground isn't frozen solid. Do you have a key for the tool shed?"

They went into the utility room to find the key, putting Isobel's tin inside as they did so. Barney whined behind the door but Zoe thought the dogs should stay indoors until they'd finished.

"I don't want to encourage him to dig up the garden!"

"I think it'll be easier without a furry little helper," Tom agreed.

Key located, they went out and unlocked the tool shed. Between them they decided on a quiet spot at the bottom of the garden where it didn't look like they would be disturbing any important plants. Tom took off his jacket and began to dig. After a few minutes Zoe, feeling uncomfortable just watching him do all the work, offered to take a turn. He handed her the spade and she pushed it down firmly into the earth, putting all her weight behind it. It was hard work and she was feeling hot in no time. When she stopped for a breather and pushed her hair back, Tom reached out for the spade again. Zoe's feminist principles insisted that she ought to carry on, but her practicality won. He was making much quicker progress than she was, and not making a macho fuss about that fact – he was just getting on with the job. As she passed the spade back to him she noticed that he had rolled up the sleeves of his check shirt, revealing muscular forearms. She looked away quickly as he started to dig again.

A thought struck her. "Do you know why the village is called Redfield?" she asked Tom. "I thought it must be on red clay but this soil is sandy, and the fields look the same from what I've seen so far."

"You're right, there are areas of clay but a lot of this would have been underwater thousands of years ago. Then there were glaciers that deposited sand in the area as well. It's not my area of expertise but one of my colleagues at school has done quite a lot of research into the geology of the area." He paused and leaned on the spade. "Have you heard of Dunwich, up the coast from here?" She shook her head. "That's an interesting bit of history. It was a busy port in medieval times but most of it has been lost to the sea. It's just a small village now. There's a bit of local folklore that says you can hear the church bells ringing from under the waves when there's a storm."

Zoe shivered. "That's spooky."

A whirring of wings caught her attention and she looked up to see a robin had landed on the bare soil a few feet away and was watching the proceedings with interest, beady black eyes on the lookout for any interesting insects or worms that might be turned up by the digging. Tom looked up for a moment and saw her enraptured face as she watched the little bird hop and peck at the earth. He gave a low, friendly whistle to the robin.

"He's so bold," Zoe whispered, afraid that she would scare him away.

Tom straightened up to stretch his back and the robin took flight into a nearby bush. He caught the disappointed expression on Zoe's face.

"Don't worry, he'll be back as soon as we've finished."

Soon they agreed that the hole was deep enough. Zoe gently placed the brown chicken into it and Tom covered it back over with earth. Zoe found a hellebore flower and bent down to put it on top of the grave.

"Rest in peace, chicken," she said softly.

Straightening up, she and Tom stood side by side in silence for a moment.

"Well I have to say, that's a contender for one of the oddest half hours I've ever spent with an almost-stranger," he commented.

"I'm not sure you can call someone a stranger any more when you've buried a body with them."

He looked at her seriously. "You may be right, Zoe. Perhaps we're friends now."

"It's certainly a memorable way to start a friendship," she said wryly. "Now I think it's time for a cup of tea." She felt suddenly shy as she asked him, "Would you like one?"

"Sounds great," he replied, smiling at her. As Tom greeted all the dogs and she busied herself with the tea things, she shook off the odd feeling. What was she worrying about? They were just being friendly. This wasn't exactly a date. Yes, he was an attractive man, but she was sure he wasn't the slightest bit interested in her romantically – and anyway she was only going to be around for a few weeks.

Tom had followed Henry into the small sitting room as they played with Henry's favourite rabbit toy, so Zoe took the tea and stollen through and put them down on a wooden side table.

Tom turned with a smile. "Thanks, just the job after a spot of grave-digging."

Zoe smiled back as she settled into a chair and curled up with her feet under her. She took a bite of stollen. "Oh wow, this is delicious."

Tom nodded, his own mouth full. "Isobel's a great baker," he said when he'd swallowed. "She brings me care parcels sometimes. I think she feels I need looking after, though I'm not sure why."

Zoe grinned. "I think it's just her way to mother everyone she meets. And I'm certainly enjoying the benefits of her Christmassy baking spree."

Tom was looking around him. "No Christmas decorations though? Not your thing?"

Zoe shook her head. "Oh, it's very much my thing normally, but I couldn't bring loads of decorations with me on the train! I've got my special snow globe upstairs on the bedside table but I'm afraid that's it. I did wonder about trying to make some sort of rustic arrangement with bits of holly and ivy but they always seem to look a lot better in magazines than in real life – well, with my skills anyway."

"I'm surprised Simone didn't leave some decorations out for you."

"I expect it was the last thing on her mind, especially with the arrangements all changing at the eleventh hour with my friend Katie's accident."

Tom nodded thoughtfully. They drank their tea in silence for a moment, and as soon as Tom's mug was empty he started to stand up.

"I'd better be getting on, got a few things to do today and I didn't mean to be out quite so long."

Zoe stood up quickly too. "I'm sorry for taking up so much of your time. Though I have to say, I'm not sure what I would have done without you today."

He smiled down at her. "That's alright. It's been… interesting."

They took the mugs and plates back to the kitchen and Tom put his boots and coat back on. As he stepped outside he looked back at her and paused for a second as if there was something he wanted to say; but then he just gave a little nod and smile and walked away down the drive.

Zoe shut the door and leaned against it for a moment. What a bizarre morning! She hoped that Simone wouldn't be too upset about the chicken. She wondered whether to email her about it but thought on balance that the news could probably wait until her return. Henry padded over, sat in front of her and cocked his furry head to one side. She smiled.

"No stollen for you I'm afraid, my hopeful friend. I'll find you a nice dog biscuit instead."

Barney heard the word "biscuit" and barked. Zoe laughed. "All right, all right! Biscuits for everyone!"

Ten

'Tiny tots with their eyes all aglow, will find it hard to sleep tonight...'

In the late afternoon, once the sun had disappeared for the day, Zoe decided to get cosy in the sitting room. The afternoon walk with the dogs had been a particularly cold one and despite a warm jumper and a cup of tea in her hands, she was still feeling chilly. It was definitely an evening to light the fire. She had all the materials to hand and she knelt down in front of the wood burning stove to build the base. A couple of larger logs went to each side, while the space in the middle was filled with screwed up newspaper and small sticks. Once she was happy she struck a match and lit the newspaper. It flared into life and began to consume the smaller pieces of kindling. Zoe carefully added larger pieces to the top until the fire was burning brightly and the bigger logs were beginning to char. She almost killed the whole thing by putting an overly large log on the top, but managed to salvage it by removing the log again and quickly adding a few small pieces.

The three dogs joined her, attracted by the growing warmth of the room. Soon they were all snuggled up comfortably together, watching the flames lick the edges of the firebox. Zoe watched the orange blaze for a while as though hypnotised. Henry laid his head in Zoe's lap with a contented sigh and she stroked his head gently.

"Definitely no ghost stories tonight, team," she said out loud. "Tom nearly got me going again earlier, talking about ghostly bells ringing under the sea. Let's find something cheerful to watch."

Miracle on 34th Street was just about to start and Zoe remembered it had been one of her favourites when she was young. It was still just as heart-warming now. She had to pause it halfway through when she realised she was getting hungry, and was just on her way to the kitchen when she heard the sound of music coming from outside, and some beeping horns. Intrigued, she quickly put on her coat and stepped out to see what was happening. Her jaw dropped as she saw the sight.

A great parade of tractors was driving slowly along the road, each vehicle festooned with brightly coloured lights so that they were lit up like Christmas trees. Some of them were sounding their horns as they went, and every so often one was blasting loud Christmas music. As Zoe stood and watched, she spotted Rob wearing a Santa hat and with a large inflatable Santa attached to the bonnet of his tractor. She waved and he spotted her and waved back cheerily. Other residents had come out of their houses too and were waving and cheering the farmers as they passed.

The closest house to the Old Rectory was a bungalow and an older couple who Zoe hadn't yet met had come to stand outside and watch the parade. The man was holding a small boy who she assumed must be his grandson. She looked over at them and the woman raised her hand in greeting. Zoe went over.

"What's all this in aid of?"

"Oh, they raise money for local charities. You'll find it online easily enough if you want to donate. It's such fun, and I'm so pleased that we've got little Ethan here to enjoy it this year!"

"Tactor!" the little boy shouted excitedly, and his grandad laughed.

"You love tractors, don't you? It's your lucky day, kiddo."

Zoe stood and watched for a few more minutes as the long line of illuminated tractors continued along the lane and disappeared into the night. She could still hear their horns and music even when the last in line had passed out of sight.

Heading back inside, shaking her head at the bizarreness of the whole thing, Zoe remembered her hunger and decided to knock up a quick mushroom omelette with some salad leaves. She took her plate through and rested it on her knees to eat while continuing the film. Another short pause was needed while she fetched some chocolate and poured herself a glass of wine. Bella gave a deep sigh as Zoe sat down again.

"Sorry Bella, I'll stay put for a bit now." By the time the credits rolled all three dogs were snoozing and Zoe felt very contented.

****

Zoe woke early on Christmas Eve. It was still dark and the house was quiet. She switched on her bedside light. Pulling back the curtain, she realised that the temperature had dropped overnight. She could see a sparkle of frost where the light touched the garden. She pulled on an oversized hoody over her pyjamas and padded downstairs to make a cup of tea. In the kitchen the three dogs greeted her with wagging tails and gentle licks of her hand.

"Good job I've got you three to keep me cheerful," she remarked to them. "I think I might feel a bit melancholy otherwise. It's Christmas Eve but I'm not sure I'm feeling very Christmassy."

Bella pressed her head reassuringly against Zoe's knee and Zoe scratched behind the dog's silky ears.

"Oh, I suppose there is the final day of the advent calendar to open." She picked it up and pulled open door number twenty-four. A picture of a robin standing in the snow completed the set of images.

"Cute. Ok, I'm going to take this cuppa upstairs and I'll be back down soon."

The dogs lay back down in their beds as she climbed the stairs again, tea and her mobile phone in hand. She got back under the covers for warmth – she'd heard the boiler click into life but the house was still chilly – and read some messages and news stories while she drank her tea. There was a message from her mum which must have been sent quite late the previous evening, with a selfie of Astrid and her friend Fiona raising their glasses and grinning at the camera. From what Zoe could see of the background it looked like they were in a pub; there was a shelf of whisky bottles and fairy lights illuminated wooden panelling on the walls. Zoe typed a quick reply – *Looks fun! Hope your head isn't aching this morning* ☺ - then decided it was time to get up properly.

She dressed in a warm cream-coloured roll neck jumper and blue jeans, and dug out her thickest pair of socks. Back in the kitchen, she decided that a warm breakfast was definitely in order this morning and she got out the ingredients for French toast. She buzzed busily around the kitchen, making coffee at the same time as whisking up the egg mixture and heating the pan. Barney watched attentively from his basket.

"I don't know if breakfast really is the most important meal of the day like they say, Barney, but it's important to me!" She sprinkled sugar over the top with a final flourish and sat at the breakfast bar to enjoy the result of her culinary efforts. Barney made his way over to sit underneath her bar stool, ready to tidy up any crumbs that might come his way.

As they headed out into the sparkling cold of the morning, Zoe found herself remembering a long-forgotten nursery rhyme and sang under her breath as they walked down the path. "Here we go round the mulberry bush, on a cold and frosty morning." Twigs cracked under her boots and the tops of the trees appeared to be steaming where the sun touched them. Every leaf and blade of grass was rimed with frost. It was bitterly cold but the effect was very pretty, almost like a Christmas card.

She spotted Poppy's cat Nova prowling through the churchyard, the black of her fur coat standing out starkly against the frosty white of the ground and the gravestones. The dogs seemed to find the weather invigorating and bounced about happily, sniffing all the interesting smells. Her hands were cold even with her gloves but she could look forward to getting cosy in the house again when they returned.

They passed a large pond on the way back from the river. A thin skin of ice had formed almost all the way across, and several ducks stood looking forlorn on its frozen surface.

Barney made a move towards the pond as though he would like to chase them, and Zoe tugged on his lead to stop him.

"Barney! That ice might hold a duck's weight but I wouldn't bet on it holding yours!"

They had one dramatic moment when Zoe slipped on an icy puddle but luckily she managed to regain her footing before she went over completely. Her heart beat frantically as adrenaline surged through her body. Bella looked up at her as Zoe stood with one hand pressed to her chest, calming the fluttering within.

"Phew! That was a lucky save. After Katie's accident I don't feel quite as invincible as usual, although surely it would be incredibly bad luck for us both to break a leg in the same month."

She was rather relieved to make it back to the house without any more significant mishaps occurring.

It was about 2pm on Christmas Eve and Zoe was curled up reading in the sitting room with a blanket over her legs when she heard a knock at the back door. It was Tom. He stood a little back from the doorstep, smart in a navy pea coat with a rust-coloured beanie hat covering his dark curls. He smiled up at her.

"I brought you something. Call it an early Christmas present if you like." He turned to pick something up then turned back to Zoe, holding a three-foot-tall potted Christmas tree.

"I had to pop out to the shops for a few last bits and they were selling these off cheap because it's so last minute now. But I thought you might like it."

Zoe's eyes prickled with sudden tears which she hastily blinked away. "It's lovely, thank you so much!"

Tom was still smiling. "Shall I bring it into the sitting room?"

"Yes please!" She opened the doors for him as he carried the little tree inside.

Tom placed the tree carefully by the French doors as the dogs frisked around excitedly.

"Perfect," Zoe declared.

Tom gave her a solemn look. "Not quite yet," he commented, reaching deep into his pockets and pulling out a string of fairy lights. Together they wound them around the tree then switched them on. The lights twinkled cheerfully as they both stood back to have a good look.

Zoe was entranced. "It's kind of magical," she admitted, gazing at the tree. "I didn't really feel like it was Christmas until this happened." Spontaneously, she turned to Tom and hugged him. "Thank you so much."

He wrapped his arms around her in return and suddenly she was powerfully aware of their closeness. His chest and shoulders were broad, his strong arms tight around her, and his hair smelled of cinnamon and wood smoke. Feeling suddenly awkward, Zoe let go, and as their bodies parted and they looked into each other's eyes she saw an intensity in Tom's gaze that left her breathless.

A ring at the doorbell broke the tension and the dogs set off into a flurry of barking as they charged to see who was there. Zoe and Tom stepped back from each other, both feeling embarrassed.

"I'd better…" Zoe began.

"Yeah, I need to go anyway, I'll let myself out the back. See you in the pub later?" He was already backing away.

"Yes, see you there."

Zoe ran to the front door, her mind full of confusion. A delivery driver wearing a Santa hat was standing there holding several packages.

"Bit brisk out here today," he greeted her cheerily. "Can you sign for these?"

He handed her the electronic device and she signed her name.

"Ta, love. Merry Christmas."

"Merry Christmas."

She retreated back inside, pushing the door shut with her elbow. Taking them into the sitting room, she realised that they were gifts from her mum and from her friend Katie. She placed them under the little tree, sparkling away in the darkening afternoon, and stared unseeingly at the reflections in the French windows. What on earth had just happened?

Eleven

'And the bells were ringing out for Christmas Day...'

A knock at the front door at about six o'clock took her by surprise. It wasn't time to go to the pub yet, and in any case she'd noticed that friends tended to come to the back door. Another delivery? She went and opened the door.

A group of around a dozen carol singers were standing outside, and as soon as the door opened they launched into a spirited rendition of 'Ding Dong Merrily on High'. The women singers were grouped into soprano and alto voices and there were a few men as well, their different voices joining in perfect harmony. Zoe was amused to spot Poppy amongst the group, her purple hair just visible beneath a hat shaped like a Christmas pudding. Clearly having some pagan sympathies didn't prevent her from enjoying the more traditionally Christian carols as well. When they finished the final line, 'hosanna in excelsis', Zoe applauded. A petite woman in the front row bowed. She wore a green elf hat with a little bell which jingled as she moved her head. Despite her small stature she exuded authority and seemed to be in charge of the little group.

"Have you got time to listen to another, dearie?"

"Yes, if you'd like to sing another!"

The woman nodded at the group and they began another song. It took Zoe a moment to recognise it – she didn't think it was one that she had ever sung – but then as the singers reached the chorus she realised that she knew it from the film *Home Alone*. The voices soared and combined in a minor key as they sang, "Fall on your knees, oh hear the angel voices." It was unexpectedly moving and Zoe suddenly felt something of the wonder and majesty of being part of a celebration that had taken place on this night for thousands of years.

As the last notes died away, the choir-mistress held out a collecting tin and gave it a shake. "No obligation, but we're collecting for a local food bank charity if you have any pennies to spare."

"Of course," Zoe smiled. "Just give me one second to find my purse."

She returned to the front door and pushed some coins into the collecting tin, glad that she had some cash to hand on this occasion. The rest of the choir had made their way back to the road ready to continue their rounds. The woman with the tin beamed.

"Merry Christmas my dear! Alright team," she addressed the group. "Off we go again!" They set off along the lane singing 'We Wish you a Merry Christmas' as they went. Zoe shut the door with a smile. What a lovely moment to be part of, she thought. She was definitely feeling a lot more Christmassy than she had first thing that morning.

Checking the time, she realised that she ought to get on with some dinner before getting ready to go out to the pub. Zoe's mum had always served fish on Christmas Eve so she had bought herself a piece of white fish which she would have with rice, green beans, and a tomato-based sauce. She switched on the radio while she was cooking and sang along with the festive tunes.

Heading upstairs after dinner, she looked for something to wear to the pub. She wanted to look good tonight – not because she was interested in Tom or anything, she told herself – it's just nice to look good when you go out. Jeans and trainers would be fine and she didn't really have many other options anyway, but she changed her thick cream jumper for a thin, clinging one in a soft green shade that brought out the green flecks in her hazel eyes. She applied a little mascara and some tinted lip balm.

She was ready to go when Isobel knocked at the back door a short while later. Steve was leaning on the gate behind her. They were all going to meet Rob and Tom in the pub again, as they had the other night for the quiz.

Zoe felt like she had butterflies in her stomach as they made their way through the old wooden door into the welcoming interior of the Mulberry Tree.

Rob and Tom were already there and had found a table near the fire. It was warm enough in the pub that Zoe immediately undid the buttons of her coat.

"What would you two like to drink?" Zoe asked. "I'll get this one."

"Oh thanks – I'll have a white wine, please."

"Pint of cider please," Steve added. "Thanks." He went to join the other men but Isobel stayed to help Zoe carry the drinks. They were served by the same young woman who had been working at the pub quiz. She gave them a tight smile but her manner was brisk, almost to the point of being unfriendly. She had seemed much more smiley the other night so Zoe was a little taken aback, but soon they were taking the drinks over to the table and she found that her attention was focused on Tom.

Tom and Rob sat at opposite sides of the table and Steve had joined them at one end. Isobel took the other end, opposite her husband, leaving an empty chair next to Tom. Zoe took off her coat and sat down, very aware of his nearness. He turned and gave her a small smile.

"Hello."

"Hi." She was excited to sit near him and at the same time felt self-conscious. Oh boy, she thought. I seem to have developed a bit of a crush. Deep breath, act normal!

She realised that Rob was asking her a question. "Sorry, what was that?"

"I said, what did you think of the tractor parade last night?"

"Oh, it was amazing! Weird and wonderful. I've never seen anything quite like it."

Rob laughed. "It's the third year we've done it, and it's got bigger and better each year. It took me ages to get all the decorations on the tractor. I think I might just leave them on now until after Christmas!"

"There was a little boy from the bungalow next to me who was very excited to see you all."

"Ah, that's nice. Yeah, the kids love it."

"I love it too!" Isobel put in. Tonight she was wearing a deep blue top with a wide boat neck and fluted sleeves, and her corkscrew curls bounced on her shoulders as she turned her head. "Do you know yet how much you've raised?"

"No, they're still getting some donations coming in but it looks like we will have done really well for the charities."

"That's great." Isobel turned to Zoe. "Zoe, did the carol singers come to see you earlier?"

"Yes! They were so good. Do they do it every year?"

Isobel nodded. "Yep. I'd like to join them, I enjoy singing, but I haven't been able to find time for the rehearsals up until now. Maybe next year."

Tom was listening. "What about you, Zoe? Do you like to sing?"

She laughed. "Only when no one can hear me! I'm not musically gifted."

"Never mind. I'm sure you have other talents." She glanced sharply at him, wondering if he was being suggestive. His expression was neutral but something in his eyes made her feel that there was a coded message in there, meant just for her. Isobel didn't seem to notice anything and the conversation continued.

The air between them felt charged with electricity. The pub was becoming increasingly crowded as the evening wore on, and Tom was forced to move his chair closer to Zoe's. Their thighs were touching under the table and she was aware of every inch of his denim-covered leg that pressed against hers. She tried to act normally and chat with Isobel and Rob, while her heart fluttered rapidly in her chest. Tom was mostly talking to Steve, who was sitting on his other side. Occasionally his hand would brush hers as he picked up or set down his drink and she would feel a little frisson at the contact.

After a second drink Zoe excused herself to go to the ladies'. She had to suck in her stomach to squeeze out of the tight corner and as Tom leaned back lazily in his chair she was convinced that she could feel his gaze on her back as she made her way across the room.

She had to wait a few moments for a free cubicle. When it was her turn it was a relief to have a quiet moment to herself, away from the chatter and all the people. She was enjoying herself but the tension was making it hard to breathe at times.

Coming out of the cubicle, Zoe washed and dried her hands and checked her reflection in the mirror. She ran her fingers through her hair and applied a fresh coat of her tinted lip balm. Popping the cap back on and returning it to her pocket, she smiled to herself. There were definitely flirty vibes between her and Tom, and she was having fun. It all seemed to be going well.

As she stepped out of the ladies', a movement to the side caught her eye. Tom and the pretty barmaid were stood together in a quiet, dimly-lit corner, heads close together as they conducted a whispered and apparently somewhat intense conversation. Tom put out a hand to stroke the girl's hair and Zoe quickly turned away with a little involuntary gasp, walking quickly back to the table away from what looked like a very intimate moment.

She sat in a daze for a minute or two while the others chatted.

"Are you ok?" Isobel asked. "You've gone a bit pale."

"Actually, I've got a bit of a headache coming on," Zoe lied. "I think I'll head home now. I shouldn't leave the dogs for too long anyway."

"Ok," Isobel replied, looking concerned. "Have a good sleep and we'll see you tomorrow."

Zoe pulled on her coat and made a hasty exit before Tom could return from whatever it was he was up to in that dark corner. She felt almost tearful as she made her way back through the darkness. Why was she being silly? Just because she and Tom had been flirting a bit didn't mean he was seriously interested in her. Or certainly not exclusively, if another option became available. And anyway, she reminded herself, in another two weeks you'll be going back home, and then what would happen to any budding romance?

Letting herself in at the back door of the Old Rectory, she was cheered by the enthusiastic reception given by the three dogs. She gave each of them a dog treat and let them into the garden for a final wee before bedtime. She decided to make a herbal tea and take it upstairs with her. Putting on her checked tartan pyjamas and getting under the covers, she let the mug of mint tea warm her hands. She thought about all her childhood Christmas Eves, when she would put out her stocking and go to bed with a thrill of excitement at the thought of Father Christmas coming to visit. She sighed. Maybe one day she would have a little one of her own and see everything fresh through their eyes. Christmas magic was definitely harder to come by as an adult.

****

Zoe woke in the still-dark room and lay with her eyes shut for a moment, not yet aware of where she was or of which day was just beginning. Like a clockwork mechanism being wound up, her brain seemed to suddenly accelerate and spring into life. Christmas Day! It was Christmas Day. Then a whole host of other thoughts followed hard on the heels of this first realisation. She was far from home, away from family, and no one was there to leave a stocking at the foot of the bed. To make matters worse, the man she was attracted to, who she had thought was interested in her, turned out to be interested in someone else. She buried her face in the pillow and allowed herself to wallow briefly in self-pity before common sense took over.

"Come on, Zoe," she told herself sternly. "Let's look on the bright side. You may not have family here but you do have a friend, and you will have company and good food. You've also got three adorable canine companions who will be looking forward to seeing you come down the stairs." She sighed. "Even if they only love you because you feed them."

Slipping on a jumper over her pyjamas, she descended to the kitchen where the three dogs were predictably delighted to see her. Bending to stroke their silky ears and allowing them to lick her hands in welcome, her mood lifted. She brightened still further when she remembered the presents underneath the little Christmas tree. Simone and Neil had left instructions for her to give their gifts to the dogs on Christmas Day too, and Zoe now took these down out of the cupboard. They could all open their presents together, after breakfast and a walk.

Zoe had planned a special Christmas breakfast of smoked salmon and scrambled eggs. She wasn't expected at Isobel's until one o'clock so she definitely needed something to keep her going. She switched on the kettle and took out the coffee, lifting the lid and inhaling deeply with pleasure before measuring a spoonful out into the cafetière. As a special Christmas treat she put a small morsel of salmon into each dog's bowl. These were rapidly devoured with noisy appreciation.

After breakfast, Zoe took the dogs out on their favourite walk along the riverside. The church bells were ringing as she walked along the footpath next to the churchyard. She was surprised by how many other people were out at that time doing the same thing; but of course, dogs needed walking no matter what day it was. Every person she passed greeted her with a cheery "Merry Christmas" which she returned with a smile. The exception was the grumpy old lady, Barbara, but even she deigned to give Zoe a curt nod on this occasion, when Zoe offered her usual sunny greeting.

She was glad not to bump into Tom; he seemed to have a habit of turning up just when she wasn't expecting him. By the time she returned to the house she may have had cold fingers but she was feeling warm inside.

Zoe made another cup of coffee, picked up the dogs' presents, and took them through to the sitting room.

"Come on Bella, Henry, Barney." They trotted after her obediently.

She decided to do the dogs' presents first. They sat watching her with interest as she gave each of the gifts a gentle squeeze and shake before ripping open the paper.

"This one's for you, Barney." She opened it to reveal a dog toy shaped like a carrot, which she offered to Barney. He took it in his mouth and gave his head a shake from side to side. More dog toys followed for both Bella and Henry. There was one more parcel addressed to all three of them, which contained dog biscuits shaped like Christmas trees. Zoe gave them each one of these which they crunched happily as she turned to her own presents.

The parcel from Katie was light and squashy, and turned out to be a beautifully soft scarf and a pair of thermal socks with a Fair Isle pattern. Her mum had remembered the name of a book Zoe mentioned in passing weeks ago, and had tracked it down and sent her a copy. She'd also sent a small box of some very lovely chocolates, with a little note attached saying 'An upside to Christmas on your own – no need to share the chocs!' Zoe smiled although tears pricked her eyes. She could hardly believe that she was in her thirties and yet this was the first Christmas Day ever that she hadn't seen her mum. As if on cue, her phone buzzed and she swiped to open a video call. There was her mum with her friend Fiona, waving at her through the screen and wishing her a merry Christmas.

"How are you, darling? Have you opened your presents yet?"

"Yes, just now. Thank you, I'm so impressed you remembered the name of that book."

"Oh, you're very welcome. I have got a couple more things for you but they were a bit heavy to post and I thought we could spread out the fun a bit if I save them for the next time I see you. Thank you for my presents too!" Astrid leaned in closer to the camera to show that she was already wearing the new earrings that Zoe had given her.

"What's the weather like up there?"

"We had just a little dusting of snow yesterday! It's all frozen now and looking very pretty. What about Redfield? I don't suppose you're having a white Christmas."

"No, it's cold but no sign of snow. It's so lovely that you've got some! Like a storybook Christmas."

"Did you have anything special for Christmas breakfast?" Astrid asked.

"Smoked salmon! It was heavenly."

"Sounds wonderful. We're about to open the Buck's Fizz then it'll be traditional turkey and all the trimmings later on."

"Isobel's doing turkey too."

"I am glad you're not going to be on your own all day, darling. It's strange enough just being away from you but I couldn't bear to think of you being lonely."

"I'm fine, Mum! Look, my furry friends are here keeping me company." Zoe swivelled the camera to show the dogs to her mother. Barney's ears quirked as he watched, not understanding what she was up to and where the other voice was coming from.

Astrid exclaimed over the cuteness of the dogs and they chatted on for a few more minutes. Zoe told her that she'd been out to the pub last night, but deliberately avoided mentioning Tom's name. Astrid and Fiona had been enjoying plenty of celebrations too, going out for dinner with friends and visiting a Christmas market.

When they had finished their conversation and closed the call, Zoe thought that it might be time to break into the chocolates, just to sample one. It was still a long time until lunch, after all.

Twelve

'So here it is, Merry Christmas, everybody's having fun...'

At one o'clock Zoe put on her coat and said goodbye to the dogs.

"Wish me luck, guys. I'm feeling a little daunted by the thought of this Christmas lunch. What weird and wonderful family traditions am I about to discover?!" Bella looked steadily at her with her dark eyes while Barney gave a little whine, recognising the signs that meant she was about to go out. Zoe sighed.

"And I'm just realising I don't even know exactly who's going to be there. I think I'll be meeting Isobel's dad for the first time but will she have invited any other 'waifs and strays', as she put it? Anyway, I'll be out for a few hours but I'll see you all soon." She gave them all a scratch behind the ears and headed out, picking up her bag of gifts as she did so.

Outside Isobel's door, Zoe found herself looking at an attractive, homemade-looking wreath of greenery and red berries, finished with a red ribbon. She took a deep breath before she raised her hand and knocked on the door. After a moment Isobel opened it and gave a squeal of delight. "Zoe! Merry Christmas!" She hugged her enthusiastically and drew her in through the door. "Come in out of the cold. Here, let me help you with your coat." She managed to find space for it on an over-full coat rack and led Zoe through into the living room.

Zoe had only been in the kitchen last time that she was in the house, so there was a lot to take in as she stepped into the room. It was pleasantly square living room, with two sofas at right angles to each other as well as a comfortable chair near to the fireplace. A real Christmas tree stood in the corner of the room, decorated with ornaments in Nordic red and white and with white lights twinkling brightly. One wall held a large number of Christmas cards hung on ribbons.

Zoe guessed that many of these must have come from Isobel's little pupils; there was certainly a large quantity of them and some looked handmade.

Steve was sat near to the door and immediately stood to greet Zoe and kiss her on the cheek. Behind him was an older gentleman who Zoe guessed to be Isobel's father. And beyond him, standing near the window and looking into the back garden, a tall figure was silhouetted against the light. The third man turned round to face them and she saw in horror that it was Tom. He was the last person she wanted to see today! Part of her was tempted to turn around and run straight out of the house, but a larger, more sensible part, knew that that was madness. Tom smiled warmly at her and she looked away quickly.

Isobel's father was now stepping forwards to shake her hand. He was smartly dressed in navy cord trousers and was wearing a shirt and tie under his red woollen jumper. His face was very kind and Zoe liked him immediately. Steve introduced him as Brian.

"It's a pleasure to meet you," he said as he clasped her hand. "Isobel has told me so much about you."

"Lovely to meet you too," Zoe replied.

"Can I get you something to drink, Zoe?" Steve asked. "Sherry, glass of wine? Or tea if you'd rather?"

"I can recommend the sherry," Brian twinkled.

A little Dutch courage to help face Tom seemed like a good idea. "Sherry sounds lovely, thank you. It's one of those things I only ever have at Christmas time."

Steve headed off to the kitchen for the drinks and Brian patted a spot on the sofa next to him. "Sit down, my dear. Tell me how you're finding life in the village."

Zoe sat. "Well, I love it. It's very different from London. Very peaceful and beautiful, although I've been a lot busier than I expected! Isobel's taken me under her wing."

Brian nodded. "Yes, that sounds like her. I think with young Lauren away, she's even more keen than usual to have lots of friends around. She's a sociable type."

"Me too", Zoe smiled. "So I'm very grateful!"

Steve returned bearing sherry in delicate little glasses and Zoe took one and thanked him.

"Are you a single lady, though?" Brian asked her. "I don't see a wedding ring."

"Brian," Steve admonished as he handed him his sherry. "Don't pester our guest with questions."

Brian held up his hands in mock outrage. "I'm just being interested! You know I like to know what makes people tick." He turned to Zoe and leaned in confidentially. "Do you know, my next door neighbour washes his car every single Sunday? Even in the winter. Fascinating. Hardly even drives the car and I can't imagine why he bothers but it's obviously important to him." He leaned back again. "Anyway, you don't have to tell me anything if you don't want to."

Zoe found that she didn't mind. "It's ok. I'm divorced, actually. We got married quite young and then grew apart."

Brian looked sympathetic. "I'm sure that must have been hard."

Zoe was aware of Tom's silent presence in the corner of the room but was determined to ignore him. "Yes, it was hard to end it and face starting again on my own. But I'm happier now."

"And did Isobel tell me that your job is something to do with computers?"

She smiled. "Yes, I design websites. I used to work for a digital marketing firm but then I set up on my own so I'm my own boss and I can work pretty much anywhere."

Brian looked impressed. "Very enterprising." He gave her knee a gentle pat and then levered himself up off the sofa. "Do excuse me for a moment, nature calls." He shuffled out through the door. Steve's phone rang and he answered it and followed, leaving Tom and Zoe alone in the room. He was looking annoyingly handsome in an open-necked shirt under a corduroy jacket, teamed with dark blue jeans.

"Are you feeling ok this morning? You left very quickly last night," he started.

"I'm fine, thank you," she replied stiffly. There was a moment of awkward silence.

"I didn't realise you were going to be here today." She just wanted to get away from him. What could she do? "I should see if Isobel needs any help in the kitchen." She turned to head for the door.

"Wait!" Tom stepped forward quickly to block her path and she glared at him. "What's the matter?"

"Nothing." Zoe didn't feel like explaining. She felt humiliated.

"Maybe I've misread the situation, but I thought we were getting on well. That, perhaps, there was a connection between us?"

Now she felt angry. Did he think she was an idiot? "I thought so too, until I saw you looking pretty cosy with the barmaid last night."

Tom's eyes widened. "Lucy?! She's like a little sister. I used to babysit her!"

His outrage was so genuine that Zoe was thrown. She wasn't sure what to think.

"I'm sorry, it just looked… The way you were stood whispering together…"

Tom shook his head. "Her gran's ill and she's worried about her. I mean Lucy's a great girl but it would be too weird. Also she's ten years younger than me, that's a bit of a creepy age gap."

His manner was completely open and artless and Zoe realised that he had to be telling the truth. She started to smile at his indignation. "I am sorry, I think I've offended you."

He grinned back. "I think I can forgive you. In the spirit of Christmas, of course."

"Of course," Zoe answered.

"So… friends?"

"Friends," Zoe agreed.

At this point Charlie appeared at the door. He had deigned to get out of his pyjamas in honour of the occasion and was wearing ripped jeans and a hoody, although his hair was as wild as ever.

"Have you seen my dad?"

"I think he went outside to take a phone call," Zoe told him.

"No worries, he's probably talking to my nan." Charlie found an open tin of Quality Street and selected a strawberry cream. "She's a bit of an old battleaxe so I might just stay out of the way so I don't have to talk to her." He offered them the tin. "Chocolate?"

Zoe shook her head. "No thanks. I think we're probably going to eat quite soon. Unless you know something I don't?"

Charlie grinned. "No, I think Mum's got it all in hand. But there's always room for an extra chocolate at Christmas!"

"I'm with you," Tom said to the boy. "Pass me a toffee."

"Ugh, you're welcome to those! I like the soft ones."

Brian reappeared and drew Charlie into a discussion about sailing, leaving Zoe and Tom to talk with each other. Zoe was still feeling awkward as she sipped her sherry. There was a silence that lasted a little too long, then they both tried to speak at once.

"Sorry…"

"No, I'm sorry. You go first," Tom said.

"I was just going to ask what the view of the garden is like."

He gestured. "Come and see for yourself. I was just watching the birds when you came in."

They moved over to the back of the room. The house was a seventies build with big picture windows affording a good view over the garden, which was a little overgrown. Frost still sparkled in the shady corners but the lawn had thawed and was glistening damply in the sunlight. A movement in the border to her left caught Zoe's eye. Something small was hopping about amongst the low-growing plants. The little bird flitted higher into the tall stems of a rose bush and Zoe recognised it with delight.

"Oh look, a wren!" Without thinking she put out her hand onto Tom's arm to draw him into the experience. She turned to glance at him then quickly dropped her hand again, embarrassed. He seemed not to notice.

"So sweet, aren't they?"

"It's so tiny, and that little tippy tail. Gorgeous. They don't seem to visit the bird feeder at the Old Rectory, this is the first one I've seen here."

Isobel came in from the kitchen, wiping her hands on a tea towel, and joined them.

"Not nearly as tidy as Simone and Neil's garden, I'm afraid. I tend to go for a light touch where gardening is concerned. I was delighted when I read about this 'no mow May' idea."

"I'm not sure I've heard of it," Zoe replied.

"Oh, it's encouraging gardeners to mow less often, especially early in the spring, to give the pollinators more food. I always liked dandelions anyway. My mum used to say there were more weeds than grass in my lawn. So now I have a good excuse for this wilderness."

"Well, it looks like you're doing a good thing for nature. We were just watching a wren."

"Oh, lovely."

Steve came back in, handed Isobel a drink and kissed her cheek.

"Everything all right?"

"Yes, everything is nearly ready and I don't need to do anything for at least ten minutes, so what do you say to opening presents before lunch?"

"Why not?" Brian answered. "When you were a little girl we had to battle to make you wait until after breakfast! Almost lunchtime seems positively civilised."

"I think I already opened all of mine," Charlie shrugged. "But here's one for you, Grandad." He handed over a gift to Brian, which turned out to be a bottle of whisky.

Various presents were passed around and everyone had something to open. Isobel gave Zoe a kingfisher-blue bobble hat – "Perfect for wild swimming!" – she grinned, and in return Zoe gave her the mug she had bought in Woodbridge a few days ago. Charlie was pleased with his edible gifts and Steve thanked her sincerely for the beer and gave her a hug.

Zoe was taken aback when Tom cleared his throat gently and passed her a small package.

"This is for you. I'm afraid it's not very beautifully wrapped. I forgot to buy wrapping paper. Although newspaper is obviously an eco-friendly choice."

"You already gave me a present yesterday!" She missed the quick glance of curiosity that Steve and Isobel exchanged over her head. "And I feel really bad, I haven't got anything for you."

"That's ok. I mean, you didn't even know I was going to be here. It's just a little something I made and I wanted you to have it." Tom's eyes were warm as he looked at her.

Zoe unwrapped the package with interest and gave a gasp as the contents were revealed. It is was a wooden Christmas ornament, a delicately carved star with her name etched into it. "Tom, it's beautiful. I don't know what to say."

He was smiling. "I thought you could hang it on your tree. I like making things."

She wanted to wrap her arms around him but felt constrained by the others around them. "Thank you," she said quietly, looking deeply into his eyes.

Charlie looked over at the ornament. "That's a good one, Tom. Did Poppy sell many in the shop?"

"Yeah, a few," Tom replied.

Zoe realised why the style looked familiar. "Oh, I saw some like this in the shop and thought they were lovely! I didn't realise it was you who made them. Do you make other things too?"

"Lots of things," Tom nodded. "Some bigger pieces, like furniture. I've got a little workshop out the back of my cottage."

"You'll have to show it to Zoe some time," Isobel interjected innocently, and luckily neither Tom nor Zoe saw the quick kick that Steve aimed at his wife's foot. There was a whole conversation passing between the married couple without any words; Isobel widening her eyes at Steve to say 'What?!' while he responded with a look that clearly meant "Don't try to match-make! Leave them alone!"

Tom was oblivious, too busy watching Zoe. "I don't know if you'd find it interesting but I'm happy to show you if you want."

She was still turning over the ornament in her hands. "I'd love to see it."

Isobel shot Steve a look of triumph. "Well, I think lunch must be nearly ready. Charlie, come and help carry dishes to the table. Steve, can you sort out drinks?"

Thirteen

'Christmas time, mistletoe and wine...'

Soon the whole party was gathered around a table groaning with food. Isobel had outdone herself. The turkey was cooked to perfection, the roast potatoes crisp and fluffy all at once. There were pigs in blankets and Yorkshire puddings – "I don't know if you normally have Yorkshire puddings with Christmas dinner, Zoe, but they're a must-have for us" – and a variety of vegetables; carrots, parsnips, red cabbage and the all-important Brussels sprouts. Steve poured champagne for everyone and they all raised their glasses in a toast before tucking in to the meal.

Zoe found herself sat between Tom and Brian. The party was small enough that they could all converse together rather than splitting into smaller groups, and they chatted amiably while they ate. Their plates were almost clean when Charlie commented; "Hey, we haven't pulled the crackers yet."

"Let's wait until everyone's finished eating," Steve suggested. "Otherwise we'll be dropping our paper hats in the gravy."

The eating carried on for a few more minutes as some people went back for an extra helping of their favourite parts of the feast. Charlie took another Yorkshire pudding, putting two pigs in blankets inside it before drowning them in gravy. Zoe went back for some more veg, while Tom had another slice of turkey.

When they'd all finished, Charlie and Steve cleared the plates so they could pull their crackers. Brian insisted that this should be done all in one go, with each person pulling two crackers at once. They all pulled hard, laughing as some of the crackers resisted snapping apart. Zoe found that she ended up holding two small empty ends of cracker.

"Oh no!" she exclaimed. "I've got nothing."

"Here," Tom said, handing a full half to her. "I ended up with two, have this one."

She took it, smiling, and extracted the paper crown and joke. The crowns were different colours and there was a bit of swapping so everyone got their preferred colour, before they put them on.

"Let's hear the jokes, then," Charlie said.

Steve went first. "Why did the turkey join the band?" He looked around at the group, but no one knew the answer. "Because it had the drumsticks!" They all groaned.

Zoe read hers out next. "What happens if you eat Christmas decorations?" She winced as she read out the answer; "You get tinsel-itis!"

"Who hides in the bakery at Christmas?" Brian asked.

"I know this one," Charlie replied. "A mince spy!"

They all agreed that the jokes were as cheesy as ever but the little gifts inside the crackers were actually quite useful. Zoe got some tiny screwdrivers which could be handy for fixing things like spectacles.

Steve topped up the glasses with more champagne while Isobel fetched the puddings.

"Now, I know not everyone like Christmas pudding so we've also got a white chocolate and raspberry cheesecake," she announced as she carefully placed the Christmas pudding and a jug of cream on the table.

"That looks wonderful," Brian declared.

"Mum's cheesecake is to die for," Charlie told Zoe. "Although I think I'll have to have a bit of both."

Isobel brought in the cheesecake and a shot of brandy to pour over the Christmas pudding. Charlie lit a match ready and they all cheered as the blue flames licked over the surface of the pudding, burning off the alcohol.

"Zoe, what can I serve you?" Isobel asked.

"I think it's got to be cheesecake, please," Zoe replied. "I've had a recommendation." She winked at Charlie.

The cheesecake was very sweet and absolutely delicious. Charlie managed to put away a decent sized piece as well as a helping of Christmas pudding. Zoe wondered if he was still growing, although he was nearly touching six foot as it was.

When everyone had finished they went back through to the living room to collapse on the sofas and digest for a bit. Steve made a pot of coffee and offered around a box of chocolate liqueurs. Zoe selected a cherry liqueur enrobed in dark chocolate. She was feeling very full but also delightfully warm and comfortable. There was a bit of a lull as Brian promptly dozed off in his chair and Charlie picked up his phone and began messaging.

"Shall we play a game?" Isobel suggested.

"Depends," Charlie answered without looking up from his phone screen. "What's the game and will we all still be talking to each other by the end of it?" He glanced up. "I'm definitely not playing Monopoly, it takes hours."

"What about the rizla game?" Steve said. He saw Zoe's puzzled look. "Well, that's what we call it. The game where you have a name stuck on your forehead, which you can't see, and you have to guess who you are. We used to play it with cigarette papers years ago but no one smokes now so we use sticky notes."

"Oh, I know what you mean. That's usually a pretty good game." She looked at Charlie. "Will you play that one?"

"Yeah, go on then."

Steve went out to the kitchen to find the sticky notes and a couple of pens. "Anything goes," he said as he came back in. "Celebrities, fictional characters or real life people who we all know."

They all came up with a name and stuck it onto the forehead of the person to their left. Zoe wrote "Santa" and pressed the note gently onto Tom's forehead. Their faces were close together and their eyes met for a moment. Zoe's heart skipped a beat but she hurriedly moved back again, task completed. Steve, on her right, firmly stuck a note to her head.

Charlie went first. "Am I a real person?"

Everyone answered yes. Isobel was next. "Am I female?" The answer was no.

They continued around the circle. "Am I a celebrity?" asked Steve. Another no.

Zoe's turn was next. "Am I male?" This time the answer was yes.

"Am I a real person?" Tom asked.

"Lots of people think so," smiled Isobel, "but I think the answer you're looking for is probably no."

"How intriguing," Tom replied. "Am I God?"

"Hey, only one question at a time!" Charlie corrected him. "It's my turn again."

They carried on asking questions, some of which became very far-fetched. Zoe was struggling to remember which questions she had asked and what the answers had been. Steve was the first to guess correctly, when he realised that he was someone they knew.

"Do I like to eat a lot?"

"Yes," Isobel laughed.

"I'm Charlie!"

Everyone clapped. "Very good," Tom said. "But I think I'm not far behind you."

"Well, it's Zoe's turn next," Steve said.

"Am I... on television?" Everyone answered yes. "I still don't have a clue," Zoe confessed.

"Ok, my turn," Tom began. "I already know I'm probably not real but some think I am, I'm male, I'm old, I'm a popular person... Am I associated with Christmas?"

"Yes!"

"I'm Santa Claus!"

He took the sticky label off his head and looked at it. Zoe gave him a small smile. "I think it was the unexpected gifts that made me think of Santa," she admitted.

He grinned. "I can certainly think of worse people to be associated with."

Isobel was next to guess correctly, realising that Charlie had stuck 'Gandalf' on her head, and after a couple more guesses Charlie and Zoe finally sorted out that he was Taylor Swift, and she was Homer Simpson. Brian had woken up by now and watched the conclusion of the game with benign amusement.

One round had been enough to satisfy everyone's need for a game for the time being, and the conversation turned to people's plans for Boxing Day. Isobel was going to join the swimming group for a morning swim.
"You should come along, Zoe. It's a Redfield tradition."
"I'm thinking about it," Zoe replied cautiously. "Still a maybe for now."
"Are you swimming tomorrow, Tom?" Steve asked.
Tom shook his head. "No, not tomorrow. I've arranged to meet up with a work friend and go for a run. I'll definitely be there for the New Year dip, though."
That changed things. Zoe was not quite sure if she was going to brave enough to get into the water, and she would feel less self-conscious if Tom wasn't there to witness her potential failure.
"Are you going to see your parents tomorrow, Steve?" Brian asked.
"Yes, that's right. We'll all drive up to Norwich after Izzy's swim."

It wasn't long before Isobel rose to her feet and stretched her arms. "I'm just going to have a bit of a tidy up from lunch."
Zoe followed her out to the kitchen, where she was starting to gather dishes together.
"What can I do, Isobel?"
"Nothing, it's fine. You're the guest."
"Yes, but I would like to make myself useful. It's been such a treat to be included today. Let me do something."
"Well, if you really want to help..."
"I really want to help," Zoe confirmed.
"Ok, I'll wash these dishes here and you can dry. There's too much to fit it all in the dishwasher and I don't like coming down to a big mess the next morning."
Isobel handed Zoe a tea towel covered in pictures of snowmen and together they set to work. The kitchen was warm and slightly steamy. Jasper followed them in,

retreating from the busier living room to the quiet corner where his bed was located, and lay down with a sigh.

"So, will you come for a swim tomorrow morning?"

Zoe looked at Isobel's shining eyes and remembered her promise to herself to be brave and try new things. "Maybe… I do have a few questions before I agree to this."

Isobel nodded eagerly, ready to combat Zoe's concerns.

"Is the water quality ok? I've read so much about sewage in rivers, it's a bit of a worry."

"It's pretty good," Isobel confirmed. "This stretch of the river is designated bathing water quality. I can't promise that it's a hundred percent clean but I've never been sick from swimming there. It's obviously a good idea to wash your hands well afterwards before you eat anything."

"Ok, that sounds positive. I guess I wasn't planning to put my face in anyway."

"Yes, I'm going to keep my bobble hat on and just go for a bit of head-up breaststroke," Isobel agreed.

"Ok. What about other safety stuff? Is there a strong tide?"

"The river is tidal and you'll feel it, but you're not going to be swept away. We swim up and down the shoreline rather than across the middle where the tide will be stronger. The opposite bank is a reserved area for nature – there are sometimes otters there! – so we don't want to disturb that area anyway. You can stay in your depth if you're worried, then you can always just put your feet down."

"I'm not exactly worried," Zoe told her. "I am a pretty strong swimmer in the pool but I know it's different in open water and I just want to be sure that I'm not going to get into difficulty."

Isobel nodded approvingly. "Very sensible. I wouldn't swim there on my own, even though I know it so well. It's always best to have a swim buddy."

"And, what about a wetsuit? You mentioned having a spare. Do you think it will fit me?"

"Yes, definitely. I bought one for Lauren a couple of years ago and you're about the same size as her. She won't mind you borrowing it. I'd suggest trying it on now but maybe not after that dinner."

Zoe puffed out her cheeks. "Definitely not!"

Isobel was trying not to smile too widely as she sensed victory was near. "And you've got your new bobble hat to go with it. So, have I convinced you? Will you give it a go?"

"Go on then!"

"Yay!" Isobel gave a little clap of her hands. "You won't regret it. Now, the group are going to be down there at eight a.m..."

"Eight! That's early for Boxing Day, isn't it?"

Isobel looked serious. "Well you know what they say, Zoe, the early worm catches the bird."

It took Zoe a moment to spot the difference. "Don't you mean the early bird catches the worm?"

Isobel laughed. "Actually it's become a bit of a family motto! When the kids were little, Charlie got it the wrong way round and then Lauren drew a picture with a huge worm towering over a tiny bird. We all thought it was funny so we always say it that way round now."

Zoe grinned. "All right, I'll set an alarm and be an early worm with you tomorrow." She stretched her arms above her head. "But now I'd better be going. It's been wonderful, thank you so much for today." The two women hugged and went back into the living room so Zoe could say goodbye to the others.

Brian was sorry to see her go. "Going so soon? We've got more games to play!"

Zoe smiled at him. "It's been wonderful but I have to go back for the dogs now. It was lovely to meet you."

"Lovely to meet you, too, my dear," he answered.

"Actually, I should really head off too," Tom said, getting up suddenly. "I'll walk out with you, Zoe."

They collected together their various belongings and stepped outside into the twilight.

The last remnants of daylight remained but Zoe made a mental note to find her torch before she took the dogs out.

They walked side by side along the darkening lane and stopped by the gate of the Old Rectory. A bird called overhead and they both looked up involuntarily. They were standing under the leafless branches of a large poplar tree which bent over the road. Neither of them could identify the bird in the dim light, but clustered in the branches were several large round balls of greenery.

"Mistletoe," Tom said, looking up into the tree. He turned to look down at Zoe and their eyes met. It was as if something clicked into place. He took a half step closer to her, his gaze flicking down to her mouth then back to her eyes. Zoe's breath caught in her throat and her heart beat faster as the distance between them narrowed to mere inches. He hesitated for a moment as if unsure of his welcome, and she leaned forwards ever so slightly to meet him in the middle. Their lips pressed gently together in a brief, soft kiss that sent shivers racing through her whole body.

"Merry Christmas," he whispered, before pulling away suddenly and stepping back. She couldn't read his expression. "I'll see you soon," he said abruptly and hurried away down the lane, leaving her standing there bewildered.

"Merry Christmas," she said out loud to herself, feeling utterly baffled. She went slowly into the house, laden with presents and parcels of food that Isobel had pressed into her hands as she left. The dogs frisked around excitedly, pleased as always to see her return, and hopeful that they would now be going out for their afternoon walk. Zoe put the perishable food into the fridge without even taking off her coat and shoes, and picked up the dogs' leads. Her head was buzzing with thoughts and she needed a walk to clear it.

Bella led the way along the now-familiar path by the churchyard edge. Zoe switched on her torch to help her avoid tripping over tree roots or snagging her hair on brambles, but there was also light coming from the church; floodlights illuminated its sides so that it glowed in the dark winter night. It had been quite the afternoon, she thought as she made her way along the path. She had loved being included with the big family lunch, jokes and games. And after the initial tricky start with Tom, it had been rather wonderful spending time with him, too. She was certainly attracted to him physically and that kiss under the mistletoe had been tantalising, but thinking practically, she barely knew anything about him. And when would she see him again?

Back in the house she settled in for the evening, closing curtains and lighting the fire. She took out the decoration that Tom had given her and hung it on the tree. She was still too full from lunch to contemplate more food until later on. The usual Christmas specials were on the TV and she nestled down on the sofa to watch. There were some messages from friends to reply to as well.

At about eight o'clock she made a plate of what she and her mum always referred to as "picky tea"; cheese and biscuits, fruit, a bit of leftover turkey and so on. She thought about her promise to Isobel to join in with the Boxing Day swim in the morning and hoped fervently that she hadn't agreed to something that she would later regret.

Fourteen

'Faithful friends who are dear to us, will be near to us, once more...'

Zoe changed in Isobel's bathroom, squeezing herself into the wetsuit. It was very tight, but she supposed that it would work better like that. She came out of the bathroom slowly.
"It fits! Excellent," Isobel smiled.
"I feel silly," Zoe confessed.
"You look great! Anyway, no one in the group really cares much about how they look when they're swimming, or how anyone else looks for that matter. I mean, swimming in a bobble hat is a pretty odd look, but it works for me!"
Isobel had a spare changing robe as well, so Zoe put this on over the top of the wetsuit to keep her warm while they walked down to the river.
When the two women arrived at the beach, several of the other swimming group members were already entering the water. Some had wetsuits but others were just in costumes or trunks. They called cheerful greetings to Isobel, who waved back as she put her bag down on a bench.
Zoe had worried beforehand about feeling self-conscious in the wetsuit, but the freezing air around her and the thought of the water was now such a distraction that her previous concerns seemed silly and irrelevant. Isobel grinned at her.
"Let's do this! We'll leave the changing robes up here on the bench," she said, beginning to take hers off.
Zoe followed suit, reasoning that the quicker she got in, the quicker she could get out again! It was almost painful to take off the robe, like letting go of a comfort blanket, but she was resolute. After the divorce she had promised herself that she would make the most of opportunities that came her way, and say yes to new experiences even if they scared the life out of her.
The tide was high and they had only to take a few steps before they were at the edge of the water. Isobel didn't pause, walking straight on until the water was lapping at her

thighs. Zoe hesitated for just a moment, took a deep breath, then stepped forwards.

The water was extremely cold – no doubt about it – but she was determined to keep going. She slowly strode deeper into the river, trying to breathe normally and not gasp and hyperventilate. Isobel was now in all the way, her bobble-hatted head bright and clear above the water as she swam slowly against the tide. Zoe continued to follow, feeling her fingers and toes turn numb as she submerged her shoulders. She was in!

Isobel whooped. "I knew you could do it! Now come on, we'll swim for a few minutes to keep warm then we'll get out again. That will be plenty for your first go."

"Keep warm?!" Zoe muttered between chattering teeth, but she obediently pushed off from the muddy bottom of the river and swam in smooth, confident strokes after her friend. The view was spectacular; the water glinted and shimmered in the winter sunlight and the moored boats bobbed gently as the tide pulled at them. It was so quiet and peaceful. Zoe felt discomfort at the cold, but also exhilaration. Her mind felt so clear; she was totally absorbed in the moment. Surprisingly the cold was bearable as long as she kept moving.

After swimming against the tide for a few minutes, they turned and cruised back the other way. This was much easier and they were back to their starting point in no time. Laughing and holding onto each other, they struggled back through the sand to the bench where they wrapped themselves in the changing robes.

"You were amazing!" Isobel praised her. "Now I know it's tricky to do but you've got to get the wetsuit off and get dry as quickly as you can."

Zoe's fingers were still numb and she fumbled awkwardly with the wetsuit under the cloak of the robe. It felt like it took an eternity but before long she had managed to remove it, rub herself roughly dry, and get some warm clothing back on.

"I'm not sure I've ever been this c-c-c-old before." she shivered.

Isobel handed her a hot water bottle. "Here, tuck this under your jumper to get your core warmed up. And I'll pour us some hot chocolate."

"I think I'm colder now than when I was in the water."

"That's called 'afterdrop'. Your core keeps cooling for a while even after you get out of the water. The hot chocolate will help."

She took out a flask and poured the contents into two double walled thermal mugs. Zoe took one gratefully, sipping the sweet creamy drink and feeling herself start to thaw a little as sugar and heat coursed through her body.

"You might want to have a bath when you get home," Isobel suggested. "Not too hot though, or it might make you feel faint."

"Good idea." Zoe was still shivering but managed to smile.

A couple of the other swimmers came over for a quick chat and they exchanged the usual pleasantries, asking how each other's Christmas Day had been and so on. They were very complimentary to Zoe when Isobel explained that it had been her first swim in the river.

"That's fantastic," one of the women commented. "It's difficult to start in the winter. I find that if I miss even a week in the autumn then the next time feels much harder."

They said their goodbyes and began to walk back through the village towards home.

"Most importantly, did you enjoy it?" Isobel asked hopefully.

"Oh, definitely! It was a real buzz. I might be persuaded to have another go when the memory of the pain fades."

Isobel laughed. "Like childbirth!"

"Or falling in love," Zoe joked weakly.

Isobel gave her a sharp sideways glance but kept her tone light. "Well, it's not always easy. But it's definitely worth it."

Zoe was about to ask whether she was talking about swimming or something else, but Isobel had already changed the subject.

A short while later, Zoe was soaking in a delightfully warm bubble bath. She listened to a podcast on her phone as she scrubbed her feet clean of any remnants of river mud. It was tempting to lie luxuriating in the water for hours, but she was getting hungry. She also needed to rinse and hang up the wetsuit that she'd left dumped by the back door. Reluctantly, she stepped out and wrapped herself in a fluffy towel. She was feeling warmer again now but made sure to choose a big jumper to ensure that she stayed that way. Her favourite hoody was a good choice; it was cut long and the sleeves had thumbholes so she could pull them well down over her wrists.

The boot room had a big traditional butler sink which was perfect for giving the wetsuit a rinse. Zoe hung it up from an overhead rack so that it could drip into the sink. Yesterday Isobel had handed her a foil-wrapped parcel of leftover turkey when she left, so she took that out of the fridge now and made herself a classic turkey sandwich. She had a piece of Christmas cake too, then took a mug of coffee through to the sitting room to make a start on reading the book her mum had sent. The lights on the little Christmas tree twinkled appealingly and she gazed for a long moment at the decoration Tom had made for her. He had really helped to make this a special Christmas.

Zoe was walking the dogs along the beach that afternoon when she saw a figure approaching. As it came closer she recognised Tom. Her emotions churned. Had that kiss under the mistletoe yesterday meant something to him? He had practically run away afterwards! His manner seemed normal enough now, as he smiled when he saw her and raised a hand in greeting.

"I wondered if I might bump into you," he said as they drew closer. "Mind if I walk with you for a bit?"

"Not at all," Zoe replied, although her thoughts were racing, "always happy to have some company."

He nodded. "You're a 'people person', aren't you?" he asked.

Zoe was confused. "I suppose so… I guess I'm disposed to like people in general, if that's what you mean."

Tom was looking at the river as they walked. "I'm not sure I am a people person, really. Although obviously there are certain people who I like. You could say I'm quite selective."

Zoe wasn't sure where he was going with this. Was he trying to tell her subtly that he wasn't interested in her in a romantic way? They walked on in silence for a minute until she felt she ought to introduce a topic of conversation.

"Isobel took me swimming this morning," she started.

He smiled. "Really? How was it?"

"Just about the coldest I've ever been in my life! But it was kind of amazing as well."

"Will you do it again?"

"Yes, I think so. It was like… a real moment of clarity, you know? I felt completely present."

He nodded. "That's what I like about it too. Everything else just melts away. No worries… it's just you and the water."

"That's exactly how I felt."

Tom was still staring at the river. "It goes all the way to the sea, you know. Well, I suppose all rivers do eventually."

"Yes, I know. I love the seaside, it always reminds me of childhood holidays. We often went down to Camber Sands on the south coast. But I can't remember when I last saw the sea. Last summer, maybe?"

He looked at her quickly. "Would you like to? I could take you, if you like? Stroll along the prom, get a coffee somewhere."

"I don't want to put you out," she said hesitantly, but her heart was singing at the thought of a trip to the seaside.

"Are you busy tomorrow?"

She searched his face. His expression was hard to read but the offer seemed genuine. She found herself studying the curve of his cheekbones and the fullness of his lower lip, and cleared her throat quickly.

"If you're sure I'm not taking you away from something you'd rather be doing, I would love to go."

His eyes held hers. "There's nothing I'd rather be doing." Zoe felt suddenly breathless until he turned away and the spell was broken.

"Shall I pick you up about ten, then?"

"Thank you, that sounds great," she replied.

They went their separate ways near the pub and Zoe took the dogs back and settled in for the evening. She still had some leftover turkey from the parcel that Isobel had given her, and decided to make a turkey curry for dinner. She fried a small onion and stirred in garlic, chilli and ginger, turmeric and cumin. Delicious smells permeated the kitchen as she added half a tin of tomatoes and put some rice on to cook. Finding some cream in the fridge, Zoe added this and the turkey to the curry. It made a beautifully coloured bowlful and she sat down to eat with satisfaction.

Just before eight o'clock Zoe fired up her laptop and logged into a video group chat. During the pandemic she and some friends had started a regular virtual meet-up so they could chat and play games together. It had been such a success that they continued even after restrictions were lifted. This evening they had planned to meet up to swap stories about their Christmases, and to play a murder mystery game.

Katie and her partner Nick were already logged in and waving at her through the screen, and they started to chat together while other friends joined the call.

"How's the leg, Katie?" Zoe asked.

"Getting there," Katie replied. "I'm sleeping better now but it's just annoying not being able to move about properly! Still, I guess there are worse times of year to be stuck on the sofa."

Zoe chuckled. "Yes, if it was summer I know you'd be going stir crazy! Are you looking after her, Nick?"

"Waiting on her hand and foot," Nick confirmed, as Katie laughed.

An old colleague of Zoe's called Jamie joined the conversation at this point. "Hey, Zoe, are you bored to death out there in Sticksville?"

"Actually, I've been pretty busy. I've met some lovely people and this morning I went swimming in the river!"

There was much exclaiming at this, with some people complimenting Zoe's sense of adventure and others thinking that the whole thing was completely insane.

Once everyone was assembled Jamie took control, in his role of designated games master for the evening. He read the first part of the script, setting up the murder scenario. Everyone had their own character to play and there were messages flying on private chats as the players tried to work out who the murderer could be. There were lots of red herrings and plot twists and turns before they eventually solved the mystery, and a sweet-faced girl named Reya was revealed to be the killer.

"Sorry guys!" she laughed.

"It's always the quiet ones," Nick joked. "That was great, Jamie. Thanks for setting it up."

They chatted on for a while about how the holidays were going so far. Reya was staying with her parents for a few days but was relieved to escape to her room for a couple of hours with the excuse that she had an arrangement with friends.

"It's just a little intense, being home," she half-whispered. "I feel like a teenager again. I keep falling out with my sister and my auntie won't stop asking when I'm going to get married!"

"I bet you're getting fed well, though, right?" Jamie asked, and Reya nodded.

"Oh yes. Can't complain about that. Not the same at your place?"

Jamie rolled his eyes. "Dry turkey, soggy sprouts and microwaved Yorkshire puddings! I wish my stepmother would just accept that she's not a good cook and let someone else do it next year!"

Zoe grinned. "Maybe you should offer, Jamie."

He laughed. "I'd definitely do a better job, but I'm not sure the emotional fallout would be worth it!"

Zoe had a smile on her face when she finally closed the video chat and logged off. It was great to catch up with everyone. She checked her phone and saw that she had missed a message from her mum.

So... did you take the plunge?! X

She grinned and typed: *Yes! It was freeeezing but I was brave! X*

The screen showed that Astrid was typing, then another message popped up. *Well done!!! Super girl. Any plans for tomorrow? X*

Going to the seaside with a new friend, Zoe typed back. She was definitely excited about the prospect of a trip to the sea. This could be a good opportunity to get to know Tom a little better, as well.

Fifteen

'Walking in a winter wonderland...'

Tuesday dawned bright and cold. Tom picked up Zoe in his car and they took the scenic route, driving for about twenty minutes along quiet back roads to the seaside town of Felixstowe. He found a parking spot in a side street and they walked the short distance to the seafront. The sun glinted off the waves, turning the grey sea to silver.

"The silvery sea," she said aloud. Tom looked questioningly at her. "That's what my dad always called it," she explained.

Above the beach was a wide prom, busy with families and couples enjoying the fine weather. There were a few bikes and scooters, and lots of dogs for Zoe to admire. They headed towards the pier, enjoying the warmth of the sun on their backs. They passed a kiosk selling coffee and snacks, outside of which a small boy was begging his mother for ice cream.

"Bobby, it's winter!" his mum was saying. "It's not the right time of year for ice cream!"

"But it's sunny!" the little boy pleaded, tugging on his mum's hand.

Zoe and Tom exchanged a quick smile and strolled on. As they approached the pier, a voice called, "Hi Mr M!"

Tom turned his head to look for the speaker. It was a young teenage girl out for a walk with her family, smiling a little shyly at them.

"Hello, Sophie," Tom greeted her, and nodded to her parents. "Having a good Christmas?"

The girl nodded in reply. Tom addressed her parents. "And how's Charlotte getting on at college?"

"Really well, thanks," the mum replied. "She's definitely enjoying it. She got a distinction on her last assignment."

"That's good to hear. Tell her I said hi, won't you?"

They said goodbye and walked on. "The older sister, Charlotte, was in my tutor group last year," Tom explained.

Zoe felt she was getting an insight into him from watching the ease with which he had spoken with the family. "What does Mr M stand for?"

"What? Oh, it's Mr Mackenzie. Tom Mackenzie. How about you, I don't know your surname either?"

"Tyler," Zoe told him.

"Zoe Tyler," he repeated, as if to fix it in his memory. She liked hearing his voice speak her name.

As they passed groups of people they heard snatches of conversation. One older couple in particular seemed to be having a rather heated discussion. Tom caught Zoe's eye but waited until the couple had passed by before he spoke.

"They reminded me of my parents. It's funny, they bicker all the time but it seems to work for them. My mum's quite fiery, you know? And my sister's just the same so they clash sometimes. I'm the sensible one," he finished gravely.

"Oh, well done you." Zoe's lips twitched as she struggled not to smile.

"What about you, what's your family like? I think you said your mum is in Scotland?"

"Yes, but just for a visit. She lives just outside the New Forest. That's where I grew up."

"And your dad?" Tom asked.

Zoe looked at the water. It was still hard to say the words.

"He died a few years ago. Cancer."

Tom rested a hand on her shoulder and squeezed it gently. "I'm sorry."

Zoe nodded and they walked on in silence for a few moments.

"Mum's been amazing. I mean, the first year was tough, but she's really… embracing life, I think that's the best way to put it. I didn't realise before how strong she could be."

"Sounds like it runs in the family."

Zoe stopped walking and looked at him in surprise.

"What do you mean?"

"Just that you seem to be a pretty strong character yourself."

Zoe shook her head. "I'm not sure where you're getting that from! It's certainly not how I see myself."

Tom held up a gloved hand and ticked off points on his fingers. "You had the courage to leave an unhappy marriage. You started your own business. You took a leap into the unknown coming to Redfield where you knew no one, and at Christmas of all times. And Isobel told me that you were amazing at the river yesterday."

Zoe felt her cheeks glowing at this unexpected praise.

Tom's blue eyes were warm as they met hers. "From where I'm standing, Zoe Tyler, you seem like a pretty impressive woman." He gave a small smile and started to walk again quickly, as though perhaps he'd said more than he meant to.

Zoe hurried to follow but then nearly bumped into Tom's back as he stopped abruptly. "Do you know how to skim stones?" he asked.

She followed his gaze down to the water's edge where a family group was gathered. An older man, presumably the grandad, was skipping stones across the waves while his small grandchildren tried to copy him.

"It's been a long time but I think I remember how."

Tom pointed towards the next bay, beyond a line of rocky sea defences. "Let's go try over there, we don't want to get in their way."

They jumped down from the prom onto the stony upper part of the beach and stumbled down to the sandier section near the sea, picking up a few suitable flat stones on the way.

Tom bent his knees, flicked his wrist and sent the first stone skimming across the surface of the water. It bounced twice before disappearing. Zoe tried one of her own but it sank without a trace. The next one was no better. She glanced sideways at Tom. "Dodgy stones," she explained. "I think you got all the good ones."

He smiled. "Can I give you a tip?"

She nodded, and he came to stand just behind her and took hold of her right hand with his own.

"It's all in the flick," he explained, gently moving her hand to show her what he meant. He stepped back and she took a breath and tried again – success! The stone bounced three times before vanishing beneath the surface.

"Three bounces! I think that makes me the winner."

"You know, I believe it's traditional for the winner to buy the coffees."

Zoe grinned. "I was going to anyway, to thank you for bringing me here. It's really beautiful." They walked back up to the prom. Further along and on the other side of the road, partway up the cliff facing the sea, was a cosy-looking café. Fairy lights were strung around its walls and each table was covered with a checked red and white cloth. Although it was busy they managed to find a table for two and ordered coffee and homemade scones with jam and clotted cream.

"So you haven't always been a Londoner?" Tom asked once the waitress had taken their order.

"I'm not sure I'd call myself a Londoner now! I suppose I have been there for a pretty long time but I've always imagined myself back in the country eventually. When the time is right."

"When I was a teenager I thought living in a village was so boring, I couldn't wait to get away to uni and be somewhere with more buzz. And I did enjoy it at the time, but when I graduated it seemed to make more sense to move back with my parents for a while and save up some money. Then I realised that I actually love it here." He paused as the waitress brought their coffee and scones over, thanked her with a smile and began to spread jam on his scone. "I am glad I had the chance to experience living somewhere else. It was a great three years."

"Where did you go?"

"Manchester. It's a great city. There's a lot that I liked about the north, especially the people. I became good friends with a guy from Leeds and we lived together in the second and third years. He stayed in Manchester so I go up once in a while for a visit."

Zoe was enjoying getting to know more about him. She took a sip of her coffee.

"Mm, good coffee. Almost a bit of a chocolatey note in there."

"Sounds like you're a bit of an aficionado."

"I do really like coffee. I've become a bit spoilt with it though. If someone offers me instant coffee I feel disappointed."

Tom laughed. "I always have some instant in the cupboard for when I run out of the good stuff! But you're right, it's not quite the same."

Zoe picked up her scone. "And how did you come to be a teacher?" she asked before taking a bite.

"I worked in an office for a couple of years and that was fine but it wasn't very fulfilling. Then one weekend Isobel pressganged me into helping out with Charlie's Cub Scout group because they were short of volunteers. They were making things out of wood and that was a skill I had. Anyway, I realised that I really enjoyed teaching and sharing my knowledge. It sort of... lit me up, you know? So I signed up for a year-long course where you train in schools. Now I'm a head of year as well as a class teacher."

"Yet you say you're not a people person. I think you might be wrong about that."

Tom sighed. "I'm not sure I explained myself very well. I just meant... I am quite independent. I don't necessarily need people around me all the time. But I've realised that I don't want to be so reserved that I don't let the right people in. Am I making any sense?"

"I think so. You're not a social butterfly but you're not Scrooge either."

"I hope not!" he laughed.

"Well you seem to keep good company with your friends. Isobel and Steve are great. And Rob," she added.

"Yeah, they're a good bunch. But what about you, how come you've ended up doing a job where you work on your own so much, when you clearly thrive on time spent with other people?"

"I didn't really plan it this way, I used to work for a company but there were lots of issues and I ended up striking out on my own. I enjoy my work but I do sometimes think about doing something different. Maybe using my skills to work for a local council? Something like that."

He nodded. "That sounds like an idea with potential."

"I am sociable by nature but I've learned to be independent too, living on my own. It is nice to have your own space. I wouldn't compromise my freedom now unless it was for a very good reason."

"Yes," Tom agreed. "But if you met the right person..."

"Oh, of course. What *wouldn't* you do, for the right person?" She spoke lightly and then hastily turned her attention to adding more jam to her scone, in order to avoid meeting his eyes.

They were both quiet on the drive back to Redfield, but it was a comfortable silence. They were nearly back to the village when Tom spoke.

"I have to go away for a few days."

"Oh." Zoe's heart sank but she tried to sound light and casual.

"My parents and my sister live in Derbyshire now – my sister moved for work and after she had her two little girls, my parents decided to move to be closer to them. I'm going up tomorrow to see them all. They like to do 'Christmas take two' so it'll be turkey dinner and presents all over again."

"How old are your nieces?" Zoe asked.

"Five and three. They're very sweet but man, do they have a lot of energy! Anyway, I'll be there for two nights, so I'll be back in the afternoon on the thirtieth. Friday." He steered the car into the driveway of the Old Rectory and switched off the engine. "So... maybe I'll see you then? Or at the New Year's Eve party, if not before."

"Sure," Zoe replied brightly, her emotions in turmoil. That was all a bit vague – didn't he want to fix an arrangement? She glanced at him and he gave a quick, tight smile. It was like the shutters had come down.

"Well, I'd better go sort out my packing." He kept his hands firmly on the steering wheel, ready to go.

Zoe nodded. "Ok. Thank you again for today."

"You're welcome," he replied, as she opened her door and got out of the car. He started the engine and reversed out, and Zoe went into the house.

Zoe sat down on the kitchen floor and allowed the dogs to climb over her legs and lick her. She hugged them all close. "I don't know, guys, I just can't read him. We certainly didn't get off to a great start when I first arrived but then things seemed to turn around completely. We had a great time at the beach today and I *think* he likes me but then he goes all reserved. I wish I knew what was going through his mind."

Barney gave a little bark.

"Yes, I know exactly what's going through *your* mind! We'll go out soon."

Sixteen

'Giddy up jingle horse, pick up your feet...'

With no plans for Wednesday and good weather outside, Zoe decided to explore some more unfamiliar footpaths with the dogs. She remembered a woodland path that she had rejected some days ago when she'd been watching ghost stories. That all seemed very silly now! Today was sunny and she fancied a woodland walk. She put on her walking boots as the dogs frisked about, recognising the signs.

They headed up the field edge together, pausing on the way to admire the view over the river. There were a couple of boats sailing along, tacking into the light wind. At the crossroads Zoe led the way into the trees. It was more a copse than a true w« wood, with a green lane running through the centre. Zoe imagined it in the summer with the trees in full leaf; it would be a lovely shady respite from a hot summer's day. She could see hoofprints in the mud and kept an eye out for horses in case she needed to move the dogs out of their way. After a couple of minutes walking she came to a place where a large tree had fallen across the path. Thinking of the horses, she had a quick look around to make sure no one was watching.

"Come on Henry, come on Barney!" She took a run up and jumped over the tree trunk as if she were a horse herself, the dogs jumping with her. Bella looked at them solemnly and walked around the end. Zoe laughed.

"I'm sure you think I'm crazy, Bella, but I enjoyed that!"

Returning to the house, Zoe felt that the walk had done her good. She caught sight of her reflection in a mirror as she hung up the dogs' leads. Her eyes were bright and her cheeks rosy from the fresh wind. She felt awake and alive. And hungry, again, she realised. Better check if there are any mince pies left!

Zoe spent some time working on the laptop in the afternoon, catching up on emails and starting some new designs. At about three o'clock she put her work away ready to take the dogs out for another walk. She thought she would go for a shorter loop this time as they'd had a good long walk that morning, and it looked like the temperature was dropping again. She pulled on her kingfisher-blue hat and her coat and headed through the village towards the pub. They could do the beach – church footpath loop but in reverse this time.

Just walking the route in the opposite direction to usual made it seem quite novel. She noticed new things about the houses she passed; different decorations seemed to stand out, and from this direction she spotted a cluster of gnomes in one garden that she hadn't seen at all when approaching from the other way. The gnomes were of various different sizes and appearances, including several particularly ugly ones, but they made Zoe smile. They were so stubbornly unfashionable; the owner obviously just loved them. She remembered that her grandma had had a collection in her garden and Zoe had always loved looking at them when she was a small child. Her own mum had rolled her eyes and said they were hideous, but her grandma didn't care.

They walked along the beach, passing a few other walkers who Zoe greeted with a "hello" or a nod. The sun seemed to have disappeared and the afternoon had become grey and still. They took the footpath up past the church and emerged back onto the lane just above Isobel's house. As Bella led the way home, Zoe heard a car door close and saw Isobel standing in her driveway.

"Zoe!"

"Hello! Are you coming in, or going out?"

"Coming in, I just had to pop to the supermarket and stock up again. How's your day been?"

"Quiet," Zoe admitted. "Just walking and working, really."

"Are you doing anything this evening?"

"Just watching telly or reading. The usual."

"Oh good. Come round and help me finish my jigsaw? It's been sitting around too long now and it's driving me mad. But I've got to finish it!"
Zoe laughed. "I could do that. Is it a thousand pieces?"
"Yes, and I'd forgotten how long it takes! I've spent hours on it!"
"All right, sounds good. It would be nice to have an actual human conversation. When shall I come round?"
"Why don't you come at six and have dinner with us? Charlie's going out so it's just me and Steve. I'm making cheese and potato pie."
"That would be lovely, thanks. I'll see you in a bit, then."
"See you then!" Isobel picked up her shopping bags and staggered towards the front door, and Zoe followed Bella up the driveway of the Old Rectory and through the gate.

The cheese and potato pie was a perfect carb-heavy winter dish. Isobel served it with green vegetables – "so it's perfectly healthy", she assured her guest – and there was apple crumble and custard for dessert. Once they had eaten, Isobel and Zoe went into the living room to tackle the jigsaw. Steve refused to help. He said that he had had enough of it already, thanks very much, and that he would stay in the kitchen. Isobel had set up the jigsaw on the coffee table, which was long enough to have the spare pieces arrayed around the edges. She was most of the way through it, but there were still lots of tricky pieces of sky and snowy ground which looked very similar.
The image showed Father Christmas and his reindeer sleighing through a snowy village. Zoe could see why it was difficult to complete; the red of the sleigh was the same as the red of a postbox and a door to a house, and there were a number of almost-identical dark green fir trees.
"I can see why you want to finish it," Zoe said. "It must have taken a while to get this far."
"Getting the four edges done was easy enough, and Father Christmas and his sleigh was ok, but these houses have been a mission."

They set to, methodically checking the different pieces and gradually filling in the blank spaces. They were able to chat as they did so, and Zoe told Isobel a little about her seaside trip with Tom. Isobel desperately wanted to ask her new friend many more questions, but she held herself back with great restraint. Steve had warned her not to meddle with other people's relationships. She was inclined to think that a *little* meddling might be required, but the trip to the seaside certainly sounded like a date to her, and if they'd managed that without any outside interference then perhaps she should just keep out of it.

After about half an hour, quite a number of the jigsaw pieces had slotted into place and Isobel was feeling cheery.

"We're getting there! Ooh, I've just remembered. One of my darling little pupils gave me a bottle of espresso martini. I think all you have to do is pour it over ice. Do you fancy trying one with me?"

"Oh, yes please."

"I'll be back in a sec." Isobel headed off to the kitchen and returned shortly with two cocktail glasses filled with a dark liquid. Ice cubes clinked gently as she set them down. Zoe picked hers up and took a sip.

"That's pretty good."

Isobel tried hers and agreed. "You don't quite get the nice creamy top that you'd get in a cocktail bar, but it's rather tasty."

"I love a good cocktail but it's an occasional treat. They're just too expensive for me to have often. If you're imagining my life to be anything like *Sex and the City*, think again!"

Isobel laughed. "I can't say I was, really! You seem far too nice and normal. Do you go out much, at home?"

"Not really. I tend to go for coffee or brunch with friends more often now instead of going to pubs and bars. I live near a swimming pool so I usually swim there once a week, and sometimes my neighbour Katie comes with me. I guess when I was married we hung out with my ex's friends sometimes, but of course that's all changed now. What about you, do you go out? 'Out' out?"

"Only once in a while. Steve and I have a longstanding tradition of going out for a date night once a month. We'll go to a restaurant in Woodbridge or Ipswich or a village pub somewhere. It helps to get away from the everyday stuff and just be together. Then there's the pub here, and swimming, where we see friends from the village."

"You and Steve seem well suited," Zoe said a little wistfully.

"Yeah, he's not so bad." Isobel kept her private thoughts to herself – that she was often amazed and delighted that she still felt so much love and attraction for a man she had been with for over twenty years. He drove her mad sometimes, of course, but she wouldn't have changed her situation for anything.

Zoe thought more about relationships as she was getting ready for bed later that night. She could see that Isobel and Steve loved each other deeply. Her own parents, before her dad's death, had been a loving and committed couple. She knew that real love existed. Her own experiences had been less fortunate, so far at least. But she still had hope.

She finished brushing her teeth and rinsed out her toothbrush. She looked at her reflection in the mirror for a moment. She couldn't help but wonder: would the spark she felt between her and Tom lead to anything more?

****

Thursday morning was a curious misty morning, the sort of day where you wondered if it was ever really going to get light. Zoe found as she walked the dogs that tiny droplets of dew were clinging to her eyelashes, and she was glad that she had put on her bobble hat. Once the dogs were safely back in the kitchen, she decided to walk into Woodbridge to get a cup of coffee somewhere by the river. The world seemed hushed and strange under the mist and she wanted to sit in a warm, bright café surrounded by people.

The river path was rather muddy but her walking boots gripped well and she could walk quickly enough to stay warm. There was little activity on the river today, just a pair of swans gliding silently by and the odd splash suggesting fish below the surface. As she drew closer to the town Zoe heard the first faint, muffled boom. She paused for a moment, wondering if she was hearing things. It came again, then again, a steady drumbeat growing nearer to her.

All of a sudden a boat emerged from the mist, a carved dragon at the prow. It was being propelled at some speed by two lines of rowers, all keeping perfect time with the beat coming from a drummer sat high at the front of the boat. With the eerie mist the whole thing seemed rather otherworldly, and the little craft reminded Zoe of a miniature Viking longboat. If it hadn't been for the modern coats and lifejackets worn by the rowers, she could almost have believed that these were ancient invaders coming to pillage a local monastery.

The rowers cut a slow semicircle across the river to change direction and head back upstream, then the pace of the drumbeat increased. The paddles whisked rapidly in and out of the water and the little boat shot forwards towards the Tide Mill. Zoe followed, intrigued, but soon lost them as they curved around a bend of the river and continued on out of sight, the drumbeat fading into the mist.

She continued on to the riverfront café that she had visited the previous week, and went up to the counter. The woman serving was wearing a sparkly grey jumper under her apron and greeted Zoe in a strong local accent.

"Yes, my darling, what can I get for you?"

Zoe ordered coffee and a caramel shortbread. She took off her hat and coat as she found a table and sat down: it was very warm and steam clouded the windows. The woman with the sparkly jumper brought her order over to the table and set the coffee down carefully.

"Funny weather, isn't it?" she remarked companionably.

"Yes, quite spooky," Zoe replied. "I just saw a strange boat with a dragon's head and I almost wondered if my imagination was playing tricks on me."

"Ah, the dragon boat's usually out at the weekends. I guess they've fitted in an extra session with it being holidays for most people this week. Have you seen the boat in the Longshed, a couple of doors down?"

"No, I haven't."

"Oh, that's well worth seeing. They're building a replica of the burial ship that was found at Sutton Hoo. I think it's open today if you have time for a look." She smiled and headed back to the counter to serve another customer.

Zoe enjoyed her coffee and snack and indulged in some people watching. There were some dogs to admire too, including a very hairy border terrier which was extremely adept at finding any dropped crumbs. When the owner, a middle-aged woman, finished her drink and took the little dog outside, Zoe heard her shout of exasperation as the terrier found and quickly demolished half a sandwich that someone had dropped on the floor.

Having finished her own coffee, Zoe put her hat and coat back on and stepped outside into the strange misty day. She looked around and saw the "Longshed" that the woman in the café had described. Sure enough, it did seem to be open, and she went to see what was inside.

It was a wooden ship; unfinished as yet, but complete enough to get a sense of the scale and of the work involved in creating such a magnificent vessel. Zoe wandered along slowly, in awe of the Anglo-Saxon ancestors who could have produced such a thing with the limited technology available to them. There were lots of information boards and exhibition items to look at, and several other people were milling around looking at these and talking with the volunteers.

Zoe recalled that she had seen a film about the archaeological discoveries at Sutton Hoo; she had forgotten that it was so close to this place. She wondered if Tom had been here. Surely he had, with his interest in woodwork. She wished that she had his number and could send him a message. After half an hour or so of exploring the shed, she dropped some coins into the donation box and headed off on the return walk to Redfield.

Seventeen

'Oh I can't wait to see those faces...'

There was plenty of time in the afternoon for Zoe to get some work done and she sat at the breakfast bar with her laptop. Working on the sofa wasn't doing anything for her lower back! She liked being in the warm kitchen close to the kettle and all the snacks. The dogs' ears perked up as they heard her open the biscuit tin about three o'clock. She regarded them severely.

"These are for humans, as well you know! But there are a few of your special Christmas biscuits left, luckily." She found the dog treats and gave one to each of her little friends.

"I think we're doing enough walking to balance out the treats," she observed to Bella. "My jeans still fit so I must be doing something right." Bella crunched happily on her biscuit, which Zoe took as tacit approval of the situation.

Switching on the TV, Zoe saw that the advert breaks were now full of invitations to shop the sales; weight loss products and schemes; and images of families enjoying summer holidays in the sun. Zoe had to smile at the predictability of it. She wasn't personally interested in spending her money on any of those things right now, but she supposed that there was something reassuring in this familiar seasonal rhythm. She wondered whether she would go on holiday in the coming year. Funds had been tight but it was so worthwhile to have a break from the everyday routine. Coming here had felt like a real holiday even though she had been doing some paid work as well. Maybe she could do some more house-sitting.

She flicked around the channels and settled on an old rom-com that she'd seen several times, but loved. She wondered what sort of films Tom liked. She wondered what he was doing at that very moment.

One hundred and fifty miles away in Derbyshire, Tom was sitting in his sister's lounge, surrounded by family but staring blankly into space.

"Tom? Tom?!"

He felt his attention pulled back into the room.

"Sorry, what was that?"

His sister gave him an odd look. "I said, do you want a top-up? You were miles away, what were you thinking about?"

"Nothing in particular," he replied quickly. "Just zoned out for a minute. Yes, I'll have a top-up. Thanks."

He managed to stay more present for the rest of the evening, but when he was lying in the guest room's bed later he let his thoughts drift back to Zoe. It was crazy to say that he missed her – he barely knew her, for goodness' sake! – but he had to admit that he was really looking forward to seeing her again the next day.

Zoe checked methodically through her clothes then sat back and sighed. She didn't know what she had been expecting to magically appear in the wardrobe overnight, since she knew exactly what she'd packed in the first place, but there definitely didn't seem to be anything suitable for a New Year's Eve party in this collection of garments. It was now Friday the thirtieth and she was running out of time if she wanted to find something different.

She had been up fairly early that morning, made a big bowl of porridge for breakfast and taken the dogs for their first walk. She had then started on some cleaning jobs. The house wasn't getting terribly dirty with just her and the dogs in residence and she didn't need to go into the closed rooms, but there was a certain amount of hair being shed downstairs! It was while running the vacuum cleaner around (trying to avoid Henry who didn't like its noise and kept barking at it) that it had suddenly dawned on her that she didn't have anything to wear for the party.

She decided to walk into Woodbridge again and have a look around the charity shops. Isobel had mentioned that there was one particularly good one near the supermarket, and you never knew what gem you might turn up there. She knew that there were some lovely independent boutiques but she suspected that they would be rather beyond her limited budget.

Yesterday's mist had disappeared. The day was bright but cold, with white clouds scudding briskly across the sky, as Zoe locked the door and set off on her walk. A group of goldfinches fluttered in and out of the bushes alongside the river path, their red faces and the flashes of yellow on their wings making them easy to identify. Zoe smiled as she watched them, then continued on her way.

She wandered in and out of the first few shops, rifling through the rails of clothes in search of the perfect outfit. The quality of the clothes was good and they had been carefully sorted by colour and size, so it was easy to find things that might fit her, but less easy to find exactly what she was looking for. Do I know exactly what I'm looking for? she asked herself. Probably not, but I think I'll know it if I see it.

Half an hour later, still empty handed, she was starting to feel demoralised when she saw a tempting display of pastries in the window of a coffee shop. It was a lightbulb moment. Oh, she realised with a start, I'm hungry! No wonder I'm finding this tricky. Time to refuel. She pushed open the door and went inside into the warm, bright interior. There were stacks of scones, pain au chocolat, mince pies, cookies, millionaire shortbread... Zoe's tummy rumbled at the sight and she realised that it was past her usual lunchtime, and although she had had a good breakfast that morning, she had then walked the dogs as well as walking into the town. No wonder she was feeling empty!

She ordered a flat white and a cheese scone with butter and chilli jam, feeling that she'd had so many sweet treats recently that she rather fancied a savoury option this time. She found a quiet corner and flicked through a local newspaper that another customer had left behind. A young waitress brought her coffee and scone over to her. The scone was large and had been heated so that the butter melted into it as Zoe spread it with her knife. A thick layer of chilli jam followed and she was ready to take the first bite. It was even better than she had expected, rich and savoury and satisfying.

Feeling refreshed, she headed out to hit the shops again. She glanced up to see that the weather had turned and the sky was now grey and steely. She visited a couple of places without success before stumbling across the one that Isobel had mentioned, near the supermarket. Looking around the rails, she realised what Isobel meant. Jackpot, she thought. Many of the items were from smart brands that Zoe wouldn't normally buy new, finding them rather out of her price range. She found the section with dresses and suits and began to sort through the rails. There was a red dress that she rather liked but it was too big. And to be honest, Zoe thought, a bit more attention-grabbing than I would prefer. Although she wanted to wear something special and feel good about herself, she didn't want to look over-the-top. She was about to give up when she spotted something in her size in midnight blue, squeezed between two other dresses so that only a little of the shoulder was peeking out. She pulled it out to have a better look.

It wasn't a dress, she realised, it was a jumpsuit. Made of deep midnight blue velvet, it had wide leg trousers and short sleeves. Perhaps it had been worn on one occasion but it looked as good as new. She took it to the changing cubicle to try on. There wasn't much room behind the curtain but she managed to shuffle out of her regular clothes and into the jumpsuit, and turned to inspect her reflection in the mirror. She could hardly believe her luck – it fitted perfectly. The fabric skimmed over her body and there was a sash belt to accentuate her waist. It was sexy without being too ostentatious. She turned from side to side and around to get a look at the back view, and tried sitting down on the seat to make sure it was comfortable. It all seemed pretty good. Turning her face to the mirror again, she gave a little shimmy. This was the one!

Zoe dressed again in her own clothes and took the jumpsuit out to the till where a white-haired lady wearing a cherry red cardigan was waiting to serve customers. She wore a name tag with the words, "Sandra – Volunteer".

"Oh, that's lovely," Sandra commented. She checked the price tag. "And what a bargain!"

"I know, such a lucky find. I'd almost given up looking and then there it was."

The woman nodded. "Ah, that's often the way, isn't it? We find things where we least expect them." Her eyes twinkled.

Zoe thanked her and stepped out of the shop, only to find that the wind had risen and the first fat drops of rain were beginning to fall. Swearing under her breath but resigned to her fate, she set off towards the river walk. At least she was wearing her sensible waterproof coat today, but she had a feeling that she would be getting soaked despite it. Her route took her through a car park and she was focused on avoiding the queue of slow-moving cars when a beep of a horn and a shout of "Zoe!" caught her attention. She looked up and spotted Rob's sandy head as he leaned slightly out of the window of his very dirty Volvo.

"Do you need a lift back to Redfield?" he called.

She hurried over, holding her hood so that it didn't blow down. "If you're offering! I like walking but I think the heavens are about to open."

"Hop in," he grinned, and she ran round to the passenger side.

"Sorry about the mess," Rob apologised as Zoe climbed in. It was certainly not the tidiest car she'd ever been in; discarded wrappers and wisps of hay cluttered the footwell, and the backseat was covered in various items, many of which looked like rubbish. "My excuse is, it's a working vehicle."

Zoe smiled at him. "I'm just grateful for your timing! Look, it's really starting to come down now."

The rain was indeed falling heavily now and as they exited the car park and headed along the road, it seemed to be turning to sleet. Rob's windscreen wipers worked overtime, pushing the icy slush away so that he could see the road. He drove slowly and carefully.

"Did you buy anything interesting?" He nodded towards her shopping bag.

"Yes, it's something to wear for tomorrow night. Mostly I just had jumpers and jeans and they didn't seem right for the occasion."

"Got to get your glad rags on for New Year. And your dancing shoes; you know there'll be dancing, right?"

"Yes." A thought struck her. "Oh god, shoes! I didn't think about that. I've only got trainers or walking boots. Maybe Isobel can lend me something."

He chuckled. "You might get away with trainers but walking boots would probably be a bit of an odd look."

"No kidding."

By the time they drove into Redfield the sleet shower had eased and a few rays of sunshine were breaking through the heavy grey clouds. Rob turned into the driveway of the Old Rectory and pulled on the handbrake. "There you go."

"Thank you so much, you've saved me from what would have been a miserable walk home." She hesitated with her hand on the car's door handle. "Have you got time to come in for a coffee? You could help me finish the Christmas cake."

"Yeah, I've got time. If you're sure that's ok with you."

"I'd welcome the company," Zoe confessed. "It feels like it's been a quiet couple of days. There's only so much conversation you can make with three dogs."

Rob laughed and they both headed into the house together.

Tom unloaded his bags from the car and carried them through into his kitchen. It had been a long drive and he was glad to be home again. His thoughts turned to Zoe, as they had so often over the past few days. *I need to stretch my legs*, he reasoned to himself. *I could stroll up to the Old*

Rectory and see if there's anyone home, maybe stop for a cup of tea if she offers. Locking the door again, he pushed his hands into his coat pockets and set off, long legs striding out in the direction of Zoe's house.

As he drew close to the Old Rectory Tom heard voices. Slowing his pace, he saw that Rob's car was parked in the driveway. He watched from the shadows under the trees as Zoe and Rob came out of the house and towards the car, talking and laughing in a friendly way. Rob held out his arms and they hugged tightly.

Tom watched with a grim expression on his face, contrasting his own reticence with his old friend's easy charm. Seems like I'm surplus to requirements here, he thought. Guess I missed my chance. Without alerting either of them to his presence he turned on his heel and slipped silently away, back the way he had come.

What a nice chap he is, Zoe thought as Rob left. Not my type at all, but he'll make someone a lovely partner. She wondered if Tom was back home yet. She was hoping that he would come by to see her. The ball was definitely in his court; she didn't know exactly where he lived and they hadn't exchanged phone numbers.

She took the jumpsuit upstairs, found a hanger, and hung it on the back of the bedroom door where she could admire it. It was about time for the dogs' second walk. Looking out of the window, she could see that the weather was still holding. She was relieved not to have to go out in icy sleet, although she did suspect that perhaps the dogs would refuse to even go out the door if the weather was too horrible. In any case, she thought she had better seize the moment.

They did a quick loop but Zoe felt that none of the dogs was keen to be out for long and soon they were making their way back into the house, relieved to be out of the cold. It was the sort of damp cold that seemed to seep into your bones. Zoe went straight through to light the fire and her three furry friends followed.

She had just got the fire going when her phone buzzed with a message from Katie. *How's it going? Any big plans for tomorrow night? I'm going to hobble out on crutches to watch the fireworks! x*

Party at the village hall, Zoe messaged back. *Not the most glam but should be fun x*

She was a bit concerned at the thought of Katie trying to manage crutches through a crowded London. Still, she did have a boyfriend to lean on, and neither of them were much bothered about alcohol so at least they weren't adding extra wobbliness into the mix.

The sleet had started again and Zoe could hear it throwing itself against the windows. The contrast between the grim-sounding weather and the cosy sitting room was rather delicious. Zoe didn't mind a bit of bad weather, even if she had to be out in it, as long as there was the prospect of getting warm and comfortable again afterwards. In fact she even enjoyed camping in a rainstorm, as long as the tent stayed up!

There had been one memorable Guide camp when she was about twelve years old, where there had been a sudden cloudburst early one morning. Zoe had woken to the sound of rain and soon all the girls were awake and chatting. Although it was early summer, the temperature really dropped and no one wanted to get out of their sleeping bags. Mercifully the tent hadn't flooded and when the rain passed, the leaders made them all a cup of tea and brought it to them in bed. Zoe still remembered it as one of the best cups of tea she had ever had.

It was about dinner time by now and Zoe reluctantly left the warm snug to see what she could rustle up in the kitchen. She had a recipe for an easy curry made with coconut milk and chickpeas. She started with chopping onion and frying it together with the spices, then adding the other ingredients. She set some rice on the hob in another pan. Even with the delightful underfloor heating warming her toes, she decided to take the finished meal back into the sitting room to eat in front of the fire. She watched some TV for a while before picking up the new book that her mum had bought her for Christmas.

 As the evening wore on, her hopes of seeing Tom faded. If he was going to make an appearance, he would surely have done it by now. Maybe he wasn't that bothered after all. She pulled back the curtain and looked out into the night but there was nothing to see except the darkness.

Eighteen

'Once bitten and twice shy...'

Zoe bumped into Isobel as they were both walking their dogs. Bella and Jasper greeted each other with friendly licks and wags of the tail while Barney jumped around excitedly.

"Are you looking forward to tonight?"

"Of course! Tell me again what's happening when?"

"We head to the hall about eight p.m., claim a table and have a drink. The ceilidh band will play for an hour or so, then they have a break and there'll be some food to help soak up some of the booze and keep everyone going until midnight. Charlie's band will play a few songs to rev everyone up again..."

"Oh, Charlie's in a band?" Zoe interrupted.

"Yes, he sings and plays guitar. They're quite good, they play in a few local pubs from time to time. Anyway, they play for a while and then the ceilidh band play another set to take us up to the big countdown. There'll be a few minutes of fireworks outside and then we all clear out. I think mostly people are ready to go home to bed at that point anyway but if anyone wants to keep partying they have to do it at home!"

"Well, I'll have to get back before midnight for the dogs," Zoe said, leaning down to scratch Henry's golden ears. "They'll be scared of the fireworks and it's not fair for me to leave them alone."

Isobel sighed. "I know, that's the problem with fireworks. I love them but generally, animals don't. Luckily though, Jasper has never seemed too bothered so I am going to stay and enjoy them this year. We've got one of those dog calming plug ins and I really do think it works – for him, at least. Also he is quite elderly now and I think he's going a little bit deaf."

Zoe laughed. "I expect that does help! I don't mind leaving a bit early anyway. It means I won't have that awkward moment of having no one to kiss at midnight."

Isobel looked surprised. "Oh, I should think there'd be a queue! And one particular eligible bachelor would definitely be fighting his way to the front."

"If you mean Tom, I wouldn't be so sure. I thought I would have seen him yesterday when he got back, but I've heard nothing."

"Oh, that's strange. You could always take the initiative and message him?"

Zoe shook her head. "I don't actually have his number."

Isobel was outraged. "Honestly, what's wrong with you two?! I can give you his number." She started rummaging in her pockets for her phone.

"No! I'm not going to make a fool of myself chasing him if he's not interested. He knows where to find me. Anyway, it's all ridiculous because I'll be going home in less than a week. Then what?"

Isobel shrugged. "I wouldn't exactly say I believe in fate, but things do seem to have a way of working out, most of the time." She could see from the stubborn set of Zoe's chin that there was no point in pursuing the argument further.

"Oh, I nearly forgot!" Zoe suddenly exclaimed. "What size are your feet?"

Isobel raised her eyebrows in surprise. "Um, six. Why?"

"I found a fab jumpsuit in town yesterday but then I realised I've only got scruffy trainers or boots to wear with it and I wondered..."

"If you could borrow some shoes? Of course," Isobel answered.

"Oh, that would be great. I'm a size six too."

"Come round when you've finished your walk and I'll show you what I've got," Isobel offered.

"Thanks so much," Zoe replied. "As I said to Rob, it would look a bit odd otherwise."

"When did you see Rob?" Isobel asked as they walked on together.

"Oh, I bumped into him just as I finished shopping and he gave me a lift home because the weather was so grim. Then he came in for a bit to help finish that Christmas cake you gave me."

"Nice. He's a good lad."

"He is. Not for me, in case you're thinking of matchmaking..."

"Wouldn't dream of it!" Isobel lied.

"Have you seen the inside of his car?"

Isobel laughed. "Oh yes, that's enough to put anyone off. It sounds awful but I think he really does need a wife to boss him around and take care of him. Like a real old-school arrangement."

"I know what you mean. How do you and Steve get on with division of labour?"

"Not too bad. I certainly do the lion's share of the housework but then I work part time, so that seems fair. He pulls his weight most of the time. And he always does the vacuuming because I hate it."

"That was one of the, let's face it, many issues with my ex. He went straight from living with his parents to living with me and he expected me to pick up after him like his mum always did."

"Ugh. Nightmare. I've tried to raise Charlie to be independent. He's pretty good at doing his share."

They walked back together and Zoe left the dogs at the Old Rectory before following Isobel into her house to try on party shoes.

Isobel had taken Jasper out a second time, for a short afternoon walk to the river, when she ran into Tom walking along the beach.

"Hey, what's going on with you and Zoe?"

Tom's expression was guarded as he looked out at the river. "Nothing. Why, did she say something?"

"Just that she hadn't heard from you. I thought you were keen on her?"

"Yeah, well, I think she's more interested in someone else." Tom met Isobel's gaze and saw the sceptical lift of her eyebrow. "What?"

"If you mean Rob, he just gave her a lift home when they bumped into each other and it was raining. She's not interested in him romantically."

Tom felt a surge of hope but tried to sound casual. "Oh, really?"

Isobel sighed and shook her head. "Honestly, if you two don't sort yourselves out soon I'm going to knock your heads together!" She took hold of his hand and squeezed it. "I know that you're naturally reserved but... get over it. She's not a mind reader."

Tom's mouth twitched in a hint of a smile. "She'll be at the party tonight, right?"

Isobel nodded. "Of course. She borrowed some shoes from me earlier."

"Oh god. I haven't even thought about clothes. You don't think I need to wear a tie, do you?"

"Definitely not. We're going to a village hall, not the Ritz. Wear smart dark trousers, a shirt with the top button undone, and that jacket I admired when I bumped into you after work the other week. Nice trainers, not your running shoes."

He smiled. "Good job I've got you, hey?"

Isobel grinned back. "I think you'd manage, but I don't mind giving you a nudge in the right direction." She looked at him appraisingly. "You really like her, don't you?"

Tom sighed. "I do, but I'm very conscious that she's only here temporarily. I don't want just a holiday romance; I want something real."

"Give it a chance," Isobel advised. "Or you'll never know what might have been."

Zoe checked her reflection in the dressing table mirror. The jumpsuit looked just as good as it had in the shop yesterday, and Isobel's silver shoes finished the look nicely. Her hair was shining and she'd gone for classic smoky eye make-up, her usual party look. She applied a slick of lip gloss and pressed her lips together to distribute it evenly. She was still feeling a little hurt that Tom hadn't been in touch, but she wasn't going to let that stop her having a good time. Maybe she'd misread the signals and he was only interested in friendship after all. It certainly wouldn't be the first time that she'd got it wrong when it came to men.

The village hall had been transformed for the occasion. A disco ball hung from the centre of the ceiling, scattering light coming from the array on the stage, and bunches of silver and gold balloons were tied along the walls. At the far end of the hall, a number of table and chairs were arranged in groups, leaving an area closer to the stage for people to dance. The bar was set up in the kitchen which was off to one side with a large serving hatch opening onto the main hall. They hung up their coats in the lobby. Isobel was wearing a mid-length emerald green dress in a satiny material which skimmed beautifully over her body.

"Izzy, I love your dress! That colour goes so well with your hair."

"Thank you! I love your jumpsuit too. I can't believe you found that in a charity shop."

There were already quite a number of people milling around chatting, and Steve led the way to the bar so they could get a drink. He was wearing navy chinos and a navy checked shirt and looked very dapper.

They stood chatting with Poppy from the shop, who was looking bohemian in a flowing peacock blue dress with long sleeves. Zoe was halfway down her first glass of fizz when there, across the crowded room, she saw Tom. Her heart thumped in her chest. Their eyes locked and he moved through the throng, gazing straight at her all the time, until he stood in front of her.

"You look stunning," he said softly.

"Thank you," she replied simply, feeling joy at his presence but still uncertain of where she stood.

Isobel subtly turned her back and kept talking to Poppy and Steve, blocking them from greeting Tom, to give him and Zoe a moment to talk alone.

"Listen, I'm sorry I didn't come to see you yesterday. Actually, I did come to see you, but I thought you were busy so I didn't get as far as knocking on the door."

Zoe was confused. "Thought I was busy? What do you mean?"

Tom winced. "Well, I saw Rob's car and I thought maybe the two of you..."

Zoe's eyebrows shot up. "Wow. Um, no. It's not like that. He gave me a lift and I asked him in for a cup of tea."

"Yeah, Isobel told me. I just thought... going away for a few days, maybe I missed my chance. I don't really date much. I don't think I'm very good at it."

"And you think I am?!"

He shrugged and she shook her head in disbelief. "Remember I was married for years? Then suddenly I'm single again but the whole dating scene is totally alien to me. I've been on a few dates over the last year but they've mostly been totally disastrous. There was one guy I quite liked. We went out a total of three times before he ghosted me. Literally never heard from him again."

Tom began to smile a little. "Maybe I've been jumping to conclusions again."

Zoe smiled too. "You think?!"

The ceilidh band finished their warm-up and the caller began encouraging people to line up on the dance floor ready for the first dance.

"So, are we going to give this a go?" Tom asked, nodding towards the dance floor.

"We can try," Zoe replied, setting down her empty glass. Isobel had already commandeered Rob as her partner and was beckoning to them to come over and join in.

They formed two lines, men on one side and women on the other, and the caller began to explain the moves for those who hadn't done this before. They had a practise without the music, slowly stepping forwards and back, round in a circle and so on, then the band struck up a merry tune and the dancing began. Zoe found it took all her concentration to follow the caller and keep in time, and there was a lot of laughter in the hall as various people messed up the steps. There was no opportunity to speak more with Tom but as they moved together, holding each other and laughing when they got it wrong, she felt closer to him than she ever had before.

The caller soon decided that they had got the hang of it well enough, and introduced a new move where the couples changed places. The ladies moved on to the right so that they danced in turn with many different partners. This presented an extra challenge and once again there was much laughter and good humoured banter about the inevitable mistakes. Eventually Zoe had been swirled right around the circle and back to Tom, and the dance ended.

They stayed on the dance floor for the next two dances, which were similar enough to the first that they made fewer mistakes this time, then Tom suggested that they head to the bar and get a drink. He kept hold of Zoe's hand as he guided her through the other dancers. She felt herself blushing and hoped that he would just think that her cheeks were hot from dancing. At the bar he gave her hand a little squeeze before he let go and she felt her heart skip a beat. Oh my days, she thought. I'm like a giddy schoolgirl!

Drinks in hand, Zoe spotted a couple of empty chairs and they went to sit down and watch the other dancers. Isobel was still going strong.

"I think it's a good job that I'd only had one drink before that first dance," Zoe commented, leaning slightly towards Tom to be heard over the music.

He smiled. "This same band were here last New Year, so it's not totally new to me."

"It definitely gets easier with practice. We were a lot better on the last one than the first."

"So what have you been up to for the last couple of days?"

"Not much, it's been quiet. Lots of walking, including going into Woodbridge. How did you get on with your family? Was the journey ok?"

"Yes, just long. The family were good. My nieces are always very entertaining. I've definitely had enough turkey for one year now, though."

Isobel bounced over, flushed and out of breath. "Come on you two, time for another dance!"

Tom stood and offered his hand to Zoe. She took it with a smile and he led her back to the dance floor. They danced together, then Zoe partnered with Steve while Tom danced with Isobel. Whirling around with bright eyes and rosy cheeks, Zoe felt joy and excitement bubbling inside her. Each time she came back to Tom there was that sense of connection as their eyes met and their hands touched. She felt happy just to be near him.

The ceilidh band finished their first set and there was a pause in the music while the buffet opened. Zoe and Tom joined the queue for food, picking up a paper plate each and moving along the table.

"Ah, the classic beige buffet," Tom commented. "Very traditional."

Zoe laughed. "Nothing wrong with a good sausage roll," she said, taking one and putting it on her plate, next to a piece of quiche and a mini Scotch egg.

"Oh, I'm not complaining. It may not be haute cuisine but I like sausage rolls as much as the next man."

The savoury snacks gave way to sweet options at the end of the table. Everything was in miniature: brownies, éclairs, tiny pavlovas that you could eat in one bite, and small wedges of Christmas cake. Zoe looked doubtfully at her plate.

"What do you reckon, pudding on the side or queue up again after the first bit?"

"On the side, I think, if you can make space."

Zoe used a chicken goujon as a dividing barrier on her plate and put a mini brownie and a pavlova next to it. Looking around, they saw that Rob had already claimed a table and they went to join him.

They had finished eating and were drinking and chatting as Charlie's band started setting up on the stage. The members of the band had a drum kit, keyboard and bass guitar as well as Charlie's lead guitar.

"They all know each other from school," Isobel explained.

"What kind of music do they play?" Zoe asked.

"Sort of indie rock, I'd describe it as. Mostly covers but they are starting to write a few of their own songs now."

The band completed their sound check and began their first song, an upbeat number that soon brought a few people onto the dance floor. Zoe was impressed.

"Oh, they're good!"

Charlie seemed to stand straighter and more confidently on the stage, looking every inch the leading man of the band. Zoe noticed a couple of teenage girls with glittery eye make-up watching him with open admiration.

The first song ended and the second had just begun when a flurry of noise and excitement by the door caught Isobel's attention and she craned her neck to see what was happening. Zoe looked over too. A tall, glamorous woman had entered the room and was enthusiastically greeting those nearest the door. The newcomer had long, streaky blonde hair which she kept sweeping back from her face, and was wearing a very short silver sequinned dress with long sleeves, which hugged her athletic figure. Zoe reflected that she would have felt deeply uncomfortable and overdressed in such an outfit, as if all eyes in the room were on her, but this woman looked entirely at ease with being the centre of attention.

For a moment Tom was oblivious, but as Rob nudged him and pointed towards the door, he turned his head and then froze. The woman began doing the rounds, greeting people at various tables, chatting and laughing. She seemed to know everyone. As she drew nearer, the woman looked in their direction and let out a little shriek of excitement before winding her way over to them.

Rob leaned back in his chair and sized her up. "Well, look what the cat dragged in," he remarked.

The woman punched him playfully on the shoulder before kissing his cheek. "Nice to see you too!" she laughed. She looked around the table. "Steve, Isobel," she said, acknowledging them with a quick smile and passing her eyes over Zoe briefly as if assessing and dismissing her. Her gaze came to rest on Tom and her smile widened. "Tom," she purred, and as he stood to greet her she kissed his cheek before resting a hand proprietorially on his upper arm.

"Nice to see you, Jemima," he replied, but Zoe thought he sounded a little reluctant. Or did she just wish that he sounded that way?

"Listen, I've got another party to go to later but I wanted to make a cameo and see a few of the old crowd first. Come and buy me a drink?"

Tom rose without speaking and Jemima linked her arm through his and steered him towards the bar. The occupants of the table all watched them go. Zoe felt a bit stunned.

"She looks like a model."

"She has done some modelling actually," Isobel said. "But she's an interior designer these days."

Rob took a swig of his pint. "She's trouble, is what she is," he remarked.

"Well obviously," Isobel agreed. Jemima was laughing and shaking back her luxuriant hair as she talked to Tom. They had been served their drinks by the barman but seemed in no hurry to return to the table. Zoe dragged her eyes away and looked at Isobel. "Trouble?" she asked.

"There's history with her and Tom," Isobel explained. "They had a bit of an on-off thing going for a while, then they were properly together for about two years. But it ended for good – oh, about eighteen months ago? At least I thought it was over for good." She frowned a little as she glanced at Jemima again.

Zoe tried not to stare over at them but sneaked a quick glance now and again. They looked such a glamorous couple. How could she hope to compete with this confident bombshell of a woman?

Nineteen

'Should auld acquaintance be forgot, and never brought to mind?'

"So, what've you been up to?" Jemima asked, twirling a strand of hair in her fingers.

"You know, the usual. Work, running, swimming. Making things. How about you?"

"Very busy with work." She rolled her eyes and sighed extravagantly. "But I did just manage a week in the Seychelles, can you see the tan?" She extended one long leg for him to inspect. "Amazing hotel. Very inspiring for my designing."

"Are your mum and dad well?"

"Same old, same old. Daddy's doctors keep telling him to slow down and reduce stress but you know what he's like."

Tom glanced over at Zoe briefly. She was determinedly not looking his way. "Jemima, why are you here?" he asked abruptly.

Jemima smiled seductively. "To see old friends. To dance..." She gave a little shimmy and took a step closer to Tom. He stepped back in response.

"I'm not dancing with you."

She pouted. "Sometimes I think that's all we've ever done. Danced around each other. Step closer, step back." She swayed forwards and back as she spoke. "Step closer..." Again Tom stepped away, shaking his head.

"Not any more, Jem. We've done this long enough."

She tilted her head slightly to one side and regarded him seriously. "You mean it this time, don't you? Something's changed."

He looked back at her steadily without speaking. Jemima smiled mischievously.

"Is it the new girl?" She looked over towards the table where Zoe was talking with Isobel and trying very hard not to look over and betray her feelings. "Very pretty, in her own way. And here was I, thinking gentlemen prefer blondes."

"Didn't you say you had another party to go to?"

"Always. There's always another party." She dropped the flirtatious manner for a moment. "Good luck to you then, darling boy. I guess I'll see you around." She embraced him, kissed his cheek, and squeezed his hand tightly before sashaying away.

"No, you won't," he whispered to himself.

At the table, Zoe glanced up surreptitiously just in time to see Jemima kissing Tom's cheek and slinking off with her hips swaying. Tom watched her go, his expression inscrutable. He turned his face back towards their table and Zoe looked away quickly. He was about to come back over when an older man engaged him in conversation. Zoe badly wanted to escape. She wondered if she could make an excuse and slip away quietly. As a holding strategy she decided to hide in the toilets for a couple of minutes while she thought about what to do.

Excusing herself, she headed for the safety of the toilets just as Tom began to make his way back to the table. She shut herself in a cubicle and leaned against the back of the door, feeling her throat constrict. She wanted to cry. Here she was having a lovely time with a man whom, she had to admit, she was very attracted to, and then his beautiful ex sweeps in and takes him away again. She took a few deep breaths. Pull yourself together, Zoe, she thought.

Now that she was in the cubicle she thought she'd better take the opportunity to use the toilet. It took a minute to struggle out of the jumpsuit and back in again. She came out to wash her hands and checked her reflection. Zoe was not gifted in hiding her feelings – her mum always said she was an open book. She couldn't do anything about the serious expression on her face but her mascara was still in place, at least. She took one more deep breath and gave herself a little shake, ready to face the room again.

She pushed open the door and almost turned on her heel and went straight back in. Tom was loitering outside waiting for her.

"Zoe..." he began.

"I think I need to go home," she said, not meeting his eyes and trying to push past him. He caught her hand but she shook him off.

"Please, Zoe, let me explain."

She stopped trying to get past and allowed herself to look up at him. He gazed earnestly into her vulnerable eyes.

"I can see why you're upset but I swear, I didn't know Jemima was going to be here and I wasn't pleased to see her. She's gone now."

Zoe looked at him mistrustfully.

"I came here tonight to see you. I wanted to see you. There's something between us."

"I don't know if I trust you," she whispered.

He shook his head. "I've never lied to you. And I promise I won't."

She looked into his open face and decided to be honest. "I'm not looking for just a fling."

He sighed. "Nor am I."

They stood looking at each other for a long moment. The band were starting a slow song that Zoe couldn't immediately place, although it sounded familiar.

"May I have this dance?" Tom held out his hand to her. Zoe took it wordlessly and allowed him to lead her to the dance floor. Tom led her to an empty space and turned, placing his hand on her waist and drawing her close to him.

"And I'd give up forever to touch you," sang Charlie, *"Cause I know that you feel me somehow."*

Zoe felt intoxicated by Tom's closeness. The gentle pressure of his hand around her waist, his cheek almost touching her own.

"You're the closest to heaven that I've ever been, And I don't want to go home right now..."

They swayed together as lights from the disco ball fractured and spun around them. Closing her eyes, Zoe breathed in

Tom's fresh, woody scent. She was aware of every inch of her body that touched his, from their entwined fingers down to her torso and legs brushing against his own as they moved to the music. She had never felt so physically attracted to someone in her whole life. The rest of the room seemed to melt away so it was just the two of them, dancing.

"And I don't want the world to see me, cause I don't think that they'd understand," the song continued, *"When everything's made to be broken, I just want you to know who I am."*

They drew apart a little so that they could look deeply into each other's eyes. Zoe felt like Tom was seeing straight into her soul. She could read her own desire reflected in his eyes.

"Shall we step outside for some air?" he asked, and she nodded. Winding their way through the crowded room hand in hand, they found the door and made their exit into the quiet darkness outside. Zoe could see her breath making clouds in the air but she barely noticed the cold. Tom turned to face her and their eyes met for a breathless second before he stepped forwards and then his lips were on hers, sweeping her up into a passionate kiss. One of his hands was on her back and the other at her waist, pulling her closer in to him. She ran her hands over his shoulders, feeling the strength of his muscles. He pushed her gently against the wall of the building for support and kissed her still more thoroughly as their hands roamed over each other's bodies. Zoe was beginning to feel weak at the knees when they broke apart to catch their breath.

The door banged open noisily as two of the revellers came outside to have a smoke, and Zoe and Tom quickly took a step apart and tried to look normal. Zoe could feel her heart thumping in her chest.

"That's a good song," she commented lightly.

"*Iris*, by the Goo Goo Dolls," Tom replied. "One of my favourites."

They looked at each for a moment and then burst out laughing.

"It's actually freezing out here," Zoe said.

"Shall we go back in?"
"Yes please!"

They went back inside hand in hand. Charlie's band had just finished the final song of their set and the audience was applauding, so Tom and Zoe were able to slip in fairly unnoticed. Isobel spotted them holding hands, grinned, and nudged Steve.

"Yeah, all right Izz, you were right. They make a cute couple."

"I was worried for a minute there when Jemima turned up! Shush, they're coming over. Pretend everything is normal."

Zoe and Tom made their way back to their friends, both trying to hold back broad smiles. Isobel acted as though she hadn't noticed.

"So the ceilidh band will be back in a few minutes," she commented lightly. "Hope you've both got enough stamina for some more dancing."

"I think I could keep going all night," Tom replied, deadpan. Zoe blushed, wondering if she was imagining a double entendre.

"Anyone need another drink?" Steve asked. "I'm going to the bar."

They shared a bottle of fizz between them and romped up and down the floor for several more dances. Zoe felt there was an extra undercurrent of tension each time that Tom took her hand or touched her waist. By half past eleven she was starting to flag and although she didn't want the evening to end, she knew she had to get home. She leaned close to Tom to speak into his ear.

"I think it's time for me to go. I've got to be back by midnight to soothe the dogs when people set off fireworks."

"Come on then, Cinderella. I'll walk you home."

"But you'll miss the big countdown."

He chuckled. "I think I can live with that. Come on."

They said a quick goodbye to Rob, Isobel and Steve, and slipped away.

It was very cold and still as they made their way back through the deserted streets towards the Old Rectory. Stars twinkled in the night sky. Zoe recognised the familiar shape of the Plough, but that was the only constellation that she knew. Tom linked Zoe's arm through his and they huddled close together as they walked. Zoe's borrowed shoes crunched on the frosty ground and each exhalation made a cloud that hung in the air before disappearing.

"Dragon breath," Tom commented. "Did you used to call it that too?"

"Yes. Oh, it's going to be so cold for the swim in the morning."

He smiled. "Well, it won't be warm, that's for sure. But the weather keeps changing. Who knows what tomorrow will bring?"

"Dragon breath..." Zoe said again. "You've reminded me, I saw the dragon boat in Woodbridge the other day. Have you ever been on it?"

Tom smiled. "Yes, a group of us from work had a go once. It was good fun once we got the hang of the paddling. My mate Joel, who I run with, tried doing the drumming at first but he was so bad we had to switch him over for someone else! He kept getting distracted and speeding up or slowing down, then we would all get out of sync and keep bumping our paddles. It was much smoother once Leanne took over."

Many of the houses they passed had lights twinkling merrily through the dark night. There were some lit windows, suggesting that the occupants were still up, waiting for midnight. All too soon they were standing at the end of the drive belonging to the Old Rectory.

"Well, this is me. Thanks for walking with me."

"You're welcome." Tom stepped closer and stroked her cold cheek with one thumb. Zoe looked up into his eyes. She felt as though every molecule of her body was being magnetically drawn to him. He gave a short sigh and pulled her against him, his lips meeting hers. They stood kissing in the darkened lane, waves of desire washing over Zoe. She wanted the moment to last forever.

Finally they broke apart.

"Do you want to come inside?" she asked huskily.

"More than you can imagine," Tom growled, holding her close. He sighed deeply. "But I'm not going to. Not tonight."

Zoe tried to stop her disappointment from showing on her face. "Oh. Ok, that's fine."

"No, it's not 'fine'. Don't think that I don't want to come inside right now and take you straight up to bed." He pressed his body closer against hers and stroked the hair back from her face. "But if we sleep together tonight we'll always be wondering if it was just New Year, the alcohol… And people will be letting off fireworks soon and the dogs need your attention." He bent his head again and kissed her gently, sweetly.

Zoe's head was spinning. For a horrible moment she had thought that he wasn't as attracted to her as she was to him. She had never wanted anyone so much in her life. But she had to admit, he was absolutely right. Damn!

Tom pulled away reluctantly and opened the gate for her. She went through and he closed it and leaned in for one final, chaste, kiss, with the gate separating their bodies.

"I'll see you at the New Year swim in the morning," he promised. "And perhaps you could come round and I can show you my workshop later, if you're still interested in seeing it."

"I'd love to see more of what you make," Zoe replied. The first bang of a firework reverberated around the still night air and she jumped. "The dogs! Goodnight, Tom."

"Goodnight," he answered softly.

Inside, the three dogs crowded closely around her as she hung up her coat and kicked off her shoes. Another bang sounded and Barney whimpered. She gave each of them a treat and sat with them in the sitting room with some quiet TV to muffle some of the noise. She stared at the screen without seeing the programme, as her mind replayed flashbacks of the evening's events. After about half an hour she thought it likely that the revellers of Redfield had lit their final fireworks of the night, and peace descended once more. She had to shoo the dogs out into the garden for their last toilet break of the day and they were all back inside within seconds.

Zoe was still feeling cold from the walk home. She made a hot water bottle then climbed the stairs to bed slowly, her body exhausted but her mind full. She put the hot water bottle into the bed to start warming it up. Changing out of her jumpsuit, taking off her make-up and brushing her teeth, her thoughts were reeling. She felt like she was still spinning around on the dance floor. She snuggled under the covers with an exhausted sigh, but despite the lateness of the hour it was some time before her brain quietened enough to let sleep come.

Twenty

'We're here tonight, and that's enough...'

When Zoe woke up, later than usual, on the first day of the New Year, the first thought in her head was Tom. That kiss last night had been so thrilling. Honestly, she'd never had a kiss like it. In her mind she replayed the evening; the dancing, the cold night air, his mouth on hers...

She lay in bed for a few moments, basking in the memory. The New Year swim was to start at ten o'clock so she had plenty of time for a relaxed start to the day. Yesterday she had taken some bacon out of the freezer in anticipation of needing a decent bacon sandwich this morning. She grilled the bacon along with a tomato cut into two, set out the bread ready, and made coffee. Soon the kitchen was full of delightful smells and the dogs were hovering, looking hopeful. The three were generally very well behaved about not begging, but clearly the prospect of bacon was too good to ignore. She cut the crispy fat off the edge of each slice and gave each of them a morsel.

Astrid phoned at nine to wish her happy New Year.

"I haven't got you out of bed, have I?"

"No, Mum, I've been up a little while. I've already had a bacon sandwich."

"I hope you're not feeling hungover!"

"No, perhaps just a little dehydrated but I'm working on it. How about you? Were you partying last night?"

"Oh, it was great fun. We went to a party with some of Fiona's friends. Lots of drinking and dancing. I feel ok at the moment but I may need a little nap after lunch."

Zoe laughed. "Sounds like a good idea!"

"And what was your party like?"

Zoe flushed, thinking of everything that had happened with Tom. "Really good. One to remember."

"That sounds intriguing. Were there, by any chance, any eligible bachelors at this party?"

Zoe decided she'd better end the conversation – quickly! "I couldn't really say. Anyway, I need to take the dogs out, just for twenty minutes or so before I get ready for this morning's dip in the river, so I'd better go. I'll speak to you soon."

Astrid was suitably distracted by the mention of the river. "Oh goodness, you are brave! All right, take care then, darling. Speak soon. Love you."

"Love you too, Mum. Bye for now!" Zoe put down the phone, feeling guilty. She hadn't exactly lied, but she certainly hadn't told the whole truth. She wasn't ready to say anything about Tom yet. And she really did need to take the dogs for a short walk before she went to the river.

As ten o'clock drew nearer, Zoe decided it was time to get ready for the swim. She wrestled her way into Isobel's spare wetsuit and put on her bobble hat and Isobel's changing robe. As she locked the back door her friend was just coming up the drive to meet her.

"Happy New Year!" Isobel called, throwing her arms wide ready to embrace Zoe.

"Happy New Year to you too! I'm very glad you've got all this spare kit," Zoe told her as they hugged. "It makes the whole thing a bit less daunting."

"Lauren swims when she's at home," Isobel explained. "But she certainly wasn't going to take all this gear to Australia! Especially as it's summer there at the moment."

"That's a funny thought."

They headed down to the beach together.

"Is Steve not coming down to watch this morning?"

"He was still getting ready when I came out. He'll bring Jasper down in a few minutes."

"Did you stay long last night after I left?"

"Just long enough to watch the fireworks, then we went home to bed. My head is definitely a bit fuzzy this morning but a nice cold swim should sort that out!"

A crowd was gathered around the benches when they arrived and Zoe looked anxiously for Tom. What was he feeling this morning? For a moment she couldn't see him at all, and she feared that he had changed his mind about her and decided to avoid seeing her. Then one of the other men moved and she saw him, talking to an older woman. His face lit up when he saw Zoe and she smiled at him, relief washing over her. He made his way straight over to her and kissed her cheek.

"Happy New Year."

"Happy New Year," Zoe replied.

If Isobel caught the vibe between them, she didn't say anything. "Happy New Year, Tom!" She gave him a hug.

The swimmers were starting to strip off their outer layers of clothing and head to the river's edge.

"Ready?" Tom grinned.

Zoe puffed out her cheeks. "As I'll ever be!"

She ignored everyone else and concentrated on her own body as she stepped towards the water. The wetsuit afforded some protection from the cold and the wind but she could definitely still feel it! She gasped as the first wave touched her toes, but breathed calmly and kept going. Last night's frost had already melted away and although the weather was cold, at least the temperature wasn't sub-zero like it had been some days. She also found that it was easier to get in this time than it had been on Boxing Day – after all, she'd already done it once, she knew that she could do it again.

A chill wind blew thousands of tiny ripples across the surface of the water and Zoe was glad that she had her blue bobble hat so that at least her head would stay warm. She kicked her legs and pulled her arms strongly through the water. Kick, pull, kick, pull... the rhythm took over until suddenly she was in the flow, feeling energised and clear-headed. The sky was bright blue with herringbone clouds high overhead. Sea birds wheeled through the air, calling to each other. Zoe felt completely at one with her body, held in the river's embrace and moving confidently through its waters. Now she had an opportunity to look around at her fellow swimmers, their brightly coloured hats bobbing above the water's surface. She felt a glow of pride at being one of this group. They were all different ages, shapes and sizes, all had different backgrounds, but in this moment they were united in purpose.

Tom appeared to her right, further from the bank. "You're doing great," he said with real warmth. "You look right at home."

Zoe laughed. "I feel great! I think the endorphins are flowing." She felt that every nerve end was singing.

They swam up and down for a few minutes, then everyone started to make their way back up the beach to dry off. Zoe's teeth chattered as she stripped off the wetsuit under her changing robe and pulled on her clothes. She was too busy with her own clothing to pay much attention to Tom, changing not far away from her, but she did catch one tantalising glimpse of his back and arms as he pulled on a t-shirt.

The pub was open early to welcome the New Year dippers with hot drinks and sandwiches for those who wanted them. Zoe ordered tea but felt a second bacon sandwich would be excessive, even for New Year's Day. Tom sat next to her.

"So, the offer to come round and see the workshop is still there, if you're interested. And I wondered if maybe you'd like to join me for lunch."

"Today?"

"If you're not busy."

"I'm not busy."

"Great. Any special dietary requirements?"

"No, I'm easy," she replied, and blushed a little.

"Ok, does one o'clock sound all right?"

"Yes, fine. Oh, I don't know where your house is."

He leaned back in his chair to gesture. "If you go up the beach a little from here – towards Woodbridge, I mean – there are a few big smart houses and then a row of cottages. That's where I live. My place is called Holly Cottage, you'll see the name on the garden gate. There's access from the road too but the beach path is probably easiest to explain."

"Wait... is it the brick cottage with the red door?"

Tom raised his eyebrows in surprise. "Yes, that's the one. You've noticed it?"

"Yes, I just..." Zoe wasn't sure what to say. *I just imagined myself living there?!* "I thought it looked cosy," she finished lamely.

Isobel was chatting with another member of the swimming group but surreptitiously keeping an eye on Zoe and Tom at the same time. They were quite absorbed in each other, she noted with satisfaction. It was about time Tom found someone. Isobel was a romantic at heart and the question marks over location and long-distance relationships were irrelevant as far as she was concerned. She had been worried last night that Jemima's sudden appearance was going to throw a spanner in the works, but that seemed to have come to nothing. She had also grown very fond of her new friend in the short time that they had known each other, and she felt that Zoe deserved happiness just as much as Tom did.

Zoe was a little flustered as she knocked on Tom's door at ten past one. He opened it wide to welcome her in.

"Good to see you, Zoe. I was just starting to wonder if everything was ok."

"I'm so sorry, I was nearly ready to go and then I found I'd left my jumper on the sofa, Barney had been lying on it, and it was absolutely covered in his hair. I'd just put a load of my clothes through the washing machine so there weren't many options. I think I got most of it off." She tilted her head to look over her shoulder at her back.

"You look good to me," Tom replied with a smile. "Anyway, welcome to my place."

Zoe looked around her. This cottage was on a very different scale to the Old Rectory, but it was entirely charming. She had entered through a covered porch and was now standing in a small cosy living room. There was a wood burner set into a chimney breast of exposed brick, a sofa covered with a throw, and an occasional chair. Bookshelves filled one alcove next to the chimney, and the other held a TV on a bespoke unit with drawers underneath. Thick checked curtains hung at the window, and original wooden floorboards were covered in the centre of the room by a large rug. There was no unnecessary clutter and everything looked clean.

"It's lovely, Tom," she said sincerely. "And very tidy."

He grinned. "Well, I did know you were coming. When I'm marking and there are books everywhere, you might not be so impressed. Come on through to the kitchen."

They passed the stairs and moved into the back of the house. What must once have been one small room had been extended to the side, with skylight windows above. It was full of light even on this winter day. A table and chairs stood in the older part of the house, and in a corner fairy lights twinkled on Tom's Christmas tree. The kitchen itself, in the extension, was modern with clean lines.

It was all that Zoe had imagined and more. "This is such a great space".

"I'm glad you approve. I'm very fond of it myself." Tom walked over to the kitchen area to check on the lunch. "I've got a tagine in the oven, I hope that's ok. I make them quite often. Good for leftovers."

"Sounds great." Zoe moved to the window by the Christmas tree to look out at the garden. There was a small patch of grass with some shrubs in a border at the end. A bird feeder hung from a tree. To the right was a long low outbuilding which Zoe assumed must be the workshop. Turning to the Christmas tree she saw several of Tom's own handmade wooden decorations amongst the green and gold baubles.

"Lunch won't be long," Tom said, straightening up. "Can I get you something to drink?"

"Just a glass of water, thanks. Actually do I mind if I just pop to the loo?"

"Upstairs and to your right," Tom directed her. Zoe climbed the steep steps and found the bathroom. Like the rest of the cottage it was compact but clean and tidy. She used the toilet then washed her hands and adjusted her hair in the mirror. She could still see quite a bit of Barney's hair on her jumper and she tried to pick off some more but quickly gave up. Coming out of the bathroom, she saw that there were two other doors, presumably to two bedrooms. She wanted to investigate further but curbed her curiosity and rejoined Tom downstairs.

He was putting plates and cutlery on the table, along with a bowl filled with slices of crusty bread, and a butter dish. He looked up and smiled when he saw her.

"Ready to eat?"

"Yes please." She suddenly realised how hungry she was. "I feel like I've got a bigger appetite than normal, these last couple of weeks. I think it's all the fresh country air."

Tom placed the casserole dish on the table and lifted the lid. "Well, this should sort you out. It's healthy too, lots of veggies."

The tagine was delicious, full of warm spices and chunky vegetables. Zoe was impressed.

"Do you do a lot of cooking?"

"I enjoy it but I don't always have a lot of energy after work. I tend to batch cook and freeze some for when I need something easy."

Zoe nodded. "I do the same thing. This is lovely. I haven't cooked anything quite like this."

"It was inspired by a holiday to Morocco that I took a few years ago," Tom said, mopping up some of the sauce with a piece of bread.

They talked about holidays, favourite places that they had visited and places that they would like to go. Soon their plates were empty but the conversation kept flowing and neither of them moved from the table. Zoe felt butterflies in her stomach as she looked into Tom's eyes. Was he going to kiss her again?

Finally there was a natural pause in the conversation and Tom picked up the plates to clear them away.

"Thank you so much, that was really good."

"You're welcome. It's nice to have someone to cook for." He stacked the plates in the slim dishwasher. "Would you like tea or coffee, or shall I give you the grand tour?"

"Oh, tour please."

He smiled. "Although when I say grand, I may be overdoing it. You've already seen the whole downstairs and the bathroom. Shall we go out to the garden?"

Zoe nodded and Tom led her to the back door. "Oh, shoes." He hurried back to pick up her shoes from where she had left them near the front door. They went out into the garden.

"Not the biggest but it's a nice sun trap in the summer."

"It's great. I think you're forgetting that I live in a flat and my only garden is a window box!"

He laughed. "Oh yes. I keep thinking that you actually live at the Old Rectory."

"I wish." She walked around looking at the plants. Tom stood on the paved area to the side, next to the outbuilding.

"And this is my workshop". He pushed open the door and stepped in, flicking on a light switch as he did so, and holding the door open for her. Zoe followed him in and looked around in wonder.

The outbuilding had a few courses of brick at the base which gave way to wooden boards above. The underside of the pitched roof was visible above the ancient rafters. Most of the wall space was covered with tools hung up in neat order, with long benches against two walls holding more tools and half-finished projects. A warm, clean smell of wood shavings filled the air.

"It would once have been an animal shed," Tom told her. "There's an uneven cobbled floor underneath these boards; rustic and nice-looking but I really needed a flat surface to stand on, and it's much easier to sweep up."

Zoe was still looking around. "It reminds me of Santa's workshop! I can just imagine a little team of elves making toys in here."

Tom laughed. "I wouldn't mind some little helpers to help keep it tidy!"

"Did I tell you I had a look in the Longshed in Woodbridge the other day?"

"No, you didn't. What did you think?"

"Oh, I loved it. It was really interesting. Really gives you a sense of the scale of the ship."

Zoe wandered over to one of the workbenches where a number of finished Christmas ornaments, similar to the one that Tom had given her, were stacked neatly in a plastic box.

"Is that a takeaway container?"

He shrugged. "I reuse things where I can."

"Very laudable." She replaced the ornament that she had picked up and turned to explore the far end of the workshop. "What's down this end?"

Tom followed her. "This is where I work on the bigger pieces." He lifted a sheet to show her the chair underneath. "Just trying to protect this from all the inevitable dust that would land on it otherwise."

Zoe ran her hand over the smooth arm and back of the chair. The shape reminded her of the classic Wegner wishbone chair, but Tom had created something more organic, with knots and knobbles still evident in the finished piece.

"It's beautiful," she told him, stroking the chair reverently. "It's like you can still see the tree it came from."

He was pleased. "That's exactly what I was going for."

Zoe was still looking at the chair. "You could make a living from this, you know. Give up teaching and just make furniture. People would pay a lot of money. I could make you a website if you wanted?" She looked up to find that his face had changed. "What's the matter?"

He was grave. "You're not the first one to suggest it. But making this my job instead of my hobby would take all the pleasure out of it. I'd be stressing about deadlines and trying to please people all the time instead of making what *I* want to make."

Zoe nodded gently, still not sure why he was so serious. "I can see that. I'm sorry, I won't mention it again."

Tom sighed. "No, I'm sorry. Bit of a touchy subject. Jemima was very pushy about the furniture when we were together, trying to get me to make things for her clients."

"Well, I suppose I see why. But when you clearly feel so strongly about it, I'm surprised she would keep pushing."

"The problem is…" Tom sighed again and ran a hand through his dark curls in exasperation, "Jemima always wanted me to be something that I'm not. She wants a certain lifestyle, you know? A house that looks like it belongs in a magazine, fancy dinners with fancy friends, a new car every other year and holidays in the Caribbean. That's just not me." He shook his head gently. "Teaching and being creative, that makes me happy. A simple life in a beautiful place." He gave a small, rueful smile. "I guess I'm just a country boy at heart."

Zoe instinctively moved towards him and took hold of his hand. He stared down at their clasped hands for a moment then entwined his fingers through hers. Gently, he pulled her closer until they stood mere inches apart, then he reached out his other hand to cup her cheek. They stared into each other's' eyes for a long moment before he leant forwards and softly pressed his lips against her own. They kissed gently at first, exploring, then more passionately. Tom pushed her against a workbench then lifted her so that she was sitting on it and could wrap her legs around him. She lifted the hem of his shirt and ran her hands over the smooth muscles of his back, and he pulled her hips closer so that their bodies were pressed firmly together. His mouth left hers so that he could kiss her neck and she shut her eyes in ecstasy. It was cold in the workshop but at that moment she didn't care.

"This is ridiculous," he mumbled into her neck, and she held her breath for a moment until he went on, "Can we go in the house?"

The sound she made was almost a sob of laughter, she was so relieved. "Yes please," she whispered into his hair. He lifted her down from the bench, and keeping a tight hold of her hand, guided her into the house and straight to the bedroom. He hesitated for a second with his hand on the door handle, looking at her to be sure that this was what she wanted too. She reached past him to help turn the handle, kissed him again, and they fell into the room and pushed the door shut behind them.

Twenty-One
'I really can't stay... baby it's cold outside...'

Some time later, lying in each other's arms under the thick duvet, Tom kissed the top of her head and inhaled the smell of her shampoo. She stroked his chest sleepily.

"I'm going to doze off in a minute."

She felt him smile. "Feel free."

"No, I can't! I've got dogs to walk."

He pulled her closer. "They'll be all right for a bit longer. Now that I've got you here, I'm not keen to let you go."

She twisted to look at him. "I see. Are you planning to keep me prisoner?"

He smiled. "You'd be very well treated." His free hand roamed down over her hip and she sighed and moved against him.

"Mmm. It is tempting. But I really think I should get dressed."

Tom paused for a moment. "Well, if you like I could come back with you to walk the dogs. And *Die Hard* is on TV tonight."

Zoe's heart soared. She tried to sound casual. "Well, if you're free..."

"I'm free."

"Me too. That sounds great."

They retrieved their clothing and dressed again. Tom put the leftover food in the fridge and locked the back door. Leaving the house and shutting the garden gate behind them, he took her hand and they walked together along the river path towards the Old Rectory.

The dogs were, as ever, delighted to see Zoe return, and when Tom joined in with stroking them they seemed equally delighted to see him.

"I feel bad, I've been out quite a lot today."

"I think you're doing a good job with them. They look pretty contented to me. Do you want to go straight back out now, before it gets dark?"

"Yes, I'll just grab the leads."

They headed out. Dusk was beginning to fall and they headed for the field edge walk to catch the last of the light. As they walked up the hill a bird called and then crossed their path with a peculiar dipping, swooping flight.

"What was that?" Zoe asked. "It was quite big."

"Green woodpecker," Tom replied.

"Oh wow," Zoe breathed. "I love how much wildlife you see here."

They skirted the edge of some woodland.

"Sometimes there are deer here," Tom said.

"What's the best thing you've spotted?"

He thought. "Hmm. Otters in the river, that was pretty special. And there's a place called Bawdsey at the mouth of the river, on the other side from Felixstowe – I once saw a seal in the river there."

Zoe shook her head in wonder. "I wish I had longer to see all these places." They both fell silent for a moment, neither wanting to talk about her imminent departure from Redfield and what it would mean for their budding relationship.

Tom spoke first. "I have to work again on Tuesday but I don't have any plans for tomorrow. We could go somewhere. There's an interesting place not far away that I think you'd like."

"That would be great. I ought to do some work really but I could put it off for one more day."

They circled back round to the house and went inside. It was lovely and warm in the kitchen.

"Cup of tea?" Zoe offered, heading to the kettle. "We never did have one after lunch." She blushed as she filled the kettle, remembering what they had done instead. Tom came up behind her and swept her hair to one side with one hand so that he could kiss her neck. He pressed his body against her from behind, pushing her against the worktop and running his hands over the sides of her body.

"Oh yes, I remember now," he said huskily.

Zoe managed to switch on the kettle before she melted completely, and allowed him to pull her around and into a long, slow kiss. By the time the kettle boiled she was quite weak at the knees but he released her with a smile and went to get the milk out of the fridge.

"Mince pie to go with your tea?" Zoe asked. "I'm afraid these are only shop-bought, not Isobel's finest, but they're quite nice."

"Yes please."

They took the tea through to the sitting room and sat close together on the sofa.

"Do you know what time the film is on?" Zoe asked in between bites of mince pie.

"Nine, I think."

"I thought maybe I could make some soup for supper as we had quite a big lunch. Does that sound ok to you?"

"Perfect."

They drank their tea and talked about the dogs, who had followed them in and were lying in their usual preferred spots.

"Do you have a favourite?"

"How can you ask me that?! It would be like having a favourite child. They're all special in their own way. Bella is so calm and sensible, I feel like she's looking after me. Henry is such a sweetie." Henry was chewing his new Christmas toy and didn't look up. "And Barney is just a ball of energy."

"I'd love a dog but I'm out the house too much with work, I don't think it would be fair. Maybe someday."

Zoe finished her tea and put the mug down on a coaster. "Have you been in this house much before? I'm just wondering if it's my turn to give you the grand tour now."

"I think I've seen most of the downstairs before, but never upstairs. I came to a dinner party once so I've seen the dining room."

"Shall we, then?"

They looked into each of the downstairs rooms first. Zoe hadn't been using the dining room or the larger reception room at the front of the house, so these had a quiet, unoccupied feeling about them. Barney followed the couple from room to room until they began to climb the stairs, at which point he lay down by the bottom step with a sigh. Tom was amused.

"Is our little shadow not allowed up here?"

"No." She smiled a little. "Special guests only."

She opened each door in turn and Tom had a quick peek at each room without going inside.

"It's a really lovely house," he said. "Great proportions."

They came to the last door.

"And this is my room," Zoe said, pushing open the door. Tom moved close past her to step inside the room and she caught an intoxicating trace of his fresh, woody scent again. He went to the window to pull back the curtain and look at the view. It was dark outside by now but following him, Zoe could see the glimmer of lights reflecting off the river's surface. He saw her behind him in the window's reflection, dropped the curtain and turned to her. He slipped a hand around her waist and pulled her in closer for a long, slow kiss. She felt a little breathless as he took his mouth away long enough to ask; "And, uh, is the bed comfortable?" She held his hand and led him over so that he could find out for himself.

Lying in bed, Tom looked over at Zoe's bedside table where a book and a glass of water sat next to her snow globe. He sat up, picked it up gently and examined it. A miniature village of houses and a church nestled in a snowy landscape, collected around a village square with a Christmas tree in the centre. There were tiny fir trees around the edges of the scene. He turned it upside down for a moment, then back so that snowflakes fell on the village.

"Pretty. Reminds me a bit of Redfield although there's no river."

Zoe propped herself up on one elbow. "I've had it since I was little. I used to think it was magical and I would make a wish on it every Christmas."

"Cute." He looked at her. "Not any more, though?"
"What?"
"You don't make wishes on it any more?"
Zoe smiled. "I grew out of it."
"Well I'd like to make one, if you don't mind."
She laughed. "Feel free!"
He looked solemn, shut his eyes and gave the snow globe another shake as Zoe watched, bemused. He placed it gently back on the table.
"What did you wish for?" she asked.
"I can't tell you, or it won't come true."
She looked at him askance, not sure if he was messing with her or being serious. He smiled and kissed her softly.
"Now, this wasn't my actual wish, but I would really like something to eat now."
She smiled. "That can be arranged. We'd better put some clothes back on…"

Tom sat at the breakfast bar watching Zoe peel potatoes and chop leeks for soup. She refused his offers of help, pointing out that he had made lunch. She did task him with finding wine glasses and pouring them both a glass of chilled white wine from a bottle in the fridge. Zoe toasted bread and cut it into little chunks for croutons, sprinkling them over the top of the soup. They sat companionably at the breakfast bar to eat. Zoe felt remarkably relaxed. It was so easy and natural, being with Tom. She felt as though they had known each other for ages. She hated the little voice at the back of her mind that whispered: what happens next, though?

They topped up their wine glasses and went back to the sitting room to build a fire and get ready for the film. They put the TV on but mostly chatted over the programmes until *Die Hard* started.

Zoe was soon totally absorbed in the film. She hadn't been sure if it was going to be one of those action films where she lost concentration because there were so many lengthy, drawn-out scenes of fights and explosions. This had good characters and she felt invested in what happened to them.

"Alan Rickman is such a good baddie!"

Tom agreed. "He's the best."

Zoe stretched as the credits rolled. "Ok, you were absolutely right. Definitely a Christmas film."

"And a good one, right?"

"Yeah, I really liked it. Would watch again."

"Great." He leaned over to kiss her. "Otherwise I really don't think this could go anywhere." He paused and continued, "Speaking of going somewhere, I suppose I'd better go home."

Zoe felt conflicted. "I'd like you to stay, but it feels a bit wrong to have someone sleep overnight when it's not my house."

"I know what you mean. I'd feel weird about it too." He sighed. "And you can't come and stay at mine when you've got the dogs to look after."

"Yep. Guess I'd better kick you out now."

He grinned. "Well, it's been a lot of fun. Still want to meet up again tomorrow?"

She nodded. There was no point in playing it cool when they had such a limited time together. She was just going to enjoy the week as much as possible.

"Can I pick you up about eleven? I should really get a few things done before we go out. We'll have a walk and then go for lunch in one of my favourite pubs."

"Sounds great."

"All right, I guess this is goodnight then." He retrieved his shoes and coat and said goodbye to the dogs. At the back door he gave Zoe one last, long, sweet kiss.

"Goodnight, Zoe."

"Goodnight," she whispered.

He pulled on his red beanie hat, gave her a final smile and was gone. Zoe shut the door and leaned against the back of it. What a day! She made her way up to bed, exhausted but happy. She already felt that she couldn't wait for tomorrow to arrive.

Twenty-Two

'All is calm, all is bright...'

Zoe felt the need to discuss events with a friend and decided to pop round to see Isobel after the dogs' morning walk. She approached the front door and had just raised her hand to knock when the door opened. Charlie was on his way out.

"Oh, hi Zoe. Are you looking for Mum?"

"Yes, I was hoping to see her. Is she in?"

Charlie nodded his head towards the lounge. "She's in there. Go on in, I'm sure she'll be happy to see you."

He let Zoe pass inside, stepped out himself and shut the front door behind him. Zoe unwound her scarf from her neck, calling out, "Isobel? Charlie let me in."

"In here," a faint voice sounded from the lounge. Zoe went through to find Isobel lying prone on the floor with her eyes shut.

"Oh, are you ok?" Zoe began, concerned. "Have you hurt your back?"

Isobel opened her eyes and stretched her arms up over her head. "No, I'm fine. Sometimes when life is overwhelming I just like to lie on the floor like a corpse for five minutes and it resets me somehow." She hugged her knees to her chest then rocked up into a sitting position. "Sorry, I probably look completely barmy."

Zoe smiled. "Well, no more than normal," she teased. "Why is life overwhelming?"

Isobel sighed. "Oh, it's just the responsibility of being in charge of everything! Work, house, general life admin. I'm slightly dreading going back to work although I know it'll be fine once I'm actually doing it. I think I'm ready to take the Christmas decorations down. The house always feels much bigger afterwards and I can clean the surfaces properly when they're not covered with Christmas cards and tinsel. It makes me feel more in control when things are tidy."

"I know what you mean. Are you at work tomorrow?"

"Yes, although it's a PD day – you know, professional development? – so the kids won't be there. We'll be going through some training and sorting out the classrooms ready for the new term. Same thing on Wednesday, and I don't work on Thursday and Friday anyway so I can get my life in order then."

"I'll be heading home on Friday," Zoe said, trying to conceal the sinking feeling that the words gave her. "Back to reality".

"I'll give you a lift to the station if you like, since I'm not working."

"Thanks, that would make the journey easier."

Isobel suddenly remembered. "How did you get on with lunch at Tom's yesterday?"

Zoe blushed. "Really well. We spent all the rest of the day together."

Isobel's eyes widened, taking in Zoe's expression. "Did you...?"

Zoe nodded shyly. Isobel whooped. "I won't ask for details, but... all good?"

"Oh yes. All good."

"Fantastic, I'm so pleased for you both," Isobel beamed.

"I really like him. We had a great time and we're going out for lunch today. It's just... has it got a chance of becoming anything more than a few wonderful days together?"

Isobel regarded her shrewdly. "Is that definitely what you want? Something more lasting?"

Zoe sighed. "You know, up until now, I don't think I was ready. It was too soon after the divorce. It was really good for me to have time on my own to figure out who I am and what I want out of life. But yes, the truth is I would like to find someone."

"And now maybe you have and it's all a bit scary."

"Maybe!"

"Well, what can you do apart from enjoy the time you've got and then figure out the rest later? I know it's easier said than done, but try not to worry. Whenever I go to yoga, the teacher spends the first couple of minutes telling us to settle onto the mat, listen to our bodies, and then listen to our minds. Are our thoughts racing? Every time it seems to surprise me to realise just how much is buzzing around in my head that I'm not even really aware of. But then she tells us to let it go, that for the length of the class there's nothing you can do about your to-do list or whatever it is you're thinking about. I think this is kind of the same thing. What happens after this week is for the future. For now, just... be in the moment."

"Good advice," Zoe smiled wryly. "Ok, I'll do my best. Thanks. I do feel better after sharing this with someone."

"Good. Now how about sharing a bit of Christmas cake? I've still got some left and I don't really want it to still be hanging around once I'm back at school."

"Go on then, just a small piece. I am going out for lunch later, remember."

Tom knocked on the door promptly at eleven as promised.
"Morning. Are you ready to go?"

Zoe already had her coat on. "Yep, all ready." She picked up her gloves and hat and locked the back door.

They drove along single track roads bordered by trees and hedgerows. It was a beautiful bright day with a clear blue sky overhead. Zoe watched a kestrel hovering high above a grassy verge.

"Do you mind driving on these tiny roads?" Zoe asked as they pulled over into a passing place to let another car go by in the opposite direction.

"No, I guess I'm used to it. And at this time of year it's easier than in the summer, because the foliage isn't so thick. You can see other vehicles coming from further away."

They came down a hill and into the village. Two horses with riders were approaching them along the road, and Tom slowed the car to a crawl to let them pass safely. The lead rider gave him a friendly salute with her riding crop. They drove on and Tom pulled into the car park of a pub. The pub itself was an attractive long, low building that looked as though it had been there for hundreds of years. A modern wooden extension had been built onto one end. There were picnic benches in the garden, deserted on this winter day, but easy to imagine full of customers in warmer months.

"We'll go for a bit of walk and then we can have lunch here," Tom explained. "An old friend of mine manages the restaurant side of the business. The food is always really good."

Zoe climbed out of the passenger seat and put on her hat. Tom guided her along a lane to one side of the pub, passing between some houses until the rough road gave way to a pedestrian-only footpath.

"What's the name of this place?"

"Newbourne. This part we're going to walk around is a nature reserve; it's actually an official Site of Special Scientific Interest. It's a good place for nature. You can hear nightingales here in the springtime. I always think it's a bit like a secret garden, although maybe more so in spring than right now."

"Did you read the book, *The Secret Garden,* when you were little? I love that story."

"Yes, me too. Everything waking up, including Mary. Life affirming stuff."

The path they were following across a meadow was rather boggy and Zoe was glad that she had chosen to wear her walking boots.

Tom led her to the edge of a stream.

"We have to go a bit off-piste to get there, I'm afraid".

A large branch was positioned across the stream from bank to bank, and he crossed this in two large strides and stood on the opposite bank, waiting for her. Zoe looked at the branch with apprehension. It was certainly strong enough to take her weight but it looked rather slippery and she didn't want to end up getting wet. She held both arms out horizontally for balance and took three cautious steps to get to the other side. She only slipped as she stepped down onto the muddy ground, and Tom caught her arm and steadied her.

"Ok?"

She nodded.

"Come on then, it's up here." He held on to her hand and led her under the dark branches of the trees to a clear pool of water which fed into the stream. The water looked completely pure, forming a deep pool over a sandy bottom, and in the very centre she could see the water actually bubbling up from beneath the ground.

"That's amazing!"

He smiled. "I thought you'd like it."

"It's really cool. I can see why it's called Newbourne Springs now."

They watched the water for a minute, then made their way carefully back across the stream to the footpath. They carried on and emerged at a small car park, then rejoined the road to loop their way back to the pub.

It was wonderfully warm inside the pub and Zoe looked around with interest as she took off her coat. Like the Mulberry Tree, this place was clearly old and featured a large redbrick fireplace which would presumably once have housed an open fire, but now held a wood burning stove and a basket of logs. A couple of older gentlemen sat close to the fireplace in comfortable chairs, newspapers and pints of bitter in front of them on a table. The décor was a modern country style with checked patterns and a mixture of painted and natural wood. It all looked very appealing.

Tom was greeting the woman behind the bar. She looked about the same age as Tom and Zoe and was medium height with a good inch of dark roots betraying the fact that her blonde hair was not, in fact, her natural colour. She had a good humoured face and her friendly manner extended to Zoe when Tom turned to introduce her.

"Zoe, this is Hannah. We've known each other since our school days. She runs the restaurant here. Hannah, this is my friend Zoe."

"Lovely to meet you, Zoe," Hannah said warmly. "What can I get you to drink?"

Zoe ordered an orange juice and lemonade, and Tom opted for the local ale.

"Just half a pint though, I'm driving."

"Go and sit yourselves down and I'll bring them over in a sec."

It was still fairly early and they had plenty of tables to choose from in the light and airy extension. They avoided those that had a "reserved" sign and sat near a window. Hannah brought through their drinks and handed them a couple of menus. Now that she was out from behind the bar, Zoe realised that Hannah had a significant baby bump.

"How are you feeling now?" Tom asked, nodding towards the bump.

"Much better now, thanks. Those first few months were hard going. It's been worse this time than it was with Rosie, and that was no walk in the park. Anyway, I'll give you a minute to have a look at the menus. There's a special board there as well." She pointed in the direction of the blackboard where the daily specials had been chalked up.

Zoe studied the menu. "This all looks good. I don't know how I'm going to choose. Are you going for a main meal or something lighter?"

"I was thinking main meal, then we don't have to do much cooking later today. I've still got lots of bits and pieces in the fridge to finish up."

"Yeah, me too. Maybe we can combine forces."

Tom smiled. "Sounds like a plan. I could pop back to mine and bring some things round to your place, if that suits?"

Zoe nodded happily. "Ok, in that case I think I'll go for the vegetable lasagne."

"Good choice. I'm going to go with fish and chips."

Hannah came back to take their order then disappeared off to the kitchen.

Conversation flowed easily as they waited for their food. Zoe felt very comfortable in Tom's company. When their meal was brought over, he offered her a chip. It was crunchy and fluffy, cooked to perfection. Zoe tried her lasagne. It was made with layers of roasted vegetables, spinach and ricotta. She held out a forkful for Tom.

"You've got to try this," she told him. "It's something special."

He leaned forwards for a taste. "Oh, yeah. Really good. I might have that next time."

The restaurant was filling up by now and a young family came to sit at the table next to them. There was a mum and dad, a small boy and a baby in a highchair. The boy immediately immersed himself in colouring but the baby was more interested in his surroundings and was twisting in his chair to look at everything. Zoe smiled at him and he beamed a gummy smile back at her. Tom looked up from his plate and saw the interaction.

"Looks like I've got competition for your affections!"

Zoe laughed. "He's certainly a cutie. But you're not so bad yourself."

"You like children, then?" he asked lightly.

"Oh yes." She hesitated, unsure whether to be more explicit, and decided that she should be open with him. "I would like children one day."

"I did wonder if perhaps you weren't keen, as you'd been married for a while but you hadn't mentioned kids."

"We talked about them – I mean me and my ex – but to begin with we felt too young, and wanted to wait a few years, and then it seemed so difficult financially so we decided to wait a few more. Then things began to break down, so I'm glad now that we didn't bring a baby into that." If this had been a casual date she would never have introduced the subject, but now that Tom had, she wanted to check that he felt the same way. "What about you?"

"Oh, I'd like children. One day." Tom finished his last chip and set his knife and fork down on his plate. "That was great. I'm just going to pop to the gents'."

He left Zoe alone for a moment. Hannah came over to clear the plates away.

"Would you like to look at the dessert menu?"

"I love puddings but I'm not sure I've got room! I don't know about Tom though."

"Tell you what, I'll bring a couple of menus over and you can just have a look. We do mini versions of some of the desserts so you could always have a little one and a coffee."

"Ok, thanks."

Hannah paused. "He must like you. He doesn't bring just anybody here."

Zoe felt a warm glow. "I like him too," she admitted.

"I've known Tom for a long time. He's done a bit of dating, of course, but he's not one to fall in love with every girl he meets. You know that saying, still waters run deep? That's Tommy. Reserved on the outside but there's deep feelings underneath." She spotted Tom returning and grinned. "Speak of the devil."

Tom slid back into his seat with a groan. "Oh, lord. What have you been telling her about me?"

"Oh, nothing, nothing." Hannah's eyes danced with mischief. "But you remember, Tommy, I know where the bodies are buried."

Zoe and Tom looked at each quickly and exchanged a smile, remembering the poor chicken.

"What?" Hannah asked, curious.

"Well, it's a funny story…" Tom began.

"She called you Tommy," Zoe commented as they left the pub and headed back to the car. "I haven't heard anyone else use that name."

Tom clicked his seatbelt into place and started the engine. "She's the only one who does. Somehow I don't mind it from her, although to everyone else I'm just Tom."

"You've known each other a long time?"

"Oh yeah, a really long time. We go all the way back to primary school."

Zoe watched the hedgerows sliding past the car windows. "I liked her." Tom reached over and gave her knee a squeeze and she smiled at him a little sleepily. "I'm so full of lunch, I think I'm going to doze off."

He smiled without taking his eyes off the road. "You can if you like, although it's not a long journey."

Zoe leaned her head back against the headrest with a sigh and let her eyelids drift shut.

Twenty-Three

'But the wind blows right through you, it's no place for the old...'

Zoe woke with a start as the car's wheels crunched on gravel. They were back in Redfield. Quickly and surreptitiously Zoe put a hand to her mouth to check that she hadn't started drooling in her sleep! Tom saw the movement from the corner of his eye and smiled.

"Hey, Sleeping Beauty. We're back."

"So I see." She stretched, as best as she could while still buckled into the car's seat.

"I thought I'd drop you here and take the car back to mine, then walk back up with whatever I find in the fridge or cupboards that looks interesting."

"Ok. Good plan."

Tom leaned over and kissed her gently. "See you in a bit, then."

Zoe undid her seatbelt and clambered out of the car, and Tom reversed back out and drove away. She let the dogs out into the garden and they pottered around sniffing and marking their territory while Zoe checked on the chickens. Everything seemed fine although there were no eggs to collect today. Barney spotted a squirrel in one of the trees and erupted into a mad flurry of barking while the squirrel, unfazed, leaped into another tree in next door's garden and continued on its way.

Tom was back within about half an hour, bringing with him various odds and ends of cheese, grapes, nuts, and half a bottle of red wine.

"Perfect, we can have…" Zoe hesitated. "My family has always called it 'picky tea', what would you call it?"

"Yeah, it was 'picky bits' for us growing up, I think. I know what you mean, anyway!"

"Good! I've got some bits to add to it too. Anyway, we won't want that for a few hours. Are you up for another walk? The doggos just need a short one this afternoon."

"Sure. Let's go now while it's light."

"I think I'm noticing the difference in the evenings already, though, aren't you? It is staying light for that little bit longer." Zoe was picking up the dogs' leads as she spoke.

Tom smiled. "Yeah, I love it. It means we've turned the corner and we're heading back towards summer. I get so much more out of each day in the summer. At this time of year it's so easy to just hunker down in the evenings and practically hibernate. In summer I get back from work and I've still got the time and energy to make things in the workshop, or go for a run or a swim."

"I really like winter as we first head into it, but by spring I am always so glad to see the lighter, warmer days back again!" Zoe confessed.

They headed out for a short loop. As they walked along the beach Tom took Zoe's hand in his own. He was wonderfully warm. She had to work hard to keep herself from grinning like an idiot at the sheer joy of being with him.

"Are you about ready for something to eat?" Zoe asked about seven o'clock.

"Yeah, I reckon. Let's make up a couple of plates and eat in the sitting room."

Zoe cut slices of bread and found some sundried tomatoes and olives to add to the items that Tom had brought over. He poured them each a glass of red wine and they took everything through to the sitting room, where they had already lit the fire. The dogs followed and lay down, on the off chance that there might be a little morsel available for them.

They switched on the TV but chatted over it as they ate. When they had finished, Tom set the two plates on a side table and put his arm around Zoe. She snuggled in close to him and sipped her wine.

"I wish I didn't have to go to work tomorrow."

"If you'd like to come round after work, I could cook something? Maybe a nice warming casserole?"

Tom kissed the top of her head. "That sounds wonderful. If I come straight round I can join you on the dogs' afternoon walk. I think it's going to be a pretty busy day so it would be nice to decompress and get a bit of fresh air."

He was absent-mindedly trailing his fingers up and down her shoulder as he spoke, with the lightest touch, and Zoe yearned to feel his hands against her bare skin. In the past she hadn't been much of a one for taking the initiative, but she was feeling bold. She placed her hand on his long thigh and gradually stroked upwards. He stopped moving his hand, distracted by what she was doing. She risked a glance up at him and saw desire in his eyes.

Zoe took Tom's glass from him and put it with hers on the side table. She knelt over him and slowly lowered herself, pressing her hips against his. He groaned and took hold of her waist, reaching his mouth up towards hers. Zoe swept her hair to the side with one hand and kissed him longingly. His hands were working their way under her clothes when a small whine broke their concentration. They both turned their heads. Three pairs of eyes were staring at them.

Tom chuckled. "Shall we move somewhere where we don't have an audience?"

Zoe felt she might explode if she had to wait much longer. "Yes, let's!"

Tom made a move towards putting his shoes on soon after nine, knowing that he had to be up promptly for work the following morning. They stood kissing by the back door for a long time before either of them could bear to open it. It was hard to say goodbye. When he had finally left, Zoe closed the door and went back to sit with the dogs by the embers of the fire.

"Oh, Bella, what am I going to do? I'm completely smitten."

Bella merely sighed and pushed her damp nose into Zoe's hand.

****

It was hard for Zoe to concentrate on her work the next morning. Every few minutes she would catch herself staring dreamily into space, reliving her time with Tom so far, and looking forward to seeing him later that evening. She really did need to get some work done though – she still had some designs to finish and there were a couple of emails to answer. She found that most of her clients took a break over Christmas too but now that the new year had begun, things would pick up and she would start getting new jobs coming in.

Although the village's bus service was infrequent, Zoe checked the timetable online and decided that it would be worth trying the bus to get her to Woodbridge so that she could visit a supermarket. She was running out of food and she wanted to be able to make something tasty for Tom later that day. As long as the bus did actually turn up as timetabled, it would save her both time and energy if she only had to walk one way.

She headed out to the bus stop a few minutes before the bus's scheduled arrival, and waited a little anxiously. Mercifully it wasn't long before the bus chugged round the corner towards her and she held out her arm to flag it down. There were just a few other passengers on board and Zoe sat and enjoyed the opportunity to gaze out at the view as they drove along the winding lanes out of Redfield. It was overly warm on the bus and the engine was rather noisy but it did make a nice change from all the walking that she had been doing.

Zoe stepped off the bus with the other passengers, near to the supermarket. As she walked towards its doors she spotted that there was also a butcher's in the parade of shops, so she stopped there first to buy some beef before carrying on into the larger shop to buy a few other bits and pieces. Heading back out with her shopping in her rucksack, she saw the shop where she had bought her New Year's Eve jumpsuit and looked longingly at it as she passed. She would have liked another browse but she really needed to get back and get on with her day.

She crossed the railway towards the Tide Mill and took the river path heading back to Redfield. The day was rather grey but relatively mild, and she strode out briskly and soon felt warm enough to loosen the scarf around her neck and unzip her coat slightly. A train clattered past along the tracks towards the station, beyond a meadow where cows grazed. She passed several people walking their dogs and acknowledged each of them with a smile and a greeting. As she moved further from the town there were fewer other walkers and she became lost in her thoughts and barely noticed the scenery around her.

Towards Redfield she reached the bench on the spit of land jutting out into the river, and here she paused for a moment to enjoy the view. There were no boats moving on the water but she could see some floating further downstream, held in place by their anchors. A couple of seabirds bobbed on the little waves near the bank. There wasn't another human in sight, and everything felt very still.

A flash of blue caught her eye. She turned her head to follow the movement, to where an old wooden mooring post rose jaggedly above the water's surface. Perched on its top was a kingfisher. Zoe held her breath in wonder. She had never seen one in real life before but she recognised it immediately; the bright, iridescent blue of the feathers on its back, wings and head, and the orange chest underneath. It stood stock still, like a statue on its plinth.

As Zoe stood frozen to the spot, watching, the bird took off in a flare of blue and dived, piercing the water's surface before rising again with something silvery caught firmly in its long beak. It flew away to the far bank of the river and Zoe watched until she could no longer see it.

"Incredible," she said out loud to herself. It felt like such a gift to see something so rare.

As Zoe made her way back into Redfield past some of the older cottages, a loud miaow reached her ears. She turned her head and saw the magnificent cat, Nova, perched atop a stone wall.

"Hello, you." Zoe moved closer to offer to scratch behind the cat's ears. As she approached, she heard another fainter sound, coming from behind the garden wall. She stepped nearer and peeked over the wall, then gasped.

Barbara, the crotchety old woman in the beige coat, was lying in an awkward position on the garden path. She was tucked in close enough behind the wall that Zoe would never have spotted her if it hadn't been for Nova's presence. Her eyes were shut and she was moaning quietly.

"Barbara!" Zoe pushed open the garden gate and hurried to the woman's side. "Can you hear me?"

"Yes, I can hear you," Barbara snapped tetchily. "There's nothing wrong with my ears. I just slipped over and I can't get up. I think I might have broken my hip."

"Oh god." Zoe pulled out her mobile phone and dialled 999 with shaking hands. She had watched this sort of scene on TV or in films many times but to be involved in it herself was so strange. She almost felt like someone else was speaking as she spoke to the call handler, explaining where they were and what had happened. Nova jumped down calmly from the wall and continued on her way.

"Is the patient conscious?" the call handler was asking.

"Yes, she's conscious," Zoe replied.

"Of course I'm conscious," Barbara put in irritably. Zoe shushed her and continued to answer the questions as best as she could.

"Can you tell me how old the patient is?"

"Barbara, how old are you?"

"Eighty-four," the woman replied, closing her eyes against the pain.

The call handler asked some more questions and confirmed that an ambulance would be dispatched as soon as possible.

"We're very busy today," he explained, "and we'll be with you as soon as we can but you may have to wait a little while."

Zoe finished the call and put the phone back in her pocket. "Barbara," she said, "the ambulance is coming but it might take a while. Where are your house keys? I need to fetch you a blanket or something."

"In my bag." Barbara waved a hand vaguely in the direction of the handbag which she had dropped as she fell.

Zoe found the bag and rooted around inside for the keys. "I'll just be a second, ok?" She unlocked the front door and stepped inside. The hallway was tidy and had clearly been recently vacuumed. A door to her right led to a small sitting room. Everything inside was as neat as a pin. There was a crocheted blanket on the back of the sofa and Zoe grabbed this and a cushion and went back outside. She laid the blanket gently over Barbara and encouraged her to lift her head a touch so that she could slip the cushion underneath. Barbara protested for a moment when she saw it.

"That's my best cushion, it's going to get all dirty on the ground."

"I'll wash the cover for you afterwards! Come on, let's at least try to make you a bit more comfortable."

Although she was still grumbling, Barbara lifted her head to allow Zoe to put the cushion into place. She sank back with a sigh. Zoe knelt next to her and took Barbara's frail, cold hand in her own.

"Is there someone that I can call for you?"

"No, there's no one." Her eyes opened. "If you need to go, I expect I'll manage until the ambulance gets here."

"That's not what I meant! Of course I'll stay with you."

Barbara's hand gave Zoe's the gentlest of squeezes. "Thank you," she said quietly.

"You're welcome. I'm just so sorry that this happened to you. Was the path slippery?"

Barbara gave a small nod. "I was so careful when it was icy, but I was rushing this morning. The slabs were damp; they can get a bit slimy with algae. I used to have a handyman come and do these sorts of jobs for me but he's retired now."

"Sounds like you'll have to find a new one."

"Hmm. Easier said than done."

"Perhaps one of your neighbours knows someone? I've found everyone so welcoming here, it's such a lovely community."

Zoe was listening out for the ambulance all the time, but she couldn't yet hear any sirens. No one had come past the cottages either on foot or in a vehicle, but as she listened Zoe thought she heard the sound of footsteps coming closer. She stuck her head up above the wall and saw Poppy walking down the lane towards her. She stopped dead and blinked at Zoe.

"Zoe? What on earth are you doing? You look like a jack-in-the-box."

"Oh, Poppy, Barbara's had a fall! We're waiting for the ambulance."

Poppy rushed towards them and through the gate into the garden. "Oh my goodness! What can I do to help?"

"I'm not sure really, I've called 999 and I found a blanket to keep her warm."

Poppy crouched down and took Barbara's other hand. "Oh, your hand is freezing! Don't worry, we're going to look after you."

Barbara looked at her with suspicion. "Shouldn't you be in the shop?"

"Well, I had to shut early, my washing machine's on the blink and I've got a repair man coming. I had to come and meet him."

"Hadn't you better go, then?"

Poppy looked surprised. "No, you're more important."

Barbara blinked hard and Zoe realised that she was on the verge of tears. Finally, the welcome sound of the ambulance's siren broke through the stillness of the quiet January afternoon. Zoe felt hugely relieved as the blue flashing lights came into sight and she was able to wave to the driver to show her where they were.

The paramedics jumped out and quickly assessed the situation. As they were talking to Zoe and Barbara, Poppy disappeared for a moment to speak to the washing machine repair guy whose van was now just visible behind the ambulance. She returned as the paramedics were loading Barbara carefully onto a stretcher and taking her to the ambulance.

"I've given him my spare key so I don't need to hang around here; I can go with Barbara to the hospital," she told Zoe.

"Are you sure?" Zoe asked.

"Yes, of course. It's all taken care of. Barbara and I may not always have been the best of friends but she's been my neighbour for years. I want to make sure she's well looked after."

Zoe put out her hand and squeezed Poppy's shoulder. "Ok, great. I'll just make sure her house is locked up." She found the keys again, locked the door, and gave the handbag and keys to Poppy.

Barbara was now safely loaded into the ambulance.

"I'm so glad you were here," Poppy told Zoe. She gave her a quick hug.

"Good luck. Let me know how you get on?"

"Yes, I will. See you soon!"

Zoe stood and watched as the ambulance turned around slowly and made its way back up the road. She felt drained, emotionally and physically, but she was so glad that she had been able to help.

Twenty-Four

'The rising of the sun, and the running of the deer...'

Zoe returned to the Old Rectory with a sigh of relief and put away her shopping. It was now well past her normal lunchtime and she was absolutely starving. The whole incident had made her feel rather shaken and a little faint. She needed to sit down and have something to eat and drink. She made a quick sandwich and a cup of tea, and sat down at the breakfast bar to eat. She felt like she should be tapping away at her computer keyboard but she wasn't up to concentrating on it at that precise moment. She had been planning to get a good couple of hours' work done before Tom arrived, but Barbara's accident had rather put paid to that. She would just have to do the bare minimum today and catch up tomorrow.

At about half past three, feeling more like her normal self, she thought that she had better start preparations for the casserole, to give it time to tenderise in the oven. Tom had told her that he would probably get away quite promptly on this first day, with no children in the school until Thursday. She would wait until he could join them to do the dogs' afternoon walk, but she needed to get started with this cooking now. Six eyes keenly followed her progress as she browned chunks of beef before adding stock and putting it into the oven for a long, slow cook.

"Not for dogs, I'm afraid." Henry tilted his furry head to one side hopefully and she laughed and rubbed his ears. "No matter how cute you are!"

Tom arrived from work just after four and was keen to head straight out for a walk. The sun had just set but there was still some light in the sky as they headed towards the field and the edge of the woods.

"We'll stay in the field rather than go into the woods, shall we? It looks quite dark under the trees."

Tom quoted softly, "The woods are lovely, dark and deep; But I have promises to keep; And miles to go before I sleep; And miles to go before I sleep."

"I like that. Who's the poet?"

"Robert Frost. We learned it at school and I always liked it. It's really about a snowy evening, but just going past dark woods makes me think of it."

"I would have loved to see some snow but I think I'm running out of time now." She fell silent, feeling awkward. They were both avoiding the subject of her imminent departure. Only a few more days to go and then Simone and Neil would be back and her work here would be done.

They carried on past the shadowy woods, occasionally hearing a mysterious creak or crack as unseen creatures moved within its depths. They had just reached the far edge of the wood when Tom suddenly flung out a hand to stop her.

"What...?" she began.

"Shh," he said, "look!"

Some fifty metres or so ahead of them in the field was a herd of roe deer, foraging for food in the twilight. Zoe and Tom and the dogs were downwind of them, and for a moment they stood motionless just watching the graceful animals, which bent their slender necks as they searched the ground for anything edible. Barney spotted them and stiffened, ready to give chase. Zoe held on tightly to his lead. As if the deer could feel their presence, the herd suddenly moved as one and made a swift dash up the hill, standing out silhouetted against the sky for a moment before they were over the ridge and out of sight.

Zoe exhaled slowly. "Oh, that was amazing. So beautiful."

"Did you count them? I think there were seven."

"No, I was just transfixed. It was magical. Almost as good as the kingfisher."

"When did you see a kingfisher?"

"Earlier this afternoon, as I was walking back from Woodbridge. I've never seen one before."

"I've only seen one twice, so you really did get lucky."

"It's been quite the eventful day, actually." She told him the story of finding Barbara lying in her garden, and the wait for the ambulance.

"Sounds like Barbara was the lucky one! You were her guardian angel today."

"I wouldn't even have known she was there if it hadn't been for Nova. I feel like there's something almost supernatural about that cat."

Tom laughed. "I know what you mean, she is something special. Are you ok, though? It must have been quite a scary experience."

"It was... intense. I did feel quite shaky when I got home but I'm ok now."

They walked on through the darkening evening, watching the stars come out. A thin crescent moon was just visible, rising over the wood. Zoe needed to switch on her torch by the time they were out of the fields and back onto the road. They didn't meet any cars in the lane and were soon making their way back into the warmth and comfort of the Old Rectory.

"Mmm, it smells good in here."

"It's beef casserole. Should be ready about half past six. Everything got a bit delayed from what I'd originally planned. The potatoes are ready to go on nearer to the time so I don't need to do anything else at the moment. Do you want a cup of tea in the meantime?"

"Yes please. I could get used to this."

Zoe had her back to him as she picked up the kettle and she froze for a moment. I could get used to this, too, she thought. But I just don't know if I'm going to have that chance.

There was a knock on the door just as they were tidying up the kitchen after eating. Zoe opened it to find Poppy standing there.

"Hello! How did it go at the hospital? Come in out of the cold for a minute and tell me about it."

Poppy stepped in and bent to greet the dogs who had come trotting forwards to say hello.

"Thanks. Yes, it was fine. Barbara was seen very quickly and she's being well looked after. They got her into have an x-ray straight away and she has broken her hip, as she thought, so she'll need to have an operation and probably stay in for a couple of weeks."

"Oh, poor her. How grim."

Tom came over from the sink, drying his hands on a tea towel. Poppy grinned when she saw him.

"Oh, hello. I didn't realise you were here. I'd better get out of your hair."

"It's fine…" Tom started, at the same time as Zoe began, embarrassed, "You're not interrupting…", but Poppy dismissed them both with a wave of her hand.

"No, no, I wasn't going to stop anyway, just wanted to let you know that Barbara is ok and that she was very grateful to you for rescuing her. She even went so far as to call you a 'nice young woman'." Poppy grinned. "Which is high praise indeed, from her! She's very proud of her independence, but I think I've persuaded her that she will need to accept some help while she recovers."

"Of course," Zoe said.

"People need people. Community… it's so important. Anyway, I'll leave you lovebirds to it." She headed towards the door. "Keep hold of her, Tom," she instructed as she stepped outside, "she's a good'un." She winked at them and strode off, whistling.

Zoe closed the door and leaned against it, looking a little sheepish. "That was a bit awkward! I hope you don't mind people knowing about us."

He smiled gently. "It's hardly a secret. I mean, I'm not one to go shouting from the rooftops about relationship stuff, but we're both adults. We don't need to hide."

"No, of course not."

"Unless you're embarrassed to be seen with me…" She looked quickly at his face and realised that he was teasing. She bit her lip.

"Should I be?" She put on the accent of a Southern belle. "Or do you perhaps mean that I am risking my reputation as a young lady of virtue, by entertaining a gentleman in my house, alone?"

Tom stalked slowly towards her as Zoe stayed with her back to the door, watching him approach. She felt captivated, fixed to the spot and mesmerized by him as he closed the distance between them with each step.

"Do you think we're shocking the village elders?" he asked, smirking.

"You tell me. Although, from reading Jilly Cooper novels I rather got the impression that folks in the countryside are at it all the time."

Tom was now close enough to reach forward and grab hold of her with both hands, pulling her towards him. She gave a little gasp at his strength as he pressed his body against hers.

"Must be all the fresh air," he said as he lowered his head to kiss her neck. "Gives you an appetite…"

Twenty-Five

'To face unafraid, the plans that we made...'

Tom was up early for a short run before work and bumped into Rob, just setting out for the farm. Rob had heard the news on the village grapevine.

"So, you and Zoe, hey?"

Tom nodded. "Yep."

"Well, congratulations, mate. She's a gorgeous girl." Rob paused. "What happens when she goes home?"

"Honestly, I don't know. I want to keep seeing her. We're both pretty much avoiding the subject at the moment, really."

Rob looked sceptical. "Reckon you want to sort that out. You don't want her to go and find someone else 'cause she doesn't think you're serious about her."

"Since when do you give relationship advice?! She knows how I feel."

Rob raised his eyebrows. "You sure about that?"

Tom shrugged in response.

"Well, like you say, I'm hardly the expert. Got a date lined up next week though."

"Good man. Where are you taking her?"

"That nice little wine bar in Gobbitts Yard, in Woodbridge."

"Cool. Well, good luck with it."

"Same to you."

They said goodbye and Tom continued with his run, but he felt unsettled. Was Rob right? What if it was a case of out of sight, out of mind, when Zoe went back to London? She was a great woman, he could easily imagine her being snapped up by someone else. He quickened his pace, trying to outrun his doubts.

Zoe woke into the still-dark morning and stretched luxuriously in her warm bed. She had had another lovely evening with Tom. She enjoyed cooking for him and walking the dogs together. It was a quiet contentment that had taken her quite by surprise. She supposed that they were living in a bubble right now, and she knew the bubble had to burst at some point, but she wasn't ready to be the one to do it.

She went downstairs to carry out the now-familiar routine of letting the dogs into the garden, and making a cup of tea. She stood by the window and watched them sniffing around the borders, cocking their legs to mark territory, and generally giving the air of being masters of their little domain. The sky was absolutely glowing this morning, making Zoe think of the old adage, "Red sky in the morning, shepherd's warning." She wasn't sure how true it was but this particular sky was extraordinary. As she stood and watched, the colours changed through red and orange, pink and yellow. It was as though the sky was ablaze, with the dark clouds higher up reflecting the light back down above the flames on the horizon.

A few small birds were visiting the bird feeder, apparently unbothered by the dogs' presence. Zoe had topped up the peanuts the day before, and a great tit and two blue tits were busily pecking their beaks through the gaps in the wire feeder to access the nutritious bounty within.

Zoe opened the fridge to look for breakfast options. At this point she was running her stores down; in forty-eight hours' time she would be making her final breakfast and packing her bags. She decided to make porridge with the milk she had left. She could pop to the convenience shop later for another pint to keep her going until her departure. She put the mixture of milk and oats on the hob and stirred gently as the alchemy of cooking gradually combined the ingredients into a thick, rich porridge. When it was ready she added a drizzle of honey and chopped a banana over the top.

There was no frost on the lawn this morning but she still put on her hat and gloves before setting out with the dogs for their first walk of the day. Her awareness that her time in Redfield was fast running out gave her a pang of sadness, but she pushed it firmly away. There was no sense in spoiling the time that she had left here. Of course Tom was a huge part of it, but she would also miss this landscape. The fields, the woods, the river. Zoe had had some great holidays in the past but she had never felt so attached to a new place as she did now. Was it because she was living here, in a way that you wouldn't as a tourist? Or was there something extra special about this place?

She took the dogs back to the Old Rectory and settled at the breakfast bar with her laptop. There were more emails to answer and she decided to speak with a couple of clients over the phone to get a clearer idea of their requirements. The morning passed quickly and at midday she decided to make a quick trip to the village shop before starting lunch.

Zoe spotted Poppy's purple hair in the window as she drew close to the shop, and gave her a friendly wave. Stepping inside, Zoe walked round curiously to see what she was doing.

"Out with the old," Poppy explained. She was dismantling the Christmassy window display, removing the toy animals and the snowy landscape on which they had stood.

"Oh, it's such a shame to see it go," Zoe commented with real regret.

"I know that technically Friday is Twelfth Night and that's when we should take the decorations down, but I'm ready to look forward to the spring now," Poppy told her. "Even if it is still a while away."

"Please tell me you're not going to start decorating for Easter now!"

Poppy laughed. "No, definitely not! But something with crocuses and snowdrops would remind us that warmer, lighter days are on their way back. Oh, did you see the sunrise this morning? Quite incredible."

"Yes, it was amazing. I tried to take a picture but my camera never quite captures how beautiful sunrises and sunsets can be. I hope it doesn't mean bad weather is on the way, though. Red sky in the morning, shepherd's warning?"

Poppy waved a hand dismissively. "Just because some ideas stick around, it doesn't necessarily mean that they're always right! Anyway, what can I do for you this morning?"

"Just a pint of milk, please."

The two women moved through the shop together, Zoe picking up milk from the large fridge as she passed and taking it to the counter. Nova appeared as if from nowhere and pressed her large head against Zoe's leg in greeting, and Zoe bent to stroke the soft fur of the cat's back.

"Any more updates on Barbara?" Zoe asked.

"I phoned the ward this morning and they said the operation had gone well. I'll pop in to see her this evening."

"That's good to hear."

"Am I right in thinking Simone and Neil are back on Friday?" Poppy asked as she rang up the price on the till.

"Yes, that's right. I'll be heading back to London on Friday morning."

"Well, I hope we'll see you again very soon. It seems like you fit right in, here." She smiled kindly at Zoe, who felt a bit choked.

"Thank you," she whispered, picked up the milk and left the shop.

Zoe had some soup and bread for lunch then picked up her work again. Tom had promised to feed her tonight, so she didn't need to do any other cooking. He was expecting her at about half past five. At four o'clock she headed out with the dogs for a short walk. She was nearly home again when she saw Isobel, who was just locking her car.

"Hi, Izzy!"

"Oh, hi Zoe!" Isobel walked over to greet her and the dogs. "How was school?"

"Oh, the usual. Just doing some training and prepping classrooms ready for the new term. I'm not back in until Monday now, though, so it was a nice gentle re-entry. How's your day been?"

"Good, pretty quiet. Just getting some work done. I'm going round to Tom's in a bit for dinner."

Isobel smiled. "Very nice. I was thinking of texting you, actually. I know you've not got long left here now. Would you like to go for a final swim in the river with me tomorrow morning?"

"Oh, yes please!" Zoe laughed. "I can't believe I'm saying yes so quickly when a couple of weeks ago I wouldn't have dreamed of doing it."

"Well, that was before you met me, wasn't it? I'm definitely taking the credit for that one."

Zoe smiled. "Seems fair. What time shall I call round tomorrow?"

"Half past nine? We don't need to go at the crack of dawn, unless you need to be working at that time."

"No, that's fine. I can fit it in whenever. Ok, half past nine it is. See you then."

"See you then!" Isobel picked up her bags of books and headed into her house.

Zoe brushed her hair and applied some mascara before walking down to Tom's cottage. She passed a couple of women who she recognised from the swimming group, and they said a cheery hello to each other as their paths crossed. She knocked on the cottage's red door and waited. It was only a moment before Tom opened it and his face relaxed into a broad smile when he saw her.

"Hello, you."

"Hi." She stepped forwards to kiss him. He pulled her into the house, kicked the front door shut, and kissed her thoroughly, his hands roaming over her body while she in turn stroked his strong shoulders and back. He let her go reluctantly but kept hold of her hand.

"Come through to the kitchen. I was just starting a risotto."

"Oh, lovely." Zoe followed him into the open kitchen-diner space. "I see you've still got your tree up."

"Yeah, I normally take it down before I go back to work but somehow I just felt it should stay up a bit longer this year. I'll pack everything away on Friday."

"I went to the shop earlier and Poppy was changing her display for something more spring-like." A thought occurred to her. "What should I do with my little tree? It's got roots, hasn't it? It should live on after Christmas but I can't very well take it back on the train with me."

Tom looked at her intently. "Do you want to leave it with me? I can look after it."

Zoe felt the tension in the air: were they going to talk about the future? Would she still be in Tom's life by next Christmas? Suddenly she couldn't bear the thought that he might not be as keen as she was, and she quickly changed the subject.

"Yes, that sounds like a good idea. So, tell me about this risotto?"

He looked a little surprised by the abrupt shift in the conversation but went with it. "Well, I've just put some butternut squash in the oven to roast and while that's cooking I'll do the risotto rice. It needs quite a lot of stirring so we'd better stay in here."

"I like it in here." She looked around as she sat down at the table. "Did you have to do much to the place when you bought it, or was it like this already?"

Tom started chopping an onion. "Oh, I did quite a lot when I moved in. When I first looked at the place it was a bit tatty and unloved, but I could see the potential. The workshop really sold it to me as well! I know a good builder and he put on the extension and we fitted the kitchen together. Apart from that it was just decoration, but still it took quite a few months of hard graft before it was all sorted. I basically lived in the workshop for that first summer because there was so much brick dust and general chaos everywhere in the house."

"Wow." Zoe was impressed. "That sounds... tiring."

Tom laughed. "Oh, yeah, it was exhausting. But all worth it in the end. I would have struggled to afford this if it had already had the extension, and even so the bank of mum and dad played a part."

"Mm. My mum and dad helped buy my flat, that's how I managed to negotiate keeping it after the divorce. And house prices were cheaper ten years ago when we first moved in. If I were starting from scratch today, I don't think I could even dream of buying my own place."

The smell of the roasting squash was now beginning to pervade the kitchen, making Zoe feel hungry. She got up and went over to Tom and wrapped her arms around his waist from behind. He twisted to kiss her, then turned back to keep stirring.

"How long will it take?" she asked hopefully.

"About half an hour. Sorry, I've not offered you a drink yet. Do you want tea, or a glass of wine?"

"Maybe tea now, then wine with dinner. I feel a bit like I'm still on holiday mode although I did get quite a lot of work done today. How was school?"

"Oh, fine. More training and meetings and so on. I'm quite looking forward to seeing the kids tomorrow."

They chatted on while the dinner cooked. When everything was ready Zoe took plates and cutlery to the table while Tom poured them each a glass of white wine. He lit a candle and placed it on the table.

"Very fancy," Zoe smiled.

Tom raised his glass. "Cheers. What shall we drink to?"

Zoe remembered the solstice celebration. "How about new beginnings? Appropriate for the time of year."

"I like that. To new beginnings."

"To new beginnings." She looked into his eyes as she took a sip of the wine.

The risotto was delicious, creamy and savoury with a hint of sweetness from the butternut squash.

"Thank you, Tom," Zoe said as she finished and placed her knife and fork together. "It's lovely to have someone else cook for me. I mean, I really like cooking, but I don't always want to do it every single day."

"I feel the same. I enjoy it but it's a nice thing to share with someone else." He stood up and took the plates over to the dishwasher.

"Would you..." Tom hesitated. "Do you want to go out and do anything? We could walk down to the pub for an hour or two."

"We can if you want to. Honestly, I'm quite happy just hanging out here."

He moved back towards her and sat down again. "I don't want you to be bored. This is all very quiet and domestic."

Zoe smiled. "I'm not bored."

"What about tomorrow? It'll be your last evening. Do you want to go out for dinner?"

She considered for a moment. "I mean, dinner out sounds great but I was thinking I could cook for you again."

He looked relieved. "Ok, as long as you're happy with that." He held out a hand across the table and she took it and squeezed it.

"Shall we go and sit in the other room where it's more comfortable?" Tom asked, and Zoe nodded.

"Sure."

They sat together on the sofa, each sitting at an angle so that they could see each other. Tom bent one long leg on the sofa cushion between them and leaned back slightly, looking at Zoe.

"You know, you're very bad for my productivity," he commented lightly. "I'm getting nothing at all done in my workshop at the moment."

Zoe realised he was teasing her. "Oh, I'm terribly sorry to be such a distraction," she replied archly. "Feel free to go out there now, if you like. I mean, it is pitch black and freezing cold outside, but if you need to get things done..."

"I think it might almost be worth getting cold if it meant you were going to warm me up again afterwards." There was heat in his voice and Zoe felt herself growing warm under his gaze. His leg was inches away from her own but they were not quite touching, and she ached to feel his body against hers.

"I expect I could do that," she half whispered, not allowing herself to move but letting the moment stretch tantalisingly between them.

"I actually do feel rather cold right now," Tom went on, a slight smile playing on his lips. He reached forwards and stroked her ankle where she had tucked her leg up on the sofa. Zoe exhaled audibly as his fingers brushed under her clothes and touched her bare skin. She gave him a look of such open lust that he grinned and moved forwards from his reclined position, stretching out over her so that he could kiss her and press his body against her own. As Tom stripped off his t-shirt and began undoing the button of her jeans, he found time to comment; "See, the advantage of being here is that there are no furry observers to interrupt us." Zoe gave a gasp of laughter as she surrendered completely to the power of their desire for one another.

Twenty-Six

'I just want you for my own, more than you could ever know...'

Zoe called for Isobel as arranged at half past nine and they walked down to the beach.

"I think we've picked the right morning for it," Isobel said as they passed through the tunnel of branches surrounding the footpath. "I just caught the weather forecast and there's a cold front heading in later this afternoon. Looks like it could be fairly Baltic tomorrow morning."

"I'll make sure I wrap up warm for my afternoon walk then! Still, I wouldn't put it past you to be out in the water even if snow was falling!"

Isobel grinned. "Well, that would be quite special, wouldn't it?"

Zoe laughed. They shed their outer layers at the bench and hastened down the beach to the water's edge. Zoe felt that she had got the hang of this now: no messing about, just get in and get on with it. The shock of the cold water touching her bare toes was as intense as ever but she breathed through it and ploughed on into the water until it was up to her chest. She pushed off the bottom and launched forwards into a smooth breaststroke.

Isobel was just ahead and Zoe swam a few quicker strokes to catch up with her. "When I first arrived and you talked about swimming in the river, I thought it was total madness! But now I think I'm really going to miss this."

"Will you try some of the outdoor swimming spots in London? There are some swimming ponds, aren't there?"

"Yes; I think I'll have to!" Zoe rolled onto her back for a moment, keeping her head above the water, to look around at the view. There was scarcely anyone around and it was very quiet. The tide was on the way out and the boats pulled gently against their anchors, wanting to ride the river down to the sea. Water lapped against the boats' hulls and a few seabirds cried overhead. It was somewhat overcast but occasionally the clouds would part and a ray of sunshine would beam down upon them.

They swam up and down for the best part of ten minutes, then decided that it was time to get out. Shivering on the beach under the changing robe, Zoe was now finding it easier to win the battle with the wetsuit that clung to her damp body. She had it stripped off in no time and was able to push her cold arms through the sleeves of a t-shirt, making sure to cover her core as quickly as possible before moving onto trousers.

"Come back to mine for a hot drink," Isobel suggested, "and then you can leave the wetsuit with me."

Jasper lifted his head as they walked in and wagged his tail in pleasure. Zoe went straight over to give him a stroke and to scratch behind his ears. Isobel put the kettle on.

"Tea, coffee or hot choc?" she asked.

"Tea, please."

"I'll make a big pot, then we can have top-ups."

The house seemed quiet. "Is Steve back at work now?"

"Yes, and Charlie's at sixth form today, so it's just me and Jasper. I love having everybody around during the holidays but I have to admit, I really relish a day alone in the house! Just being able to do exactly what I want without any interruptions." She poured water into the pot and brought it over to the table.

"So, I'm dying to know... How's it going with Tom?"

Zoe smiled involuntarily. "It's... rather wonderful," she confessed. "I can't believe how comfortable I feel with him."

"It certainly seems like you've been seeing a lot of each other."

"On the one hand I feel like we've moved really quickly – you're right, we have been spending every spare moment together – but on the other hand, there's a lot we still don't know about each other. We've not actually been able to spend a whole night together yet." She giggled. "What if he snores?!"

"And the million dollar question... what happens next?"

"Oh, don't. I think we'll have to at least broach that subject tonight. I suppose we'll take turns to shuttle back and forth for weekends. If that's what Tom wants too." She sighed deeply. "I *think* he wants to keep seeing me."

"Of course he does!" Isobel was incredulous. "You definitely should talk though. Communication is key."

Zoe looked at her doubtfully. "Didn't you ever have any worries about how much Steve liked you, in the early days?"

Isobel shifted uncomfortably in her seat. "Well, I suppose I did for a bit. He was quite popular with the other girls. And it wasn't just that. I was only young, I wasn't looking for a serious relationship, let alone a husband! It was pretty terrifying to realise that what I'd imagined as a distant future was actually available to me, and that if I didn't grab it with both hands I might let this amazing man slip through my fingers."

Zoe looked wistful. "It seems like you made a good choice."

Isobel grinned. "Well, I am *very* clever, you know." They both laughed.

Tom texted to say he would be later than expected, and it was almost half past five when he knocked on the door. Zoe ran to open it, wiping her hands on a tea towel as she did so. The dogs crowded around, equally keen to greet the new arrival.

"Everything ok? I thought you were expecting to be back quite quickly tonight."

"Bit of a nightmare, actually. A pipe burst and flooded part of the main school building and half the playground. They're going to have to shut the school tomorrow to clean up and let it dry out over the weekend."

"Oh no!"

"Yeah, it's a real nuisance. Especially on only the second day of term! There'll be some cross parents out there but I'm afraid there's nothing the head can do, it's just one of those things. I had to stay and help as much as I could, and get some materials ready so that I can set some work online for the kids to do tomorrow. On the positive side, I won't need to be at the computer every minute of the day so if you like, I could drive you to the station and see you off."

Zoe was happy to take every extra minute with him that she could. "Yes please. I'll let Izzy know that she's off the hook."

Tom followed her over to the kitchen worktop to see what she had been doing. "What are we having tonight?"

"Chicken breast stuffed with goats' cheese and wrapped in bacon."

"Oh, man. You're spoiling me."

She smiled. "I like cooking. Anyway, this is ready to go in the oven whenever. If I put it on now it'll be ready in about half an hour – does that sound ok?"

He put his arms around her. "Perfect. Now what could we find to do for half an hour while we wait for it to cook...?"

He kissed her deeply, pulling her body tight against his, and she melted into his embrace.

Half an hour later, they managed to make it downstairs in time to turn off the oven before the chicken dried out. Zoe felt completely sated. Every muscle felt relaxed, her limbs felt languid, and she was sure if anyone could see her right now, they would be able to read in her eyes just how fulfilled she felt at that moment. They sat at the breakfast bar to eat companionably, side by side.

Zoe had been somewhat dreading this final evening, knowing she would have to say goodbye at the end of it, but now she had the promise of seeing Tom again tomorrow when he took her to the station. She could defer the pain of their final parting for a little longer.

"So, how was it having the kids back in school today?" she asked him.

"Yeah, good. Spent some time talking with my tutor group in registration about what their favourite Christmas presents had been. Video games seemed to feature strongly."

"How old are they?"

"Year Seven, just in their first year of high school, so they're still quite sweet. It's about Year Nine that things tend to get a bit more difficult with hormones and general stroppiness."

Zoe laughed. "I can imagine! It doesn't feel long ago that I was that age. I remember it painfully well. What was yours, anyway?"

"My what?"

"Your favourite present."

"Oh. Hmm, tricky question. Well, it may sound a bit boring, but my sister bought me a task lamp for my workshop with a magnifying attachment. It's not something I'd thought of getting for myself and it will be really useful."

"That's the problem, isn't it? If you'd thought of it, you probably would have bought it sooner, but then your nearest and dearest struggle to think of anything good to buy for you."

Tom grinned ruefully. "I know we men are notoriously difficult to buy for. What about you, what was your favourite this year?"

Zoe hesitated. "Honestly? It was the decoration you gave me. The fact that you made it just for me... it was really special." Tom put down his fork and put his hand over hers, his eyes warm. Zoe wondered fleetingly whether they would still be seeing each other next Christmas, and added, hurriedly; "And I didn't get you anything!"

"Well, I think I can forgive you for that." Tom smiled and picked up his fork again to spear a piece of chicken.

"What about your best present ever?" Zoe asked. "Was there anything from childhood that really stands out?"

"Oh, a remote controlled car," Tom answered promptly. "I loved that thing. I would make obstacle courses to drive it around and sometimes I would tie one of my sister's Barbies to it and give them a ride. She wasn't too happy about that, though."

"Mine would have to be the doll's house I got when I was about four. It was so wonderful and unexpected. Apparently I said to my parents, 'I didn't know I'd been *this* good!'"

Tom laughed. "That's sweet." He finished his last mouthful of dinner and set down his cutlery.

"Did you swim this morning?" he asked.

"Yeah, we did. It was lovely. Really quiet, no one around but me and Izzy."

"Nice."

"I went back to hers for a cuppa afterwards. She said..." Zoe hesitated. Was this the moment to bring up the future? It was time to bite the bullet.

"What?"

"She said communication is key. And we should talk about what happens next. With us." Zoe's heart was in her mouth. She looked down at her plate, not wanting to meet Tom's eyes.

"She's right, as usual. Well, obviously I want to see you again."

The sense of relief was overwhelming. Although her rational brain had been saying *of course he wants to see you again*, the irrational part had been afraid. It was wonderful to hear the words spoken out loud for the first time. She looked up to find him looking at her earnestly.

"I hope that's what you want too?"

"Yes, of course it is." She placed a hand on his leg, reassuringly. "It's about an hour and a half on the train from Woodbridge to London Liverpool Street so it'll be a bit of a trek but it's not like I'm on the other side of the country."

He nodded. "Ok. Well, you'd probably like to be at home for a bit, having been away for so long. Shall I come to you next time? You can show me around your neighbourhood."

"Ok, yes."

"I'll have a look at train times and we'll work something out. I think next weekend may be tricky. It might have to be the one after."

"No worries." Zoe spoke lightly but her heart sank. Two whole weeks? She ached at the thought of being apart from him for even a day.

"Ok, sounds like we have a plan." Tom gave her a quick smile but it felt as though there was a distance between them already. She wished that she hadn't brought it up at all. At least now she knew that he definitely wanted to see her again. But they didn't have a firm plan and they hadn't really fixed anything. It would be too ridiculous to ask if they were now 'boyfriend and girlfriend'. They weren't teenagers, for goodness' sake. But was there really any commitment here?

Tom finished his last mouthful of food and set his knife and fork down on the plate. "That was great, thank you."

"You're very welcome." Zoe had kept a few scraps of bacon back to give to the dogs, and now that the humans had finished eating she put these treats into their bowls.

"I bet you'll miss these three," Tom said.

Zoe's eyes filled with tears which she hastily brushed away, her back to Tom. "Yes. There's a lot I'm going to miss about Redfield."

He came up behind her and put his arms around her. "It'll be ok," he whispered, and suddenly she felt that he was right, it would be ok. Everything would work out. She couldn't control every outcome, but they'd find their way somehow. She twisted round in his arms to face him and they kissed, their actions clearly speaking what they couldn't yet find the words to say to each other.

Twenty-Seven

'On the Twelfth Day of Christmas, my true love gave to me...'

Zoe woke up feeling flat. It was hard to believe that her time in Redfield was already coming to an end. It had been such a wonderful three weeks. Her train was due to leave at ten thirty and Tom was going to pick her up at ten, to leave a little extra time for any possible traffic issues. At least she would get to see him one more time before distance separated them. Possibly for ever, she thought morosely.

She went downstairs, let the dogs out into the garden and switched on the kettle. Once she had made coffee she put on her coat and took her drink into the garden. She wanted to make the most of every last moment in this special place. Even on a cold, grey day, the wintry garden had a bleak beauty. Walking around slowly, she thought how many memories she had made in such a short time. Here was the chicken run where Tom had helped her to search for the lost chicken. Here was where he had helped her dig a hole. Here was the tree where Barney had barked at a squirrel. Here were the bird feeders where she had watched the birds visit every day.

Zoe had completed most of her packing on the previous day, so there were just a few belongings still to put away and then some tidying up to leave the place clean and in order. She ate breakfast, washed up and wiped down the surfaces. The dogs had eaten their breakfast too by this time and she fetched the leads ready to take them out for the last time.

They headed out along the route that they had taken on that very first evening, past the side of the churchyard and out onto the beach by the river. Zoe now knew exactly where to watch out for rogue tree roots on the footpath but there were always new things to discover too; she spied the green shoots of snowdrops beginning to push their way above the ground in the churchyard. The river itself was a constant presence yet was constantly changing as the tide ebbed and flowed. Heavy clouds obscured the sun this morning, making the water's surface a steely grey, but she found that the view was always interesting, no matter what the weather.

Here was where she had waded out into the river for her first swim. Here was the pub where they had won the quiz. Here was the corner where she had first bumped into Tom, on her very first evening in Redfield. So much had happened in such a short time. And to think that she had been expecting a quiet Christmas!

Back at the house, Zoe had a final check round for anything that she might have forgotten. It was now a quarter to ten and Tom would soon be round to pick her up. There was just one thing left to do, and Zoe hated to have to do it. It was very hard to say goodbye to the three dogs. Zoe knelt to hug each of them in turn and tears fell from her eyes onto their soft fur.

"Oh, you guys! I'm going to miss you so much."

Henry put his paws on her knees and licked a salty tear from her cheek.

"Thanks, Henry," she laughed through the tears. "Be a good boy, now. And you, Barney." She turned to Bella. "Thank you for looking after me, Bella." Bella leaned her head affectionately against Zoe's shoulder. "Your humans will be back this afternoon and my work here is done. But I'll always, always remember you."

Zoe had taken her bags outside to wait by the gate for Tom to pick her up, when her phone rang. "Zoe, it's me. I've just gone out to the car and it won't start. I think the battery's dead."

Zoe's heart sank. "Oh no! My train leaves soon. I guess I'll have to see if Isobel can take me after all."

"I'm so sorry," Tom said despairingly. "I really wanted to see you to the station."

Zoe tried to put on a brave face. "Maybe it's better this way. I hate long drawn-out goodbyes. And it's not like I'll never see you again." Even as she said the words she felt her heart break a little. What if that was exactly what happened? Although they had said they would meet up in a couple of weeks, she felt suddenly lost without him by her side.

"I'll call you later," he said.

"Ok, speak to you later. I'd better get on to Isobel quickly."

He hung up and she dialled Isobel's number. She was only too happy to help.

"Of course, you know I'm not at work today. I'll put my shoes on now and see you outside in a minute."

"Thanks, Izzy, you're a lifesaver."

Within a few minutes they were on their way to Woodbridge train station. Isobel had taken one look at Zoe's miserable face and given her a huge hug. "Don't fret. It'll work out."

"Yes, I'm sure we'll get there on time."

"You know that's not what I meant. He is a good man, Zoe. He's not going to forget about you the moment that you're out of sight. And for a long distance relationship, you won't be *that* far away."

"I know. It's just... Well, we haven't defined it as a relationship at all yet. It's been such a whirlwind but now I'm not sure where I stand." She sighed. "I just feel like my heart is aching. Don't tell him any of this, by the way!"

Isobel kept her eyes on the road. "I won't, it's not my place. Have faith. Things will happen the way they're meant to happen."

Having ended the phone call, Tom swore and kicked the car's tyre in exasperation. He went back inside the house, shut the door and pulled off his coat. As he went to hang it on a hook on the back of the door, he saw Zoe's scarf was hanging there. She must have left it behind the other day. He reached out and stroked the soft fabric for a long moment. He picked up his phone and dialled her number but there was no answer. He tried again – still nothing.

Then, almost not knowing what he was doing, he left the house again and began to run.

It wasn't far to the Old Rectory but by the time he reached it, Isobel's car was just disappearing out of sight. Without hesitation Tom turned around and kept running, heading for the river path.

Isobel pulled into the station car park and stopped the car in a drop-off space. She got out to help Zoe with her bags and gave her another big hug. "Come back and see us soon," she said.

"I promise I will," Zoe answered through a feeling of tightness in her chest. "Thank you for everything."

"Hurry now! You don't want to miss the train."

Zoe hurried, waving to Isobel just before she went through onto the station platform. It felt like an age had passed since she had arrived here three weeks ago. She showed her ticket and stepped onto the platform. It was very cold and there was no sun visible through the clouds, which had a strange yellowish tint to them. There were a few other passengers already waiting, standing around in small groups or sitting on benches.

Examining the electronic noticeboard, she realised that her train was delayed by ten minutes. Great, she thought. Ten extra minutes of standing in the freezing cold feeling utterly dejected. She was glad she had her bright blue bobble hat and decided not to sit down on a bench as she thought that would make her even colder. Instead she stood huddled in her coat, shifting her weight from foot to foot with the idea that a little movement would keep her warm. The minutes passed slowly as she watched the clock counting down the seconds to the arrival of the train.

A sudden loud clatter of steps from the footbridge over the line made her look up, and her mouth dropped open. Tom was standing at the top of the bridge, leaning on the parapet and panting. He wasn't wearing a coat but looked hot, steaming slightly in the cold air.

"Zoe!" he yelled.

She took a step towards him, disbelieving.

"Don't get on the train," he called down to her.

"Tom? What are you doing?"

"I couldn't let you go without telling you how I really feel," he shouted.

"I told you I don't like long goodbyes." Zoe glanced around to see the other passengers around her watching, amused by the scene. "If you've got something to say, do you think maybe you could come and say it down here?"

He shook his head. "They wouldn't let me onto the platform without a ticket. Zoe, you can't leave. I was too scared to face up to my feelings before but the truth is, I've fallen in love with you. I love you."

The rest of the world faded away as Zoe looked up at him, standing there on the bridge baring his soul.

"I love you too," she replied simply, her heart full.

"Stay. Stay with me. You don't need to go back to London today."

Zoe was beginning to laugh now. "This is crazy! I do have a life of my own to get back to, you know. Well, how long do you want me to stay for anyway? Until tomorrow? The whole weekend?"

Tom smiled. "How about forever?"

The other passengers on the platform were grinning and nudging each other. "Say yes!" one old lady with white hair advised Zoe. The train was now approaching the station.

Tom was still standing on the bridge. "I'm going to come down. Will you come out and meet me?"

Zoe nodded and everyone on the platform cheered and clapped. She made her way back out of the station to find Tom standing waiting for her. She walked slowly towards him and he caught her up in a passionate kiss worthy of the movies. It was a long moment before he let her go and they beamed at each other.

"You know, you could have said all this over the phone instead of embarrassing me in front of all these people," Zoe admonished him.

"I did try. You didn't pick up."

Zoe frowned and dug her phone out of her bag. "Ah. Missed calls. I guess it was on silent and I didn't notice over the vibrations of the car. The car..." She remembered, and took in his appearance. "Your car? Did you run here?!"

"It's a shorter route along the river path than by road. I thought I might just catch you. Had to give it a shot, anyway." He grinned ruefully. "Although I now know why I don't usually run in jeans."

"Maybe we can get a taxi back," Zoe suggested.

Something small and white flickered past her right eye and Zoe looked up and gasped. Tiny flakes of snow were swirling down from the sky and settling around them.

"I don't believe it!" she said in wonder. "It's like one final piece of Christmas magic."

Tom smiled and took her hand in his. "Christmas is over, Zoe. But the magic..." And with that he bent his head to hers. The guard's whistle blew and the couple stood kissing with snow falling all around them, as the train pulled slowly out of the station.

Acknowledgements

I would like to thank my first readers, Nora Hydes and Claire Blakey, for their support and encouragement. I might not have made it this far without you!

Thanks to Claire Trott for letting me borrow Nova.

Thanks to my family for always being there and for understanding when I talk about fictional characters as though they are real people.

And special thanks to you, reader, for picking up this book! I hope that it brought you joy.

About the Author

Caroline Green lives in Suffolk with her husband and two children. In her spare time you will often find her out for a run with friends, or curled up with a good book. She enjoys wild swimming, but only when the weather is warm! *A Riverside Christmas* is her first novel.

Printed in Great Britain
by Amazon